I Love You,

Nora Whispered

by

Kathy L. Salt

2020

I Love You, Nora Whispered © 2020 Kathy L. Salt
Triplicity Publishing, LLC

ISBN-13: 978-1-970042-10-8
ISBN-10: 1-970042-10-9

Printed in the United States of America

First Edition – 2020
Cover Design: Triplicity Publishing, LLC
Interior Design: Triplicity Publishing, LLC
Editor: Megan Brady - Triplicity Publishing, LLC

Also by Kathy L. Salt

Stargazing

Out of Hand

A Tale of Spiders and Canned Soup

As always thank you to my wonderful beta readers, Marco and Tasha. I want to thank my Mom and Dad who were always up for discussing every aspect of the book - thank you for being my biggest cheerleaders. I want to thank my editor Megan who worked really hard on it. Lastly I want to thank my wonderful wife, who always pushes me to write.

For my grandmothers.

Prologue

1928

"Miss Waterhouse!"

Katherine had never felt so exhilarated in her entire five years. Behind her, she could hear her minder calling but Katherine didn't care. If Ms. Bree hadn't wanted Katherine to run off, she should have locked the gate when leaving Katherine alone in the garden to play.

Katherine had tried the gate every single day the entire summer and for the first time, it had moved open when she had pushed on it. She knew where the horses were and that's where she was heading now. She ran from her safe, fenced-in garden with her swing and her mother's flowers, past the main building and the servant's quarters, all the way down to the stables.

Katherine had been in the stable before. She was the only child of Simon Waterhouse, one of the most prominent Olympic horse trainers in all of England. Her mother had taken her to the stables or her father had taken her. Sometimes they took her after church. Sometimes they took her before dinner. Sometimes they took her because they had business there. They didn't take her because she asked; never because she wanted it. This was the first time she had ever been there without an adult.

She slowed down when she reached the stable door. She took one quick stride into the peaceful dark within and stopped completely. She had never felt so small before. In front of her, two horses held their heads over the box edge but she knew there was more there. Her ears filled with the gentle sound of horses chewing and her nose filled with the best smell she knew. Stable. Warm horses. Leather.

Together it was an intoxicating cocktail, a smell she already loved.

"Katherine!" A hard hand closed around her shoulder, making her wince. She yelped at the pain, making one of the horses kick out at the wooden wall. The stable filled with sharp horse cries.

"Why did you run off?" Ms. Bree leaned down, her eyes bulged and her face red in a way Katherine had never seen before. "The horses are big and you're small."

Katherine gulped at the words. She knew that the horses were big but she disagreed that they were dangerous for her. *I am not small. I am not.*

Ms. Bree looked like she wanted to say something else but eventually, she closed her eyes and took a deep breath. When she opened her eyes, the fire had gone down and she looked more like herself again. Katherine's minder and only friend.

Katherine's shoulder ached from Ms. Bree's hard grip and her eyes filled with tears. She gulped again and noticed that she had been holding her breath, waiting for Ms. Bree to yell at her. Instead, Ms. Bree let go and pulled her into a hug that smelled just as comforting as the stable.

"You scared me so."

Katherine leaned back and looked Ms. Bree in the face. She pursed her lips and stared into her eyes. *Please say yes.*

"I just want to ride one. Please, Ms. Bree." She clasped her hands together, begging. "Please, please, please, I want that more than anything."

Ms. Bree laughed.

"Is that why you ran?" She pinched Katherine's nose. "You, silly girl. You're not wearing the proper clothes."

"But I don't have any proper clothes." Katherine crossed her arms over her chest. "My stupid mother doesn't give me—"

"Miss Waterhouse." Ms. Bree put a finger over her lips. "You will not speak badly about your parents. You know the rules."

Katherine nodded. It did hurt somewhere deep inside her stomach to call her mother stupid.

"What are you doing here?" Her father came to them from inside the stable. His gait made a familiar step, step, click made from the cane he had. A constant reminder that he couldn't ride himself anymore. Not since the war. Katherine had heard the story a million times. It made her hate that cane.

"The little miss wanted to ride the horses," Ms. Bree stood up, keeping a hand on Katherine's shoulder. The hand was left there to keep Katherine in place, both mentally and physically. Katherine looked up at her. The grip wasn't hard and she easily wormed her way out of it and ran to her father.

"I want to ride horses." She stood up on tip-toe, smiling the most angelic smile she could and clasped her hands behind her back. "Please, father."

Her father's laughter sounded like a bark. It was so loud that the horse next to them jumped.

"You truly are my daughter, aren't you?"

It seemed like a positive question that required a positive answer and Katherine nodded like a good girl. She used all the self-discipline she had to not jump up and down in excitement. It was perpetually hard to know how her father would react and she didn't want to scare the horses.

"I tried to tell her—" Ms. Bree started but her father lifted his hand to silence her.

"I'm sure you did your best, Ms. Bree," he said. "But trust me, when you've been bitten by a love of horses there is nothing you can do."

"Did they bite you, father?" Katherine took his hand, searching it for bite marks.

"No, dear. I just mean that I love horses just as much as you." He turned back. "Swanson?" One of the stable boys came from around the corner.

"Yes, sir?"

"Tack up Samson's Heartbreak. My daughter is going for a ride."

Katherine's heart started a strange staccato rhythm. Fear and excitement ran through her body and it felt as if ants started running down her legs. She couldn't believe it was finally happening. *Finally.*

"Sir, no disrespect," Ms. Bree said. "But her clothes. Shouldn't she wear a riding habit?"

"She's just going to walk around the arena with Swanson leading the horse." Her father squeezed Katherine's hand. "She'll be fine." He took Katherine's hand and led her down the stable. He was still talking to Ms. Bree, so Katherine tuned his voice out, focusing on the horses instead.

"He's ready," Swanson called after just a few minutes. "I just gave him a rudimentary brush down."

"That's fine. Lead him down to the arena," her father said. "We're coming."

They walked down to the arena, Katherine still hand in hand with her father. Ms. Bree followed behind. Katherine watched the horse being led by Swanson in front of them. *Samson's Heartbreak* her father had called it. It was just a regular horse. Brown. Katherine couldn't wait to touch it. To sit on top of it. To feel that power underneath.

"Tie the stirrups together before the saddle," her father said. "She won't need them anyway." Katherine looked as Swanson took the leather stirrups and put them over the horse's back, in an X, just in front of the saddle.

"Hold this." Her father gave his cane to Ms. Bree. "Are you ready?"

Katherine couldn't believe it was finally happening. Her dad put his hands on her waist and lifted her up in the air. He placed her on the saddle and told her to hold the reins.

Katherine could only squeak as a reply. Being on top of a horse was nothing like she had imagined. It wasn't like sitting on a fence. Or a chair. Or a sofa. She was definitely sitting on a living being. She felt Samson's muscles underneath and when he took a few steps forward, Katherine thought she was going to fall off. The whole situation felt very unsafe, very out of control. If Samson's Heartbreak decided to run away with her or to buck her off there was nothing she could do. She grabbed the edge of the saddle, her mouth dry, unable to find her balance. How adult riders managed to canter, gallop and jump, she had no idea.

Swanson held the horse by the bridle and made a smacking sound with his lips. They started walking forward. It went slowly. Almost painfully slow. And still, every step was a trip from hell. Katherine couldn't let go of the feeling that any moment, Samson would start running and she wouldn't be able to stop him.

"Are you having fun, Miss?"

She nodded, unable to get any sound passed her tight, thin lips. Her fingers turned white as she continued holding on to the edge of the saddle. Her knees were starting to shake from the strain of trying to hold herself up.

She couldn't relax. She could hardly breathe. After a few more strides tears started flowing down her cheeks. This was not what she had imagined in her short life at all. This was not how dreams were supposed to come true.

Was this really it?

Chapter One

Twenty years later

Katherine laughed out loud at the long strides of the thoroughbred underneath her. She wasn't allowed to canter her father's prize-winning horses but she didn't care. She was far away from the stable where no one could see her. No one had to know. She gave Tampas more rein and he flew over the field, not even stopping when they were both heaving and sweating. He wouldn't tell anyone. Katherine was sure that Tampas enjoyed their cantering as much as she did.

A fallen alder tree caught her eye and she almost steered Tampas towards it. The thought of flying over it was tantalizing. It would be so easy to just... *No*. Katherine swallowed and instead pulled on the reins. Tampas neighed and threw his head from side to side, seemingly annoyed with slowing down.

"Calm, calm, little one." Katherine squeezed her legs around him. "Some rules I dare to break but not this one. You know what my father would do if anything happened to you?" She couldn't imagine what would happen if it did. And as much as Katherine enjoyed the *thought* of jumping, she had never jumped.

The ground underneath them was changing and she slowed down even further until Tampas was walking. There were roots on the ground and she didn't want to risk him tripping.

"I don't think he really believes I am only walking you." Tampas lifted his head and blew air through his nose as a response. "You're right. I shouldn't really worry about it." She laughed and kicked him into a trot. Surely a trot wasn't dangerous over the roots?

As she got closer and closer to home she felt herself revert back to who she was there. Her smile disappeared, her brow deepened, her shoulders stiffened. She would have done anything to stay in the forest with Tampas. She much preferred that over getting married and moving away like most of Katherine's peers had done a few years ago. Katherine had opted to stay at *Waterhouse Acre Stables* and convinced her dad to let her exercise the horses. He didn't let her canter, not *officially,* but he did trust her to take them out.

She was lucky to have such a forest close to her home. The underground was mostly soft where she chose to canter. Someone long ago had made a path with macadam, perfect for riding on. The path was surrounded by tall oaks and smaller deciduous trees. This was her home. She couldn't imagine being happy anywhere else.

She slowed down into a walk before turning around by the big ash tree that she had loved her entire life. Suddenly she was back home. Back home to the big brown stable, the fenced-in yards, the horses. Her parent's house, the white picket fence, and her old swing. The servant's quarters. Her mother Sandrine was walking towards the main house with bags after a day of shopping.

She rode up just outside the stable and dismounted in one swift move. She already missed being in the saddle. *Buggar.* She wiped down some dust on the side of her brown jodhpurs and smoothed the crinkle of her jacket. She plastered a smile on her face as her father came around the corner.

"Did he behave?" He didn't even greet her. Instead he looked at his prize-winning possession, or would-be prize-winning possession, with ever-critical eyes.

"Yes, he did." She tried to feel brave when he touched the sweat that shone on Tampas's neck.

"And how about you?"

"Huh?" She looked from Tampas's neck to meet his eyes instead.

"Did you behave?"

She stared at him—not *up* because she had matched his height at the age of 18— yet he still towered above her. She knew that she had broken the rules and he knew it too. The only question was if he would bring it up. Ban her from riding again. He hadn't so far.

He sighed and nodded. "Mr. Bricken is bankrupt." Mr. Bricken was her father's competition, pushing out more prize winners than they in the past couple of years.

"So?" She started leading Tampas towards the stable, waving dismissal at the stable hand coming to help. She wanted to groom him herself. Her father followed. "Shouldn't that make you happy?"

"They're auctioning off their horses. Foals, yearlings, mares, all of them. It's a great opportunity for us to get some cheaper horses." He smiled ruefully. "Can you imagine? Me finding my next champion among Mr. Bricken's stable?"

"That would indeed be glorious." She smiled as well, knowing all about Mr. Bricken's and her father's competition. "So why do you look troubled?"

"Our lawyer is coming here from London today. I can't cancel with him and I can't send Peters alone or with one of our stable boys." Peters was their in-stable veterinarian.

"Let me go." She much preferred spending the rest of the day around horses rather than getting dressed in her ordinary clothes and listening to her mother and drinking tea. "You trust me, right? I'll look at gums, listen to intestines, check coat and eyes." *And don't make me take one of the stable boys, please. Peters was fine.*

"Parentage." Her father sounded thoughtful. "You know the good names and bloodlines."

Katherine's heart skipped a beat. Was her father actually considering letting her go? She nodded eagerly.

"Yes. Of course. You won't be disappointed."

He smiled a crooked smile.

"What will the others say? That the Waterhouse family has gone mad, sending their daughter alone to an auction?"

Katherine rolled her eyes.

"I won't be alone, Peters will be with me. And things aren't like they were when you were young, father. It's 1947, there are loads of women in charge at auctions."

Her father didn't look completely convinced but he nodded slowly.

"You will change before you go, right?" he said, casting an eye on her outfit.

Katherine nodded.

"Is there anything specific you want me to look for?"

"I want you to look for yearlings. Not something ruined by Bricken's training and not something so young we can't start training within the year. You decide, let Peters examine them. If there is nothing wrong with them, bid on them. But try to be smart." Katherine kept her mouth shut at her father's remark about Bricken's training. Even though they didn't see eye to eye on method, Bricken had continuously pushed out winners.

"How much?" She took Tampas's bridle off, tied him up and unsaddled him. "And how many horses do you want?"

Her father waved at one of the stable boys to bring the brushes and once they came, he asked the boy to take care of Tampas. Katherine looked in contempt at the blonde boy who reached for *her* horse. She didn't have the gall to take out her frustration on her father, but the help... they were free game. She had been looking forward to brushing him and having some post-riding cuddles. She sneered at the boy and felt a rush of joy when he paled and avoided her gaze.

"Come on now." Her father put his arm around Katherine's waist and led her out of the stable. Thoughts of the auction filled her head again. She repeated her question as they walked towards the house, quicker and quicker as her father pushed her forward.

"Don't give more than 30 sterling for a yearling or ten for any interesting foal. I'm mainly interested in older yearlings. I was at the bank last week and withdrew 90 pounds. You can have all of it but I would prefer it if you spent less of course, depending on what's there."

They got to the door. The wind blew through the garden, taking the summer scents from the flowers and flowing over them. Crickets sang in the bushes.

"There is an Arabic thoroughbred, not sure how old. It's a foal from Winter Champion, one of the champions from last year. If you can get him, I'll be happy. Especially since he is a stallion, we can take foals from him later. Be willing to go to 35 for him."

Katherine sucked in air through her teeth. Thirty-five pounds was a lot of money, especially for a horse that wasn't even broken yet.

Her father noticed her puzzlement.

"I know. But to get hold of Winter Champion's bloodline, that would be top class."

"Why not try to buy Winter Champion himself?"

"I doubt Mr. Bricken will sell him off like a common cow. He is probably already sold to somebody willing to give more money than I."

Katherine nodded. They went into the house and she headed upstairs right away to get dressed. She felt safe on horseback, but she felt equally safe in her room.

Her parent's house was a large stone cottage from the early 1900s. Her room had wallpaper with small flowers on it which could be seen between the paintings of horses her parents had given her for various birthdays. She pulled the band out of her hair and put it on top of her desk.

She unbuttoned her jodhpurs and folded them carefully before putting them in a box she had just for horse stuff. She didn't mind the smell but the maid complained and her parents had made her get a box to appease the maid. She went to her bookcase and picked up her copy of *A Horsebuyer's Guide* and skimmed some of the pages while walking over to her wardrobe.

She read the words *a pretty, shining coat,* before throwing it on the bed. She critically looked at her wardrobe. The basket filled with tan stockings looked menacingly at her. She hated stockings and preferred trousers. Even though times were changing, she didn't own any proper ones currently. She figured trousers were not proper attire. Eventually she settled on a grey skirt with a white shirt on top. She grimaced as she pulled on the stockings, then thought to herself that she was at least going to an auction and could thank her father by being properly dressed. She pulled a brush through her black hair and applied some red lipstick, but refused to touch the thick foundation and the itchy rouge her mother had given her for her birthday. She glanced at herself in the mirror and smirked. She did like the way she looked.

She grabbed the book again, and her purse, and went downstairs.

Chapter Two

Martha and Nora Lakes lay on top of the bed. Martha's eyes were closed but Nora's were open, watching her. How Nora was going to survive with Martha gone she didn't know. Her best friend. Her big sister. Her protector.

"What did you say the stable was called?" She closed her eyes again, not wanting Martha to see the sadness in her eyes. She sighed.

"Waterhouse Acre Stables." Martha reached out without looking and patted Nora's head as if she was five and not 19. "Why? Planning to call on me?"

"Oh yes." Nora giggled. "Right away. I won't let you sleep a single night without me." They had always shared a bed and the thought of them being apart now was strange. "Do you have to go?"

"You know I have to." Martha lay on her side and supported her head in the palm of her hand. "I need a job. And it's not like London is brimming with opportunities for an unmarried woman like me."

"I'm sure there is something." Nora bit her lip. "Maybe some rich man can have you as his secretary and then marry you."

Martha laughed out loud. "Yeah, like I would want to marry him. I have to get out of London. You know I do. You know I haven't liked it since we came back."

Nora did know, and in some way, she also missed their year as evacuated in the countryside. It had been easier to breathe out in nature than in the middle of London.

"And we'll see each other all the time. There are more trains every day."

With what money? But Nora didn't say anything. She didn't want to whine. Or complain. She knew that Martha would be sending most of her paycheck back to the family anyway. She wasn't only doing it for selfish reasons like loving horses or the British countryside; she did it for all of them. Nora knew that and still, being alone worried her. No one else in the family cared. It was only Martha who didn't see her as a burden.

"Do you have any plans for the summer? Maybe you should find yourself that secretary job and a rich husband."

Nora felt her cheeks heat. Not from embarrassment at the idea of marriage but embarrassment because it was so clearly a joke. No one would offer her employment. No one would ever marry her.

"Sure," she said mirthlessly and sat up, quickly touching the corner of her eye to catch the tear before it fell. "So, when does your train leave?"

"This afternoon. I promised mother I'd have lunch with you all first." Martha stroked her on the back, acknowledging her sadness without saying a word about it. "I kind of promised that we would make sandwiches. I bet they're still at washhouse."

At the same moment, a shrill yell came from downstairs.

"We should go before they kill each other," Nora said.

*

Their downstairs combined kitchen and living room were encased in chaos. John and Emily had promised to watch the rest of the brood when they played outside but Emily was nowhere to be seen. Rose and Robert were arguing. Eunice had scrubbed his knees and was crying and Anne, the youngest, was trying to blow on them, assumingly to make the pain go away. John was standing in the middle of everyone, looking desperate.

"Where is Emily?" Martha picked up Eunice and tried to soothe him. Nora came after her, limping as she walked. "Wasn't she supposed to help you watch the rest?"

"She left." John looked like he was about to cry. "I tried to watch the others, I did."

"We believe you." Martha looked at Nora. "Do you have any idea where Emily might have gone?"

Nora shook her head. Emily, their fourteen-year-old sister, had a mind of her own. Nora felt a twinge of guilt that they had asked her to watch the others while Nora and Martha spent some time alone. They should have known what was going to happen.

Martha picked up Eunice while Nora attacked Rose and Robert. She couldn't wait until school started again and the children would go back to school. When Martha left, she would be all alone. She and all the children. With an occasional visit from Mary or Thomas who were still living in London with their own families. Edward, the brother between Martha and Nora, had died in the war.

Nora sat down, pulling Anne onto her lap, only half listening to what Rose was saying; she was watching Martha. Her best friend. Her sister. The only one who valued her. Martha was now carrying Eunice on her hip, reassuring John and somehow managing to stir in a big pot at the same time. She didn't even look when she told Robert

16

to start cutting an onion and he listened. When she left, Nora knew she had to pick up the slack as the oldest child living at home.

"Go help," she told Rose. "Help Robert at the cutting board." Rose shook her head, stubborn in a way only a twelve-year-old can be. "But Robert is helping. It's unfair if you don't."

"So why aren't you helping?"

"Don't talk to Nora that way." Martha swatted her hand at Rose but her voice remained calm. "She is doing what she's supposed to. Overseeing you sorry lot."

Nora felt her cheeks heat, embarrassed even in front of her younger siblings. She grabbed some plates and huddled around the table to put them in place. Their door slammed but she hardly looked up when their father walked into the room, greeting everyone.

She sat down at the table, the people talking around her. She ate quickly, hoping to slip from the table and go upstairs again.

*

The crickets were chirping as Martha and Nora walked to the station, Martha's bag between them. Nora pulled at the grass on the side of the road as she walked by. Her left foot was hurting but she tried to ignore it. She wanted this time alone with Martha.

"I'll come back for you, okay?" Martha touched her hand to Nora's. "If it's possible for me to keep you there. I'll come."

"Maybe I could work."

Martha smiled at her, a soft, gentle smile that Nora hated. The only thing about Martha she hated. She knew what it meant. *No, you can't. You are injured. Accept that you're useless.* She knew that Martha loved her. It didn't help.

*

They had said goodbye quickly and Nora had hurried home, sneaking into the hallway and up the stairs. The rest of the family had been in the sitting room but no one had reacted to the sound of her footsteps or the closing of her bedroom door. She fell down on the bed, laid on her back, and crossed her arms. She pursed her lips. She wondered what Martha was doing now. *She is probably still on the train.* She tried to imagine what it looked like; the seat, the interior walls of the train, how it would feel to have the engine under your feet. No images came to her.

Chapter Three

Katherine's father had taught her to drive a couple of years back and having her own car was freedom. Peters, the veterinarian, was going to meet her there, so she waited for no one.

She relaxed behind the wheel, keeping the window open, enjoying the air flowing through the entire car, and pulling at her hair. *This is lovely,* she thought, as she broke before train rails. A train passed by. Quickly.

I want to go by train sometime. It seemed to go much faster than a car. Or a horse. As she drove again she wondered if there was any way she could convince someone to let her try driving a train. She just wanted to go fast.

She parked by the stable and got out.

"Miss Waterhouse!" Peters came up to her, all smiles and sparkling eyes. He leaned forward to kiss her cheek but she held out her hand for a shake instead. It was no secret that Peters was fond of Katherine, a sentiment she didn't share. She didn't mind it though. He wasn't too forward or bothersome and she enjoyed the attention. It told her that she had options.

"Peters." She nodded politely. "Have you checked out the horses?"

"There are three yearlings which I suggest we bid on. Some of the foals are in bad shape." He shook his head. "That's what happens when you invest all your money in a war that eventually ends."

Katherine nodded. A lot of people were struggling since the war had ended. Even Katherine's parents had sounded worried behind closed doors. But they were still okay, family money had them covered. Katherine alone was the beneficiary of at least one will.

"Show me."

Peters led her to the pens. The horses were divided into different pens according to age. It was clear that whoever was in charge didn't really care anymore. Stallions were pushed together, their rears branded fresh and old bite marks. The yearlings looked worried and restless, neighing at her when she came near. The worst thing was the pen with the foals; they huddled together in one of the corners, every single one with a scared and lost look in their eyes.

Katherine swallowed. She wasn't one to cry, even out of the public, but what she was seeing was making her insides ache. She wanted to buy all of them. Give all of them a home. In the end, all she had was 90 pounds and a hurting heart.

"Let's try to get four yearlings and one foal." Peters was standing behind her, waiting for her directive. He didn't protest her plan. She had to get a foal. She had to save at least one of them. She didn't care what her father would say when they came home.

The auction was about to start. Katherine turned around to walk to the show arena when a small roan caught her eye in the pen with the mares. She was smaller than the others and she had bite marks on her legs, but her eyes were clear as she looked straight at Katherine.

"And her." She pointed. "Whatever money we have left we will use to bid on her."

"On her?" Peters flipped through the prospect they had received on arriving. "Nightingale Prancer. Four years old. Not broken. Are you sure?"

"I will break her myself." Katherine went up to the fence and made a smacking noise with her lips. "Come here, girl."

The roan took a few tentative steps towards her when another mare, a big brown thing, pushed her way to Katherine's hand, looking for treats. Katherine removed her hand, disgusted.

"Greedy thing."

"We will see what's left after we have bought the others. Come on." Peters put a hand on her back and ushered her to find seats in the arena.

Katherine had lost her interest. It was a meat market. Soul-selling and foul-smelling.

They went to sit down and waited for the bidding to start. In spite of the number of people there, the actual bidding wasn't exciting at all. Katherine and Peters got all the horses Katherine had set her heart on, including the roan. Altogether she spent 86 pounds.

Peters went to collect the yearlings and paid a young boy to get the foal. Katherine went to get Nightingale Prancer. The roan was now alone in the enclosure, standing in the southern corner, her head hanging.

Pitiful creature, Katherine thought. Nightingale Prancer really didn't seem like much. When Katherine put the hand on the gate a man standing to her right snickered.

"You spent money on that?"

She didn't reply. Instead, she closed the gate behind her. The roan hadn't looked up.

Please don't be dying or something. Buying a sick horse would have been a shame Katherine would not have

21

managed to live down. She hoped that Nightingale Prancer just had worms and perhaps was slightly undernourished but otherwise fine.

She clicked her tongue and made a cooing noise.

"Hello, Nightingale." She stopped a few feet away and kept still. "I'm here to take you home."

At the sound of her voice, Nightingale Prancer looked up with wide eyes. She threw her head up and down and took a step to the side, turning her rear slightly towards Katherine.

"There, there." *Don't kick me, please.* In spite of better judgment, Katherine raised her hand and took another step towards Nightingale Prancer. The roan was trembling now and the sight made Katherine's insides ache. "Who hurt you?" It didn't matter that Nightingale Prancer was shaking or scared, a small crowd was gathering on the other side of the fence, and Katherine was sure at least some of them knew whose daughter she was. She couldn't embarrass her father like this.

"I apologize." She leaped forward and grabbed hold of Nightingale Prancer's halter. The mare neighed and threw her head up but didn't make any other move to get away. It hurt Katherine to scare a horse like this, but she didn't have time to do things at Nightingale Prancer's pace. Katherine attached a lead to the halter and turned away from her, hoping that the roan would follow her.

She had to pull at the lead a bit but Nightingale Prancer followed her out of the enclosure. Katherine had thought that she would give them problems when loading into the transport but the roan walked right in, next to the foal and the other yearlings. Her head was down and she looked defeated. When Katherine tied her up on the stick, the roan closed her eyes and looked to be asleep.

Katherine swallowed back tears, a strange sensation. *I'm going to take care of you,* she thought, resisting the urge to pat Nightingale Prancer between the ears. She wasn't sure it would be received as comfort and she didn't want to scare the horse any more than necessary. She gave a pat to the foal who pressed himself at one of the yearlings only to be nipped at. Katherine was on the verge of suggesting she would take the foal in the backseat of her father's car.

"Soon we'll be home," she told all the horses instead, hoping that the trip wouldn't be too bumpy. *At least Peters is the one driving,* she thought to herself, since he wasn't known for driving recklessly. In fact, Katherine was expecting to arrive at least fifteen minutes before him.

Peters closed the hatch behind the horses and Katherine went to pay. She ignored the gaggle of men still watching her. *Probably thinking I made strange choices because I'm female.* She sneered, not at them, not at anyone, perhaps at herself, and sat down in the car. She started it and left, not looking back. She couldn't wait to be back at Waterhouse Acre Stables and unload the horses. She knew her father. He wouldn't approve of Nightingale Prancer and she hoped to find a place in the stable for her before Peters and the horses arrived.

Chapter Four

The train was unbearably hot in the summer. The air stood still and a single fly buzzed by the window, hitting it occasionally. Martha stood up and let it out, gaining an ugly look from the elderly woman sitting opposite of her.

"What?" she asked, even though she knew it was rude.

"You're letting all the cool air out." The woman pursed her lips.

Martha laughed, *what cool air?* But she didn't reply. Instead, she sat back down in her seat. The woman had probably had a point though when she thought that it might be even warmer now than it had been before. She closed her eyes and thought about the place she was going. She wondered if there would be an opportunity to be near the actual horses and not just muck dung. Maybe brush them or help with tacking or… *anything.*

Martha only noticed that she had fallen asleep when the train whistle blew and the locomotive came to a halt.

"Last stop, ladies and gentlemen." The conductor walked between the seats. He stopped next to Martha's seat and peeked at her over his glasses.

"Last… stop?" Martha straightened her back. She thought frantically and repeated the stops in her head. *Market Harbourough, Leicester, East Midlands Parkway, Nottingham, Sheffield, Darnall, Woodhouse, Shireoaks…* She was supposed to get off in Shireoaks. And here she was, in Worksop, a little town in the middle of nowhere.

24

She grabbed her bag and got off the train with the others. Worksop had a very small train station with just a small bridge between the two platforms. It was nothing compared to King Cross that Martha had left a few hours before. If she looked at the tracks both ways, all there was, was greenery.

She went into the station and found a little hole in the wall where a young girl sat, chewing gum and looking into a small book.

"Hello," Martha braised herself for some arguing. She only had two quid in her pocket and she doubted that was enough for another ticket, but maybe if she made up some reason, maybe...

"Hello." The girl couldn't be more than 14, and how she had gotten this summer job, Martha didn't know. "What do you want?"

Rude.

"There was a problem with the train and I missed my stop. I need to go to Shireoaks. To get to my new place of employment, Waterhouse Acre Stables." She didn't know if saying the name of the stable would help.

"There are no more trains today," the girl said, still not looking up from her book. "I'm closing up in five minutes. Do you want to buy a ticket for tomorrow's train at seven? There is a hotel down the road."

"I can't afford a bloody hotel." Martha pushed away from the wall and placed her arms on her chest.

"How about a map then?"

"What?" Martha turned toward the girl again.

"We're selling maps for 20 pence. Maybe your stable is on there. You could walk I suppose."

Martha placed her hands on the ledge and leaned forward.

"Can I look at it before I buy it?"

The girl smirked.

"Of course not. What do you take me for?" She held out her hand, the cruel smile never disappearing from her face. "That will be 20 p."

"You could have said please." Martha gritted her teeth but she was desperate and probably late already. She dug into her pocket, found the coins, and placed them in the girl's hand.

"Thank you, ma'am." And with that, the girl pulled down the hatch and a click told Martha that it was locked.

Martha scoffed but quickly opened the map. It was a map of Nottinghamshire, with Nottingham most clearly marked. From Nottinghamshire, Martha located Mansfield and Worksop. Not far away from Worksop, she could see Shireoaks written in small letters. She couldn't believe her luck when she saw what it said in cursive, almost closer to Worksop than Shireoaks, *Waterhouse Acre Stables*. She assessed the distance from Worksop. She had no idea how long it would take her. She hadn't been taught to read maps, except for the most rudimentary skill. In London only tourists used maps. Like her pa always said, *all Londoners are born with the London map drawn on their heart*.

Martha knew they were expecting her at Waterhouse Acre Stables. She needed to start moving if she would have any chance of reaching the stable before dark.

Chapter Five

The paperwork had held her longer than anticipated, so by the time Katherine drove from the auction, Peters had already set off. She was then stopped by a train crossing. *The trains are so slow,* she thought. The government had created *British Railways* earlier that year, promising easy access through all of Britain. Katherine didn't really see what the point was. They polluted the countryside with the soot, the noise, and of course train tracks everywhere. Cars were better. *Probably better for nature too,* she thought spitefully, as she continued to wait for all the carts to pass. At this rate, Peters would arrive before her and her father might discover Nightingale Prancer before she had a chance to prepare him.

Finally, all of the train cars had passed and Katherine could drive on. She stepped on the gas, trying to drive as fast as the car would go. She could see the stable up ahead now, but she had lost sight of Peters and the truck after the train. That meant he had already arrived and Katherine had no idea what was waiting for her when she got there.

She parked the car by the main building and walked down to the stable. She braced herself and forced on an icy expression. She needed to sound calm and professional and be able to explain to her father why buying Nightingale Prancer with *his* money wasn't a huge mistake.

The gravel sounded abnormally loud under her feet as she walked around the corner. She could see the truck.

The back was open. Her father was standing on the other side of the truck and she could hear his voice.

"Why did you let her—?" His tone wasn't angry but tired.

"Hello, Father."

He turned around, his facial expression neutral.

"Hello, Daughter." He sighed and his shoulders relaxed a bit. There was a worn-out look in his eyes. "Do you have anything to tell me?"

"You gave me 90 pounds." She stuck her chin up. "I got four yearlings and a foal. Just like you wanted. I had enough for her. She… there is something about her, father. She…"

"She is clearly ill," her father interrupted her. "Have you looked at her? I understand that she touched your heart or your conscious, but I trusted you to make sound, logical decisions. I trusted you with our money. I trusted you with our reputation." His tone softened but it made Katherine irritated. Like she was a silly girl to be pitied. As if he was sorry for giving her too much responsibility because she clearly couldn't handle it. She would have preferred if he had argued.

"I'll pay for the veterinarian fees with my own money." She was trying to convince him she made a good decision. "And I think it'll be good for me to have my own horse."

Both her father and Peters looked at her, waiting for her to continue.

"You want me to learn properly, yes?" Katherine could almost see the wheels turning in her father's head. "This isn't a horse that you'll be trying to make a profit from. This could be my horse. A horse to teach me things."

"It's an unbroken four-year-old." Her dad put his arm around her shoulder, an awkward action since Katherine was taller than him. "She can't teach you anything."

"We will teach each other." The more she talked about it, the surer Katherine became of her decision. It would be fine. It would all work out. "Just let me keep her, please, father."

Her father sighed. "What can I say?" He pinched her cheek, something he hadn't done for at least fifteen years. "Of course, you can keep her. I don't stand by your decision. I think you made a mistake. But making mistakes is part of being young."

I'm twenty-five years old. Katherine forced a smile, but inside she was fuming.

"Now go and take her out," her father said. "We already took the others and she nipped at one of the stable boys. Since she's yours, it's time to start taking responsibility. I'll tell Albert to clear one of the boxes for her. Before we know she's clean, I don't want to introduce her to the rest of the herd."

"I need to get a lead." Katherine forced a smile and pressed a quick kiss to her father's cheek. She went into the stable to find a lead with forceful strides. Her heart was beating in a weird staccato rhythm. *Danger, danger, danger.* When she passed by the blonde stable boy, she reached out and pushed him into the wall without stopping. He made a surprised sound as he fell to the ground and Katherine felt herself relax. She knew he wouldn't complain. Without looking back, she fetched the lead and went out again.

Once outside again, she walked to the end of the truck and headed into the darkness within. It took her a few moments before her eyes adjusted but when they did, she could see the outline of Nightingale Prancer. She was standing exactly where Katherine had tied her up, just an hour earlier. Her eyes were closed.

"Hello, girlie."

Nightingale Prancer opened her eyes and turned her head as far as the rope would allow.

"It's just me." *Your new owner.* Katherine walked towards the horse as slowly as she mustered. She touched the tips of her fingers to Nightingale Prancer's muzzle and reveled in the hot air that came out of the big horse nostrils. "We're going to get along. I promise."

She put her hands around the lead and undid the knot. She clicked her lips together and walked out of the truck, Nightingale Prancer willingly coming after her.

The horse didn't seem as nervous anymore, moving less like a ballerina and calmer.

Outside the truck, her father was still waiting. He was just standing there as if waiting to appraise his new horse. *My* new horse, Katherine thought to herself. She straightened her back as if walking properly would better his view of the horse. Nightingale Prancer stopped in the sunlight outside and raised her head, high. She turned from side to side as if taking in her new home.

Katherine gave her a second, then she pulled on the lead again and they continued towards the stable. She held her breath as they got closer to the door. She had seen other horses refuse to enter stables. Scared of the dark or scared of the cold or just scared of places they hadn't been before; some horses were pasture-raised and had never been in stables before. Katherine had no idea what kind of life Nightingale Prancer had lived before or if she had ever been inside a building at all.

Luckily Nightingale Prancer just lifted her head and took a deep breath and walked right in. Her ears flicked when the sound of their steps changed from gravel to the *click-clack* on the cement floor.

"Here, Miss!" One of the stable boys called out. "I prepared this box for her. What name should I write on the door?"

"Nightingale Prancer." Katherine led the roan into the box, turned her towards the gate, and asked the boy to close it. Once they were safely closed in, she took the harness off. "This is your new home."

Nightingale Prancer put her head to the ground and smelled the straw she was standing on. Katherine took the opportunity to put her hands on her back. She pressed down as hard as she could, feeling the bones.

"You're way too thin." She bit her lip.

Nightingale Prancer lifted her head and turned around to smell Katherine instead.

"Well you are," Katherine said. "I'm going to have to feed you properly." She took a step back and looked at the legs and the rest of Nightingale Prancer's body. Her coating was dull and her tail too thin, and she had a couple of bite marks on her flank and dock. Katherine squatted down. "Don't kick me now, I'm not scarier just because I'm on the ground." Nightingale Prancer neighed but didn't move as Katherine put her hand on the horse's leg and let her hand travel from the top to the bottom. Just above the hoof, the flesh and skin felt spongy. *Probably worms,* Katherine thought and hoped. She stood up again.

"I'm going to get some brushes. I will be right back." She also got a bucket of hay that Nightingale Prancer could focus on while she tried to brush her.

Even though her strokes were gentle and careful, Katherine wasn't sure that Nightingale Prancer enjoyed it at all. The horse didn't close her eyes and relax like other horses did when brushed. Every time Katherine lifted the brush and put it back, her eyes went wide and her whole body tensed. She never complained more than that and Katherine was adamant that she was going to continue for a little while longer.

In this box, among the horses, with horsehair all over her clothes and the sound of horses perpetually chewing filling her ears, Katherine wanted to stay forever.

Katherine didn't know how much time had passed. She spent a long time on Nightingale Prancer's coat and when the roan finally seemed to relax even a bit, she tackled the tangled mess that was Nightingale Prancer's mane. The noise died down as the day ended and people went to eat dinner or off to the nearest pub for a drink.

Finally. Katherine relaxed as well and started scratching Nightingale Prancer's forehead. She thought that the roan was warming up to her.

"See," she said. "We're going to be the best of friends. And no one will be allowed to hurt you. Or starve you. You're going to eat yourself trim and then I'm going to teach you things and you will teach me things and then we'll be unstoppable." She wanted to cheer out loud when Nightingale Prancer leaned her chin on her shoulder. "You will see. Everything changes now. This is our new life."

With that, there was a small knock on the box door and two bright eyes and a freckly nose peered over the edge of the gate.

"Hello! My name is Martha Lakes. I'm so sorry I'm late. There was a problem with the train and I got off in Worksop but I've been walking all day and is this

Waterhouse Acre Stables? It said so on the sign, but you never know. You'll put a good word for me with Mr. Waterhouse, right?"

Chapter Six

Martha could feel her mouth running and no matter what she did, she didn't seem to be able to just *shut up*. The woman in front of her was absolutely lovely, almost as lovely as the horse she was cuddling with. She was tall with dark hair and dark, almost black eyes. Eyes even sharper than her cheekbones, which was saying something. She was thin and tall, so much that she looked like somebody had taken a normal-sized person and stretched her out.

Martha was tired. Her joints ached, her feet hurt and for the past hour, she had had a headache. She had walked for so long she had almost thought the stable was a dream. It was late now and the yard outside had been voided of people. Martha had been about to go up to what looked like the servants' quarters and knock when she had heard a voice from inside the stable. Female stable workers did exist and that's what the woman in front of her must be. Her clothes were covered in horse hair and her hair was in disarray. Martha ignored that the long fingers that were still tangled in the horse's mane looked uncalloused and not like the hands of a working woman.

"I'm Miss Waterhouse." The woman sounded irritated.

"Oh." Martha's smile didn't falter. "Well, nice to meet you then. Is this your horse?"

Miss Waterhouse looked surprised at Martha's inability to take a hint. She was wrong though. Martha could take a hint, she just had never met a person she couldn't charm with her ever-present enthusiasm and candor.

"Yes," Miss Waterhouse said.

"Nice." Martha looked at the horse. She frowned at the sight. "Has anybody mentioned you need to feed her more?"

The woman raised her upper lip, giving the impression that she was growling. Martha had touched a nerve.

"Of course, I know." Her voice was low causing the horse to hit her head backwards, clearly unnerved by her owner's behaviour. "I got her today. I'm going to have a veterinarian look at her tomorrow." She touched her hand to the horse's neck and said, "Sorry," in a much gentler voice.

She opened the box and got out, standing in front of Martha.

"That's good." Martha felt herself talking again, almost without wanting to. "At my old stable one of the horses just died one day. Poof. Dead in the box. We still don't know what happened. He wasn't even skinny or anything before hand. I'm thinking it was a heart attack but the stable manager didn't know what that was." Martha paused, thinking. "And I don't even know if horses can get heart attacks, do you know?"

Miss Waterhouse's eyes went big and she opened and closed her mouth a couple of times. Then her eyes narrowed again.

"Do you need me to show you to the worker's quarters?" The tone of the voice didn't give any room for declining. "I will let my father know at dinner that you're here."

Martha nodded. Miss Waterhouse turned around, started walking and Martha followed.

"At my old work we were invited to dinner." Martha couldn't help herself. "We had to dress up of course but I liked that. Stable boys and the riders and everything. You should have seen my sister Nora's face when I told her—"

"Well, you're going to find that that isn't something that happens here," Miss Waterhouse interrupted her.

"Oh, you misunderstood me." Martha couldn't be stopped. "I don't wish for that to happen here at all. It was awfully dull, having to mind your manners, having to wash behind the ears and your hands and to use a napkin and to…" Martha closed her mouth when Miss Waterhouse turned around and looked at her. It was clear in the other woman's face that she didn't know if Martha was joking or not. In truth, Martha wasn't sure of that herself either. Her headache was growing and she was longing for a warm, dry bed to sink on. She just couldn't help that messing with the uptight Miss Waterhouse was a lot of fun too.

"I hope I can bring my sister here," she said instead. "My sister Nora. She's an invalid and can't really work but maybe she could brush horses or something. Or sing to the people working. She has a nice voice. Well, or so I think. It would be lovely if she could just visit sometime. She is my better half. Well we're not married of course. But she is everything I'm not."

Miss Waterhouse muttered something in response. They stopped in front of a small, brown house near the stable. Miss Waterhouse lifted her hand and knocked on the door. Hard. She more or less hit the door with her closed fist. It was clear she wanted to get rid of Martha. Badly.

Chapter Seven

Nora was awoken by a big bang. She opened her eyes and listened intently. Ever since the war and the IRA bombings she had been waiting for it to happen again. Bombings, chaos, death. Her body went stiff and she fought against the instinct to hide under the bed. *Nothing is happening. Everything is fine. Nothing is happening. Everything is fine. Everything is happening. Nothing is fine.* She suffocated a noise in the back of her throat. She was ready. Any moment, her ma or one of her siblings would run through that door. Doom would be upon them.

She listened intently, waiting for screams or more bangs. All she could hear was the pounding of her own, frightened, heart but after a while she could also make out the birds outside and… yes, that was definitely Rose and Emily arguing downstairs. She let out the breath she didn't know she had been holding. She sunk back into her pillow. They were okay. They were free to live one more day.

She turned her attention to the fighting downstairs. There was a door slamming. Instead of annoying her, the sound filled her with jealousy. Arguing with a sibling was such a normal activity. An activity that wasn't for her. People didn't take her serious enough to argue with her. She knew theoretically that Rose and Emily were her sisters as much as they were each others' but it didn't feel like. It was as if the Lakes family were somebody else's family and she was a distant cousin they had taken in. Or perhaps the family ghost, haunting the upstairs.

I Love you, Nora Whispered

Nora put her legs on the side of the bed. She held her breath as she forced herself upright. Her left leg had been giving her trouble lately, and she hoped it wasn't an omen that her condition was about to get worse. She gritted her teeth and worked against the wish to slam her fist into her useless thigh. She could hurt herself and it wasn't worth it. She wobbled over to the dresser while hoping that her muscles would wake up soon and that the stiffness would go away. She grabbed a blue dress that lay prepared on the chair in the room. One of Mary's hand me downs. At the thought of Mary, Nora smiled. Mary was their older sister and she lived with her husband in another part of London. She had *married up* as their mother would say.

Maybe Mary won't mind me showing up today. Just because Emily and Rose didn't feel like Nora's sister, it wasn't the same with the older siblings. Mary, Thomas, Martha, Edward — if he had been alive — they were her real siblings. The ones who remembered what life was like before Nora got polio. Maybe she had even argued with them. *Maybe over toys.* She smiled at herself in the mirror when she applied lipstick, a gift from Mary for her last birthday. *Or over the last potato.* She pulled a brush through her hair and thought she looked presentable enough.

Nora walked down the stairs and found Anne crying on the stairs, both knees scrubbed.

"What's wrong?" She sat down on the same step.

"I fell and they didn't notice." Anne pouted like only a four-year-old could. "My knees hurt."

"I'm sorry, darling." Nora pulled Anne into her lap and rocked a bit back and forth. *At least Anne doesn't know that I'm an invalid yet.* "Where is ma and pa?"

"At work." Anne dried her nose on Nora's shoulder but Nora didn't mind. "Ma yelled at me before she left."

"I'm sure she is just stressed." Nora didn't tell her little sister that she had been increasingly worried that her mother was pregnant again. She didn't know if it was possible considering her mother's age but all the signs were there. "I'm thinking of calling on Mary, do you want to come with me?"

Anne looked up from her safe place under the crook of Nora's chin.

"Yes!" She smiled through the tears. "Can we go right now?"

"Let's just have breakfast first."

*

Mary lived in a flat close to the St. Pancras station. Nora wished that they could have taken the tube there but she was saving her money, even though it would have been fun for Anne to ride the underground. Instead Nora told Anne all about the London underground as they walked to Mary on foot.

"So, there are people under our feet?" Anne stamped her foot on the ground and jumped back and forth, dangling in Nora's arm. Nora staggered but managed to keep upright. She kept her grip on Anne's hand tight.

"Here it is." She stopped by the building where Mary lived. "Come on."

They walked into the building. Nora sighed when she saw the stairs, unsure if her body could take it but Anne pulled her towards the elevator.

"No, Anne," Nora said. "I don't know how to operate it. What if we break it?"

"We won't."

Anne walked up to the elevator and pulled at the door. She couldn't properly reach the handle and looked at Nora until Nora opened it. On the other side of the door there was a metal grid that you could pull back to allow entry. Nora and Anne entered. The elevator shifted and made a groaning sound. Nora couldn't let go of the feeling that she was dangling on a wire and her heart lurched in her chest. Edward, her late brother, had told her how elevators worked. It didn't seem safe at all.

"Press the right button," Anne ordered her.

Nora grimaced at her. "Yes, captain." She looked at it and guessed that she was to press the button close to the 3 since Mary lived on the third floor. The elevator made a clunking noise and then started going upwards. It was slow but Nora's heart kept thumping. She preferred the stairs no matter how hard it was for her to climb them. She squeezed Anne's hand harder, hoping that her little sister wouldn't notice how scared she was.

The elevator came to a halt with a groan and the door clicked to let them know it was possible to open it. They exited the elevator and walked up to what Nora remembered to be Mary's door.

She knocked and crossed her fingers, hoping that Mary would be happy to see them. The door swung open and a scent of warm, freshly baked bread hit them like a tidal wave.

"Nora! Anne!" Mary's eyes glittered and she opened her arms, pulling them both towards her ample form. Mary was like freshly baked bread herself, warm and comforting. Her cheeks were red and her blue eyes sparkled. She was the fairest of the Lakes children but she had their pa's chin, their pa's eyebrows and their pa's nose.

"What a pleasant surprise," Mary took a step back. "Come in, come in. Benjamin! Your aunts have come to visit."

Nora giggled to herself. Benjamin wasn't even one year old yet. She didn't know why Mary talked with him as if he was older. Then again, Benjamin was the happiest baby Nora had ever seen, so maybe there was something to it.

"I've just made bread," Mary said. "So, you chose the right time. Did you bring the others? Oh, why didn't you? Emily is getting so pretty, I wish she would let me do her hair, you know? Then again, the temper on her. Perhaps it is better that you came, Nora. The only one who is even remotely quiet. Then again, I love noise. Have I told you…"

Nora fell on to one of Mary's chair, smiling at Mary talking. It was as if Martha was home. She helped Anne sit on the chair next to her and just hummed and nodded at the appropriate times. Mary's mouth continued moving as she served them both tea and put bread and butter on the table.

"I wish I had some ham or cheese," she said in between stories, "but I haven't been able to go to the market all week. Benjamin has been fussing, haven't you, baby?"

She put Benjamin on her lap and he looked up at her with a smile on his little face. He gurgled and clapped his hands together. That he would have been fussing Nora couldn't see but she just nodded.

"Do you want us to go to the market?"

Anne nodded fast, bread crumbs all over her face. "We can help."

"No, no, no." Mary shook her head. "But I'd love to go together. We need to get out a bit." She shook Benjamin and tickled his belly. "Don't we, baby?" She leaned down and kissed his cheek.

Nora chuckled at the sight. *I want to be that kind of mother.* A wave of sadness washed over her and she swallowed against the sudden onset of tears. She forced the smile to stay on her lips. She didn't think she would ever become a mother. Not being who she was. She took a deep breath and drove the sadness away.

"Let's go."

*

When Nora and Anne came back home several hours later, Rose, Robert and Eunice

were playing in the front yard, trying to walk on the fence. As they approached they stopped what they were doing and approached them.

"Where have you been?" Robert said.

"At Mary's," Anne responded in Nora's place. "We went and bought stuff."

"That's not fair," Rose said. She crossed her arms in front of her chest and looked intently at Nora. "Why didn't you invite us?"

"You didn't show any interest this morning," Nora mumbled. She wondered how her

twelve-year-old sister could make her feel so silly but there they were. She didn't add that the outing wouldn't have been half as pleasant if she had brought anyone other than Anne.

Rose didn't answer, just pursed her lips.

"Is ma home?" Nora didn't wait for Rose to answer, just pulled Anne through the gate and into their home.

They walked into the kitchen, finding their ma by the stove.

"There you are." Their ma sounded and looked tired but she smiled at them. Nora stopped in the doorway and just observed. She looked at the swollen ankles, the slightly rounder belly. Her ma was pregnant. Either that or ill and no matter how horrendous her siblings were, Nora rather her ma was healthy and pregnant than the alternative.

"Ma?" She walked up to her, letting go of Anne whom left to find dolls. "Ma, are you...?"

Her ma looked down.

"It's clear to see isn't it?" She bit her lip and looked younger and unsure for a moment. "At my age. Should I be ashamed?"

"Of course not." Nora pulled her into a hug, being careful to not touch the hot spatula that was in her ma's left hand. "Of course not. Have you told pa yet?"

"I'm planning to tell him tonight." Her ma chuckled. "He has never not been happy, though, so why would he be displeased now." She hit her forehead. "Child number twelve! What am I thinking?"

"You should be proud, ma." Nora blushed a little as she said the following words. "You have a husband who loves you and God has clearly blessed you and..."

Her ma slapped playfully at her hands. "Such things you say." She sighed again. "I don't know how we're going to afford it. We're struggling as it is."

"I know." Nora chewed on the inside of her cheek. "Maybe I could work. Like Martha. And perhaps John could—"

"John is to stay in school until he is 17. He is my only child to pass the 11+. He could go far. No. Maybe I could ask Thomas to remember his family from time to time."

"Maybe I could work." As soon as Nora had said it, she wished she hadn't. They had been having such a good time and now her mother's face filled with pity and her smile changed from caring to condescending.

"Dear Nora." She brushed a stray hair from her face. "You know that we value you. You must know that. But I don't think that you're employment material."

"I could be a secretary." Nora stood still. Her ma's words turned her into a statue. Frozen in time. It was as if somebody else was in the kitchen. Talking. Nora was somewhere else.

"But who would hire you." Her ma's voice sounded far away. "I know you could do it but getting a job is about presentation. They would judge you in many ways, my dove. How you look, how you talk, how you walk." She could see her ma touching her cheek but she couldn't feel it. "You know I love you but no, we need to be realistic."

Nora's eyes filled with tears. She turned away from her ma and staggered towards the stairs. At this time when she wanted to walk with dignity, her body failed her.

"I'll be down for dinner." She walked up the stairs and found her way to hers and Martha's room. *Sometimes I hate everything. I hate my ma. I hate my sisters and brothers. I hate London. I hate my life. I hate everything. I know it's a sin but sometimes I want to die.*

Chapter Eight

Martha's mouth filled with saliva when she entered the servant's quarters. Mrs. Chapman, the housekeeper, had brought the leftovers from The Waterhouse's Family dinner. It wasn't often that that happened but Martha didn't question why. She was so hungry and her entire body ached from a whole day of labour. She found an empty seat that had a clean plate and sank down by the long wooden table where the workers ate their meals. She was later than the others and most people had already left; Martha would have left sooner but she had been brushing some of the horses for longer than necessary. Except it was necessary to Martha. Very necessary.

"You're dirty." Mrs. Chapman hadn't left yet and instead poured stew on Martha's plate. "If I wasn't so tired, I would have made you go and clean up."

"Good thing that you're tired then."

Mrs. Chapman shook her head at Martha's word but didn't say anything more. Martha smiled. Mrs. Chapman seemed strict but she was harmless and she seemed to have a soft spot for young women.

As soon as the plate was in front of her, Martha picked up her spoon and started devouring the stew. As soon as the tangy, rich flavour of tomato, beef, and potato hit her tongue, she closed her eyes and almost giggled in delight. The best time to eat was after physical labour and there was nothing like it.

"There was a letter for you." Martha placed a white envelope next to Martha's plate. When Martha picked it up she saw that Mrs. Chapman had been right. Her fingers left brown streaks on the white paper.

Martha let go of the envelope and brushed her hands on her trousers before grabbing it again. She could see that it was Nora's handwriting on the outside and she was eager to see what was new in London.

Dear Martha,

I trust this letter finds you well. Ma is pregnant again. I don't know who is more surprised, I or she or pa. They haven't told the others yet. It's strange to be the oldest in the household now. I think that's why ma told me. It's nice that she confided in me. It made me feel normal. Emily and Rose have started arguing a lot. I think it's because Rose is almost turning thirteen now. They are too close in age. They both act like they're older than me. Anne is so sweet though. She is the only one that makes me feel normal. She and I called on Mary. Benjamin is the happiest baby I have ever seen. I wish I had a photo of him I could send you. Maybe we could go and visit once you come to London. I miss you so.

What is it like in Waterhouse Acre Stables? Is it like your old place? Is your employer nice? Do you think there is any work for me?

Please, Martha, is there a way I can come and live with you? Ma is worried about having another mouth to feed. I don't want to be a burden anymore; I don't want to be a burden on anyone. I told ma I would try to find a job, maybe as a secretary, but she told me that no one would hire me. Please help me prove her wrong.

Your sister,
Nora.

Martha closed her eyes, sighing, her heart feeling heavy. She could feel Nora's desperation through the letter. She could see her in her mind's eye, sitting on her bed, tears travelling down her cheek, her hands shaking. She could also see her, finishing the letter and going downstairs for dinner and pretending like everything was fine.

I need to help her somehow. Martha looked up at Mrs. Chapman. She was standing with her back to Martha, doing something over the sink, maybe washing something. There was water splashing.

"Mrs. Chapman?"

"Yes, dear." Mrs. Chapman turned around, wiping the hair from her forehead. "What is it?"

"Do you need help in the kitchen?" Martha chewed on the inside of her cheek. Unsure what to say. "I have a sister. She is twenty years old and needs work. She can do dishes or maybe stir... umm... in pots." Martha felt her face grow hot, she hated asking for favours like this. *For Nora.* Her sister was worth feeling a bit embarrassed.

"Is she back in London?" Mrs. Chapman looked thoughtful. "Why doesn't she find kitchen work there if that's what she wants?"

"She misses me." Martha smiled weakly. "And I miss her." She sighed. "She is rather poorly and I think being away from the bad air in London would do her well."

"She is ill and you want her to work in my kitchen?" Mrs. Chapman pointed at her plate. "Don't forget to eat your food."

Martha took a quick spoonful.

"She isn't ill. She is bad at walking, mainly. She had polio as a child and she has something called post-polio syndrome."

"I can't just say yes, child." Mrs. Chapman turned back to the sink. She placed a clean pot on the side. "I can't just say yes. I don't make the decisions on who gets hired, that's for Mr. Waterhouse to decide."

"Do you think I could talk to Mr. Waterhouse?" Martha hurried to finish her plate so that when Mrs. Chapman faced her again, her food would be eaten up.

"No." Mrs. Chapman smiled at her. "I will talk with him. I don't know your sister but I've been thinking about needing an extra pair of hands. It probably won't be a very high salary but if you two can share a bed, we can probably offer her room and board. Are you sure she isn't too poorly to do dishes? It can be hard and heavy work."

"I'm sure." Martha nodded. She wasn't sure exactly but if she could just get Nora there, everything would work itself out. She wanted to cheer. She had never expected her issue could be resolved so fast. *I can't wait to write to Nora and tell her.* Martha almost felt like taking the next train to London just so she could tell her in person.

"Now don't go writing to your sister before I've had a chance to talk to Mr. Waterhouse. He still has the final word."

Martha nodded in agreement, hoping that she looked innocent. Of course, she was planning to start a letter as soon as she returned to her room. In her mind she was already standing on the platform in Shireoaks, waiting for Nora's train to arrive. She could see them lying on the bed in her little room, talking late until the night. They could walk into Shireoaks together on the weekends, looking at clothes or going for milkshakes. If they even sold

48

milkshakes in Shireoaks. She chuckled at herself. *I'm getting ahead of myself.*

"Thank you so much!" She stood up. "And thank you for dinner. It was lovely."

"That's alright, dear." Mrs. Chapman yawned. "I'm going to head in now. Goodnight."

Once she had left, Martha got up, washed her plate in the sink, and then headed to her room. In her mind, Nora had already moved in and she started to think of what they needed to make it work.

Another pillow, she thought, looking at her narrow bed. It would probably be better for both of them if they slept with their heads on separate ends. She would need to make room in her wardrobe of course. And maybe they could have another chair on their small wooden table. Martha smiled at the word *their.* It would be their room now, not only hers.

Martha took her towel and her bathroom kit; she knew she had to get clean before heading to bed. She didn't dare to think of Mrs. Chapman's reaction if she found out Martha had made the white linen sheets muddy brown.

Chapter Nine

"I saw Nightingale Prancer out in the field today." Her father's words broke the silence the Waterhouse family had been enjoying for the past hour.

They were sitting in her father's study. Her father was smoking, her mother was reading one of her books on politics and Katherine was mending a pair of broken reins she had found in the saddle room earlier, thinking that she could use them with Nightingale Prancer.

"Yes, father?" She sighed. She had preferred the silence. Lately, she never knew what would be coming from her parents' mouths.

"She was looking healthy," her father continued. "Her stomach doesn't look as swollen and her coat appears shinier."

Katherine nodded but didn't look up from the leather between her fingers. She stuck her tongue out in the side of her mouth while pushing a thin, thin needle through the reins.

"The veterinarian de-wormed her," she said when the stitch was done. "And I've been brushing her both morning and night hoping to help her circulation. It seems to be working."

"Certainly. She has a delightful small head. Do you know anything about her parentage?"

Katherine looked up now, her thoughts spinning. If her father was interested in Nightingale Prancer it could only mean one thing. He was *interested* in her. For breeding most likely, she thought. Their gazes met.

"Don't worry," he chuckled. "I'm not going to steal her from you. But maybe in a few years, we could let her carry a foal or two. Depending on her lineage, of course."

Something about the way he was talking about her horse rubbed Katherine the wrong way. She looked down on the reins again. *You were angry I bought her just a few days ago.*

"I'm sure her family tree is with the other papers I got at the auction." She didn't answer the rest of his question. "I'm planning to start breaking her in soon."

"Do you know what you're doing?" Her father's smoke reached her nostrils and she inhaled the familiar smell. It calmed her and she almost asked for a cigar before stopping herself.

"I will learn," she said firmly.

Her father didn't push it. Instead, he kept smoking and staring into the fire. Katherine almost smiled. Sometimes her parents complained that she was too quiet or didn't say what she was thinking; how could she be anyone else when her parents were the same? She was a direct product of who they were. She looked over at her mother, who was reading by the window. Katherine smiled when she noticed the title of the book, *Women who work.* It was strange how her mother could be so feminist in her way of thinking but still against her own daughter's freedom. Even though her mother didn't say it outright, Katherine knew that if she put on a dress tomorrow and found a respectable fiancé, her mother would celebrate.

It came down to prestige and money. Sometimes Katherine wondered if it would have been easier if she had been born poor but quickly dismissed those thoughts. She knew how fortunate she was. Katherine didn't lack for anything and certainly wouldn't in the future either. If her parents ever dismissed her, she knew she would remain in one will. Her father's aunt had always liked her.

"I'm impressed," said her mother, getting her attention again. Sandrine Waterhouse had lived in Britain for almost thirty years and still spoke with a slight Italian accent. "You're showing a lot of love to that horse. Spending all of those hours down there. I appreciate your candor and will. I don't know how you do it."

Katherine grimaced. Her mother's compliments often sounded more like complaints.

"I just wish you could be more presentable. I'm sure you understand," her mother continued. "Not just brown and grey or cream. Those horrid riding habits aren't flattering on any woman."

Katherine rolled her eyes and focused harder on the needle. *Here we go.*

"How are you going to find a man this way?"

"Sandrine…" Her father interjected. "You don't need to—"

"Stop it, Simon," Sandrine said. "Our daughter is twenty-five years old. She needs to hear the truth. She needs to make a life of her own. And for women in England that means finding a husband."

"Men like horses." Katherine pursed her lips.

"Yes, men like horses," Sandrine said. She closed her book. "But men also like women who behave like women. Who dress like women. Who smell like women and not manure."

Katherine exhaled through her mouth. Her mind had gone numb. She was ready to agree with her mother just to make her be quiet. She looked at her father.

"You have sponsored so many young riders," she said. "I remember all of them. You teach them and train them and use them to make you money in competitions. Why can't you do that for me?"

"You still act like you're a little girl," Sandrine continued. "When I was your age, I was already a mother to your brother and pregnant with you. I don't want you to waste your youth or lose any opportunities."

"You already said I'm not young anymore. There is no youth left to waste." Katherine stood up. "I'm going to bed." She wasn't going to bed. She was planning to head straight out to visit Nightingale Prancer.

"Don't be cross, my darling." Her mother stood up as well and headed to her. She grabbed both hands and squeezed them. "I'm not saying it to be cruel. I love you so much and I want nothing but the best for you. In another world, an ideal world, you could play with horses all your life but that isn't the world we live in. I don't want you to wind up alone."

It was hard to stare into her mother's eyes. She could see love and wisdom, and she knew her mother meant well. Yet she still couldn't just deny her very nature. Putting on a dress and pretending wouldn't change who she was.

"What do you want me to do?"

"Mrs. Smith called me today." Her mother had a response prepared. "Charlotte and Cecilia are having a birthday party next week and on Tuesday are going shopping for clothes in Shireoaks. I suggest you go with them, find a nice new dress for yourself and then attend their party."

Katherine squinted. She was sure that it was her mother who had called Charlotte and Cecilia's mother rather than the other way around. However, she was relieved. She had been friends with Charlotte for a long time and Cecilia, Charlotte's twin sister, wasn't that bad either. This was better than her mother inviting eligible bachelors for dinner, which had also happened many times in the past couple of years.

"Of course, mother." She smiled and noticed to her surprise that it was a genuine one. "If that would make you happy."

She said goodnight to her parents. Rather than going upstairs to her bedroom, she snuck out the kitchen door. She lifted the hem of the dress she had worn to dinner so that it wouldn't touch the mud in the garden. She opened the stable door and made sure to close it behind her. She waited until it was firmly closed to turn on the light. The stable was completely silent, except for some deep horse breathing. When light flooded the building, a few horses put their heads over the box wall.

Katherine chuckled and tickled the nearest mule. "Sorry, Swayze. It's not time for breakfast yet." Swayze, a large brown thoroughbred, blew warm air at her face and then retreated back into his box.

Katherine walked all the way to Nightingale Prancer's box, opened it, and locked it behind her. She let go of her dress then, not caring anymore, and threw her arms around Nightingale Prancer's neck, leaning her face into the mane.

"You smell so good," she spoke into the warm fuzzy skin. "I hope you know that."

Nightingale Prancer neighed as if acknowledging that yes, she did know that. Katherine smiled. She leaned back and started scratching the horse's forehead.

"Tomorrow we should go for a walk," she said in a low voice. "There is a hill in the forest we should climb up. There is no better way to build muscles than climbing.

According to my father anyway." Nightingale laid her head on Katherine's shoulder making Katherine smile. She stayed there, giving and taking comfort until late in the night.

Chapter Ten

Nora walked down the stairs. For once her limbs were working for her and she felt almost normal. The smell of breakfast put her in a good mood too. Most mornings Rose and Emily, who were up first, left bread out for the rest of the siblings to pick on. This morning was different and the whole house smelled of baked beans and fried eggs. Nora's mouth watered as she got closer to the kitchen.

Her mother was there, standing by the stove.

"Good morning, darling." She pressed a quick kiss to Nora's cheek. "I hope you slept well."

"Good morning, ma." Nora stared at the food in the pan. "What's the occasion?"

Her mother chuckled.

"Well, apart from the fact that I'm fancying a cooked breakfast, I want to tell the rest of the family today. I sent out Emily and Rose to buy fresh bread, but that isn't all. John brought home his grades yesterday and they are very worth celebrating. And there's more." Her ma's smile grew wider and she reached into her apron pocket. "This arrived earlier. I couldn't resist opening it even though it was addressed to you."

"Ma!" Nora grabbed her letter but wasn't angry. Not having much privacy was something she was used to. She hoped that Martha - who else would write to her? - hadn't put anything cruel about the family in it. "What did she say?"

She half-listened to her mother as she put her own eyes on the words.

Nora!

The news I have is too important to start with all the usual pleasantries, et cetera, et cetera. After your letter, I asked the housekeeper if she had any use for you. She did and asked Mr. Waterhouse about it. They're offering you employment! The salary is low and you'll have to live with me as no other rooms are available but board is included. Please say yes and come here! It's going to be lovely. Please find enclosed enough money for train fare here. Don't do like me and fall asleep on the train and miss your stop. You want to get off in Shireoaks not...

Nora stopped reading. She folded it with shaking hands, feeling sick. She couldn't handle the happiness and excitement that coursed through her veins.

"Oh darling, you've gone completely pale," she heard her mother say. "Please, sit down." She felt herself sitting down, letter in her lap, and her ma's warm hand pressing against her cheek. She had a job! Employment. She was going to make her own money. She was getting out of London. She swallowed.

"Ma, get me water please." Her mouth was dry.

A cool glass was put into her hand and she drank from it in big gulps. Her vision and breathing returned to normal and she looked up at her mother who was again standing by the stove. Her hips had widened a bit, and soon it would be impossible to hide her pregnancy. It was probably good that she was telling today and not waiting longer.

As the rest of the family gathered in the kitchen, John and Robert came down with the younger children and

Rose and Emily came back from the store. Their pa appeared from somewhere in the house. He kissed everyone's forehead before sitting down at the head of the table. As the conversation continued around her, Nora focused her thoughts on herself again. She still couldn't believe it. She looked at the people around the table. She had no qualms about leaving *this*. No one was talking with her. No one was even looking at her. No one would miss her. For once, the thought didn't make Nora sad. She wouldn't miss them either.

*

Nora packed her two regular dresses, her church best, her underthings, some shirts, and a dress. She also packed Martha's old working trousers that had been passed down to Nora. Her bible. Her diary. Her collection of strange necklaces Mary had made during her teenage years. She didn't even own a bag that fit it all so she was borrowing her pa's in the meantime. She looked at her meager belongings and wondered what she should pack. She had put everything she owned on the bed.

Nora was feeling a bit nervous now. She smelled the familiar scent of mildew and Emily's obscene perfume that spread everywhere. She heard Eunice and Anne playing in the corridor just outside her room. If it even was her room anymore. She knew that as soon as she and her bag had walked out the door, Emily and Rose would claim this room as her own, just like she and Martha had done when Mary had left.

Martha. Nora smiled. Even though she didn't know what was waiting for her on the other side, Martha would be there. Even if the work sucked, they would at least be together. She started packing the bag. It was a military standard rucksack. She wondered if she would get any looks when carrying it. It was an unusual bag for a young woman.

Maybe people will think I'm a young widow, carrying my late husband's bag, she thought. Then Nora shook her head. She focused on Martha and how lovely it was going to be to see her. In Nora's head it was going to be like they were young; talking late at night, sharing clothes, making fun of people they met. Well, Martha talking and Nora listening. This made Nora wonder about the type of people she might meet at Waterhouse Acre Stables. She took a deep breath. *How am I going to manage this? Working?* Nora had almost no faith in herself. *Whose idea was it that...* She gritted her teeth. She needed to focus. Somebody had employed her. She had every chance of doing a good job. But to do that she needed to stop thinking so much. She needed to calm down and stop being such a dreamer.

*

The whole family followed her to the Kings Cross Station, in contrast to how it had been when Martha left. Her pa insisted on carrying her bag. Her ma wanted to see her off. John, Emily, and Rose said they were meeting some friends later and might as well tag along too. Robert and the youngest couldn't stay at home by themselves. Nora felt like one of those celebrities Emily had told her about. When she got a hug from all of them, she wondered if maybe her place in the family had been more real than she had known.

"We will miss you. Our Nora." Her mother pressed a kiss to her cheek and Anne wanted another hug.

"Make us proud," her pa said. He put his arm around her ma. "I can't believe we have five children who have left the nest now." His wife swatted at him.

"You still have seven at home, counting the new baby," Rose said and rolled her eyes. "Hardly something to celebrate."

"Well, I'm going to get married soon," Emily quipped. "You all just wait."

"You are fourteen years old," their mother said and shook her head. "Here, hold Anne and stop talking rubbish."

Nora chuckled. Maybe she didn't hate them after all. Her family was insane. But it was her family. They were hers. It didn't matter if she left.

And leave she was going to do. Even if she had wanted to stay, her train was coming. And what a relief since Rose and Emily had started arguing.

"I have to go," she said. "Give me my bag please."

Her pa handed her the bag and they all waved as she hurried to her train as fast as she could. She turned around and didn't look back.

Nora had only ridden on trains three times in her life. Martha, Nora, and the others had been evacuated to the countryside during the war but Nora didn't remember those trips. She had been so scared. The third time it was a small trip to visit their aunt in Blackpool just a few years ago. This was the first time Nora was traveling all by herself.

The train was full and Nora got stuck behind a large family who was trying to find seats for everyone. Her knees were starting to hurt and she knew she had to sit down soon.

"Excuse me." She tried to maneuver to a seat but was stuck behind the rotund back of the father of the family and no one heard her. She turned around and tried the other way. Eventually, she found a free seat and sank into it, relieved.

The train whistle sounded, the conductor fired up the engine and soon they were on their way. The bumpy ride and stuffy cabin were making Nora feel sick. Or maybe her nerves were making her feel sick. She couldn't be sure. She closed her eyes and tried to sleep but the lumpy seat was too uncomfortable. Leaving London on her own was scarier than she thought. *Maybe I should have stayed at home.* Sure, her family vexed her but at least they loved her. At home, she was safe. There, she knew who and what she was. The unknown opened up before her and she swallowed, her throat feeling dry. The trolley lady came through and Nora was dying to buy some water or tea. Unfortunately, after buying her ticket, she had no money left.

Nora's thoughts returned to Martha. *Martha. Soon you're going to see Martha.* They had organised a phone call with their neighbour who had a telephone and Martha had promised to meet her at the station at Shireoaks. The trip was only a few hours. *I can survive this. I can do this.*

"Excuse me miss." A voice made her open her eyes. "Are you alright?"

It was a young woman, with red hair and sparkling blue eyes. Her skin was completely unblemished as if she hadn't seen a day of work in her life.

"What?" Nora's mouth was dry.

"You look awfully pale. You probably want some water, yes?"

"Leave her alone." Another woman elbowed the red hair in the waist. "Your water is warm. Nobody wants it."

"No, I'd love some water. Please. Thank you." Nora's tongue was almost sticking to the floor of her mouth. She would have drunk lake water if that was all that was offered.

The redhead handed her a small bottle.

"You can have all of it. We have what we need." She smiled at the other woman in a very familiar way. There was something so intimate in her eyes that made Nora look away.

"Thank you," she said again as she focused on the water. She sighed. "I feel much better."

"No problem. See, Marjorie? It's always nice to offer water, even if it's warm."

Marjorie shook her head and looked the other way. She looked very different from the redhead. The redhead had hard angles, where the other woman was soft, dark where she was light.

"My name is Nora," Nora tried. She knew that the other women hadn't invited more conversation but there was still an hour to her stop and she wanted to pass the time.

"Leonora," the redhead said. "And this is Marjorie, excuse her bad mood."

"Oh…" Nora shook her head. "No worries." She looked down, feeling awkward. She wasn't used to making conversation with strangers. Martha usually made friends for them and Nora tagged along.

She looked up, wondering if Leonora was expecting her to keep talking, then realized that Leonora wasn't looking at her. Instead, she was looking out of the window and the world going by. Marjorie looked bored with her nose buried in a book.

Nora settled back in her seat. Before she knew it, the conductor announced her stop. She got up, nodded goodbye to Leonora and Marjorie, grabbed her bag, and exited the train. *Martha, here I come.*

A lot of people got off in Shireoaks and Nora waited for the crowd to disperse, expecting to spot Martha. The crowd cleared and Martha wasn't there, just a homeless man and a reuniting couple. No one was waiting for her. Nora's heart skipped a beat. She was in the middle of the country, alone at a train station. Without money. Without any way to contact Martha.

With much struggle, she managed to get the rucksack up on her back and she walked along the platform, hoping to meet someone who looked approachable.

Shireoaks was small. Much smaller than London, that was clear. In London, there were little shops everywhere. People everywhere. She had never known that she would miss that. There was always someone to ask for help or directions.

"Martha." She called out. She had nothing to lose. She groaned. "Where are you?"

She walked on. There had to be some stores. Something. She walked by a postal office that seemed closed for lunch. Then she found a small clothes store that seemed open.

She took a deep breath. *No time to be nervous or shy.* She opened the door and went inside, a little bell ringing.

Chapter Eleven

"Oh, another customer." Mrs. Mann, who owned Shireoaks' only clothing store went to the door, leaving Katherine and her friends in the changing rooms.

Katherine hated Shireoaks and she hated Mrs. Mann but she didn't hate the green evening dress she had found there. It was a bit too low in the front but it complemented her figure and made her feel tall, beautiful, and powerful. Her friends had already found dresses for their upcoming birthday parties and had headed out to buy them all milkshakes while Katherine decided on the dress.

"Oh, Miss Waterhouse." Mrs. Mann put her head through the sheet.

"What?" Katherine sighed. "I'm going to change, could I have some privacy?"

"Of course, miss." Mrs. Mann went up to Katherine and started undoing the strap in the back even though Katherine had not asked her to. "There is a young woman, a Miss Lakes, in the front. She said she's coming to work at your father's stable."

"What?" Katherine pulled away from Mrs. Mann. "Thank you. I will take care of the rest myself. Tell her to wait, I'll be right there." She didn't want help taking the dress off. Mrs. Mann's long nails felt like claws on her back.

Mrs. Mann nodded and left again, giving Katherine time to change. Once she had put on her regular clothes again, a proper brown dress and black panty-hose, she grabbed her purse and went back to the front of the store.

Mrs. Mann had said Miss Lakes. *Martha's sister?* Katherine tried to keep her distance from Martha since her arrival a few weeks ago but failed incredibly. Katherine didn't think she could survive another one.

"Ah here is Miss Waterhouse." Mrs. Mann was talking to somebody with their back turned to Katherine. At Mrs. Mann's words, she turned around and Katherine's breath stuck in her throat.

Miss Lakes looked nothing like Martha. Martha was fairer, taller, and looked sturdier. You could see the family resemblance in the left dimple and the lively brown eyes but that's where the likeness ended. There was something about the way Miss Lakes was standing that gave the impression that she was in pain, as she leaned slightly to the side. She had dark, shoulder-length hair that fell around her face, a small pointy nose and black, thick eyebrows that gave her face character. She smiled at Katherine, a small tentative smile and a rosy blush spreading on her otherwise pale cheeks.

Katherine cleared her throat, realising that none of them had said anything for a while. Miss Lakes hadn't either. She had just looked at Katherine, waiting for her to speak first with an open look in her eyes. Katherine just knew that when she spoke, Miss Lakes would listen to her in a way that no one had listened to her before.

"Miss..." she had to clear her throat again. "Miss Lakes?"

"Call me Nora." Nora's voice was soft and pleasant. She held out her hand and Katherine stared at it. "You're supposed to shake it." Her smile didn't look teasing but rather as if she wanted to help.

"My name is Katherine." Katherine shook it. "Katherine Waterhouse. My father owns Waterhouse Acre Stables."

Nora looked relieved.

"I'm coming to work in the kitchen. I'm Martha Lakes's sister. The housekeeper, Mrs. Chapman is expecting me." Nora took a deep breath and again, Katherine got the impression that just standing up was painful for her. "Martha was supposed to meet me here but she didn't show. Could you help me get to the estate?"

"Of course, I could." Katherine nodded. "I have a car." She had to be ill or something. She shook her head quickly, trying to clear it. "I'm here with my friends though, so we need to tell them we're leaving." She turned away from Nora, needing to not look at her for a moment. "I want to pay." She put the green evening dress on the counter and Mrs. Mann wrapped it up.

"That's beautiful." Nora stepped up to the counter to have a look.

"Yes, it is." Mrs. Mann had decided that it was her turn to talk. "And it's Miss Waterhouse's color too."

"Thank you." Katherine grinned. People were talking too much now and she wanted to get out of there. She grabbed the bag that Mrs. Mann handed her and they left the store.

They had only taken a few steps down the street when Katherine noticed small painful grunts emitting from Nora with every step. Her gait was uneven, like one of her legs was shorter than the other and she struggled under the military rucksack she was carrying on her back.

"Do you need help?" She didn't want to ask but felt she had to.

"No, no, no." Nora's face was redder now. "It's just been a long trip and sometimes my body doesn't like moving. Or walking. My bag is surprisingly heavy." She looked up at Katherine. "You don't think something has happened to Martha, right?"

Katherine reached over Nora's head and grabbed a hold of the strap of the bag, not caring about the flailing hands, trying to stop her.

"I'm sure your sister is fine." She put the bag on her back. "My father had a sponsor coming today, looking at some of our yearlings. Maybe he needed her help with that."

"She said she was coming." Nora was walking much better now that she wasn't carrying the rucksack.

"Well, you found me. So, all is good. Let me just find my friends, then we'll go back to Waterhouse Acre."

They found Charlotte and Cecilia at the local café, with three milkshakes in front of them. They looked with curiosity when Katherine entered with Nora in tow.

"This is Nora Lakes," Katherine said before they could ask. "She's going to work in the kitchens back home. Apparently."

"Nice to meet you." Nora's words were so soft they could hardly be heard but Charlotte must have heard them.

"Hello," she said, then looked at Katherine. "Does that mean you need to go?"

"Yes. I don't want to make Nora wait."

"It's no problem. Really. I can—"

Katherine sighed. She didn't want to stay. She had bought a dress, socialised for a while, and was ready to go back home. She wanted to take Nightingale Prancer out for a walk. Not sit in Shireoaks and drink milkshakes.

"Try your milkshake at least." Cecilia pushed it in her direction. "They're very popular in America."

Katherine sat down with a small growl, a sound she hoped no one heard. She put Nora's bag down on the floor.

"Do you want me to order one for you?" Cecilia looked at Nora. "They have vanilla and chocolate or blueberry."

"Oh." Nora's face went bright pink. She put her hand in her pocket as if counting pennies there. "No, I, umm…"

"I'll pay for it," Katherine surprised herself by saying. She didn't like to see Nora embarrassed. "You can see it as an advance on your salary." Before anyone could react, Katherine had gotten up and walked to the counter. It was only when she got there that she realised that she didn't know which flavour Nora wanted. She looked behind her. Charlotte and Cecilia were talking to Nora. Katherine was happy to see her face had returned to her normal color, but her ears still had a bit of a salmon hue.

"One chocolate milkshake please." *Everyone likes chocolate.* Katherine also had to admit that Nora's hair reminded her of the dark chocolate truffles Mrs. Chapman made on her birthday.

She paid and returned to the table, handing Nora the milkshake.

"Thank you," Nora mumbled, turning a bit red again. She looked down at the table and put her lips around the straw.

Katherine had to look away, her heart pounding. She grabbed her milkshake and sucked hard. Maybe she was having heatstroke. Or maybe she was ill in some way. She wasn't acting normal. Her body wasn't acting normal.

"Are you alright, dear?" Charlotte put her hand on Katherine's. "You look a bit flushed."

"Yes, yes." Katherine exhaled slowly. "I'm fine. Maybe a bit warm."

"The heat has been unbearable." Cecilia nodded. "Where did you say you were from, Nora? London?"

Nora nodded, her mouth still around the straw. Her eyes had widened a bit and she let go of it, smiling.

"This is the best thing I've ever tasted."

I'm glad you like it, but Katherine didn't say what she was thinking. It wasn't appropriate to fraternize with staff after all. Even if she had indeed bought her a milkshake. She swallowed, working hard to not stare at Nora. *Well, everyone can make mistakes.*

"London must be terribly hot." Cecilia fanned herself with her hand. "All that bad air."

"It is very hot," Nora said. "My ma owns a washhouse. It is so hot and humid there, most of us refuse to go in. I don't think the air is bad though." The last words were almost whispered. As if Nora wanted to defend London but didn't dare to do it loudly.

Cecilia nodded and left Nora alone. Instead, she bumped her shoulder into Charlotte's.

"I can't believe our birthday is almost here, can you?"

*

Less than an hour later, Katherine had managed to excuse herself and was finally walking towards the car, still carrying Nora's bag. She noticed to her joy that Nora seemed to be walking even better after sitting down.

"So, what's wrong with you?" she asked when they got to the car and she unlocked it. "I can tell you're walking strangely."

Nora sighed.

Katherine opened the door for her and waited for her to sit down before closing it. *Now you're opening the door for her like a gentleman?*

When they were both in the car and Katherine had started the engine, Nora opened her mouth.

"I'm not useless." She looked straight ahead. "I can work. I can't do hard labour but I'm good enough to work in the kitchen."

Katherine chuckled. "I didn't say you were useless." They drove away from the parking place. "Don't worry, I'm not asking as an employer. I'm just curious."

If Nora was looking at her, Katherine couldn't tell. She was looking straight in front like her dad had taught her to do.

"I had polio as a child," she said eventually. Her voice was small, as if ashamed. "Two of my sisters and one of my brothers had it too. We all recovered. Well, none of us died. After a few years of recovering, I started getting other symptoms. A doctor my pa took me to called it *post-polio syndrome* even though he said he had never seen it develop in a child before." She sighed. "My body didn't grow as it should. I had some muscle atrophy. I'm weak." She sighed again, a broken sigh that made Katherine's insides knot. "I get tired often." She stretched. "Doesn't mean I can't work."

"Of course not." Katherine didn't know what to answer. She had never met someone who had had polio before. "I'm going to drive you down to the servant's quarters. I'm sure we can find Martha and see why she didn't meet you."

"Thank you," Nora said. "I don't know what I would have done if I hadn't found you."

Chapter Twelve

Katherine was a strange person. Nora knew that they were arriving soon and took the last moments to study her properly. The woman in the driver's seat was taller and darker than most British women. Her hair was almost black and her sharp cheekbones gave her face an angular look. Nora had to admit that she was handsome. *Or beautiful,* she corrected herself. All she felt was gratitude. When she had met Katherine she had been tired, hungry, and in pain. Katherine had carried her bag, bought her a milkshake, and was now driving her in a car. Katherine had saved her.

"I've never known a woman to drive a car." Nora couldn't even remember ever being in a car before. She had seen them of course, but she didn't even know anyone who owned one.

"Well, some women do." Katherine sounded tired. "Here we are."

Waterhouse Acre Stables towered before them with green pastures, clean white fences, and several buildings. Nora glued herself to the windows. She tried to count the horses she saw out in the pasture.

"So many," she said.

"My father owns thirty-four horses." Katherine's smile was audible. "I own one."

*

"Nora!" As soon as the car was parked, Martha came running. There were streaks of dirt on her cheeks and

72

on her clothes. She opened her arms and ran right into Nora, hugging her and lifting her up in the process. "I'm so sorry, little sister." She put her down and took a step back, not letting go of her hold of Nora's waist. "One of the fences in the pasture broke and we had a jailbreak situation."

"Is everything fine?" Nora stared worryingly over the pasture. Everything looked calm.

"Yes," Martha nodded. "But it took us several hours. When I finally got access to a clock, it was already too late. I went to Mrs. Chapman and she said I could borrow a bicycle. I was going to fetch one when you came." She turned to Katherine. "Thank you so much, Miss Waterhouse! Please feel free to take money for gasoline from my salary."

Katherine's facial expression changed from blank to annoyance and her color turned a bit darker. "No, that's alright." She turned to Nora. "I trust you'll find your way now? Your bag is in the trunk."

"I'll get it!" Martha went over to the trunk, leaving Nora and Katherine staring at each other.

"Thanks again." Nora smiled and to her surprise, Katherine almost matched it.

"You're welcome." She nodded and then she left, not looking back.

"She's a bit annoying, isn't she?" Martha came up behind her. "Come on, let's go."

Nora didn't answer as she followed Martha up a small path between two buildings. She didn't know how to respond when Martha called Katherine, ahem, Miss Waterhouse, annoying. Luckily, she didn't need to. Martha didn't stop talking.

"As soon as Mrs. Chapman said that you could come, I've been counting the minutes. I hope you're going to like living here. The horses are amazing and most of the staff are a fun bunch. I've enjoyed it but I'm going to enjoy it even more now that you're here."

She dragged Nora into the servant's quarters, introducing her to any random person that was in their way. There were so many faces and so many names, making Nora's head spin, giving her a headache. She wanted to lie down and sleep for a long while and process the last couple of hours. It was almost dinner time. When the thought occurred to her, Nora's stomach grumbled.

Martha giggled. "You sound hungry. Don't worry, we're almost at dinner. As soon as we've left your bag in our room, I'm going to introduce you to Mrs. Chapman. I have to go and feed some horses before we're going to eat but before you know it - we'll be eating."

Nora nodded. She didn't know what to say. She knew what she wanted to say. She wanted to say that she didn't have the energy for all of it. She also knew that she couldn't say just that. She was a worker now. She had employment. She finally had an opportunity to prove herself. She couldn't start her first day by failing.

Mrs. Chapman was a short, skinny lady, in a brown dress and grey hair in a bun. She talked with a Scottish accent in a biting way, as if continuously daring Nora to defy her or talk back. Nora nodded silently, agreeing, and showing that she was listening with each new thing Mrs. Chapman said. Nora was to get up at five in the morning and start the kettles. She would brew tea and make coffee for the stable workers. On Sundays, she would head to a nearby farm to buy fresh bacon and eggs but most days she would toast bread and boil beans in tomato sauce. Mrs.

Chapman didn't trust her with the Waterhouse's breakfast but for the rest, and herself, Nora knew what to do. During the day she would follow any orders that came up; sandwiches for Mrs. Waterhouse if she had her ladies meeting during the day, an extra pot of tea for Mr. Waterhouse if he asked for it. Sometimes Miss Waterhouse came looking for apples for the horses. It was only when Miss Waterhouse was mentioned that Nora was really listening. In the evening Nora would get a break as Mrs. Chapman didn't need or want help with dinner. But after dinner, Nora was expected to wash all the utensils and dishes from the Waterhouse's dinner. She would occasionally have help, but the girl who had previously done her job was busy planning her wedding and Mrs. Chapman preferred if Nora learned to do it by herself from the beginning.

"You can start tomorrow," Mrs. Chapman finished. "I can see that you're tired and I prefer to have you fresh and ready for tomorrow. Can you find your way back to the servant's quarters?"

Nora nodded. "Yes, ma'am." She said goodbye and goodnight to Mrs. Chapman and made her way back to the servants' quarters.

She hardly heard what Martha was talking about all through dinner. Then she excused herself, going back to their room. She lay down in bed before even changing out of her clothes. She was asleep before her head hit the pillow.

Chapter Thirteen

When Martha woke up she first wondered why it felt so crowded. She turned her head to the other side. Nora was lying next to her, eyes open, staring at the ceiling. *I wonder what she's thinking about.* What did Nora think about their new home? Their square room. Their table with the two chairs. The window that faced the forest. The little brown carpet on the floor.

"How are you feeling?" Martha couldn't stay silent anymore.

Nora turned to face her and propped her head up on her elbow.

"I don't know. Awake." She smiled. "A bit hungry." She grabbed Martha's hand. "A bit nervous. I'm worried I won't be able to do everything Mrs. Chapman is expecting of me."

"Don't worry." Martha sat up. "But speaking of Mrs. Chapman, we should probably get up. I need to feed the horses and —"

"What time is it?" Nora's eyes widened and she flew up into sitting position.

"It's quarter to five." Martha yawned. "I don't understand why the horses have to be fed so early." *Yeah, yeah, it's because the first training session is at eight.*

"Quarter to five!" Nora pushed on Martha's legs until she could pass. "Mrs. Chapman is expecting me at five!" She grabbed her bathroom kit and ran out of the room.

Martha shook her head and chuckled to herself. She wasn't worried. She didn't think that Nora would be late and if she was, Mrs. Chapman was slow to anger. Martha had understood early that even though Mrs. Chapman liked to pretend she was strict, she was actually harmless.

"Well," she said to no one. "Time to get up." She needed to feed the horses before eating breakfast and she was already hungry. *It's lucky I love my job.* It didn't even feel like work. Getting to spend every waking moment in the stable was everything she had dreamed of and more.

*

At noon both Martha and Nora were taking a well-deserved break. Nora made them sandwiches for lunch before meeting Martha outside. Martha had enjoyed a morning of cleaning out the boxes and tacking up the horses that were going to train that day. Now they were sitting on a bench by the paddock, watching Miss Waterhouse and her horse, Nightingale Prancer. Nightingale Prancer was one of the most beautiful horses that Martha had ever seen. Nora seemed to be thinking so too. Her eyes were glued to the couple walking before them, following their every move. Martha hadn't even known that Nora liked horses. *It couldn't be Miss Waterhouse Nora is looking at, could it?* Martha wasn't sure. She took another bite of her sandwich and put her gaze back to the horse and rider. Even if it was, she hoped that Nora would reconsider where she put her affections. Miss Waterhouse was not worth it.

"I don't understand how somebody so unpleasant can be so good with horses."

Miss Waterhouse was walking Nightingale Prancer in just a bridle and reins, probably trying to get her used to having a bit in the mouth. Martha found the process exciting. She had never followed the breaking of a horse so closely. She wondered when Miss Waterhouse would add a saddle or start sitting up.

"She's not unpleasant." Nora finished her sandwich with a final bite, dusting the crumbs on her skirt down to the ground.

"Have you seen how she talks to people?" Martha said. "She never smiles."

"She drove me here," Nora said. "She carried my bag. She bought me a milkshake." She shook her head. "She wouldn't have done that if she was all bad."

"If you say so." Martha wasn't sure. Maybe Miss Waterhouse had done that to impress her friends or something. Nora had said there were friends there.

Miss Waterhouse led Nightingale Prancer closer to where they were sitting.

"Bring me the lunge, please." Miss Waterhouse set her eyes on Martha. "I'm going to see if I can make her trot and canter."

Martha nodded, handed her sandwich to Nora, and got up.

"Right away Miss Waterhouse." She sneered, wondering if the stuck-up Miss Waterhouse could even tell that she was mocking her.

*

Nora looked different now, Katherine thought. When they had met in Shireoaks, she had looked flushed and tired. She looked more energetic now, her eyes clear and her face a bit more nuanced color. Her hair was brushed and not messy like it had been. She was wearing a small white apron around her waist.

She looks nice. Katherine cleared her throat, wondering where that thought had come from.

"This is your horse?" Nora asked. "I remember you mentioned that your father owns thirty-four horses and you own one."

Katherine smiled. She looked at Nightingale Prancer's soft mule and pressed a quick kiss to it.

"Yes, this is Nightingale Prancer." *Love of my life.* Katherine almost laughed at her silly thought. She was so besotted with this horse. More than she had ever been with a living being before. "She is untrained so I'm trying to break her in."

"Breaking in sounds terrifying." Nora got up from the bench and walked over to the white fence of the paddock.

She still walked with a limp, even though it wasn't as prominent as last night. She leaned over the fence. Before Katherine knew what she was doing, she walked up to the fence with Nightingale Prancer.

"Breaking in is just a term," Katherine said. "It just means teaching to carry a rider. You can touch her if you want."

Nora's mouth fell open and she reached forward with her left hand. The tips of her fingers touched Nightingale Prancer's head.

"She is so soft," Nora said. "You're so lucky she's yours."

Katherine filled with ridiculous pride; having Nora call her horse soft felt as important and big as a Grand Pris. *You're being silly.*

"Here is your lunge, Miss." Martha handed the rope over the fence. Katherine hadn't even seen her coming.

"Thanks." She threw a look at Nora who smiled at her. She took off the reins and attached the lunge to the bridle, then threw the reins at Martha. "Come on, girl." She led Nightingale Prancer to the middle of the paddock again.

She smacked her lips together and waved a whip behind Nightingale Prancer's behind. She would never hit a horse with a whip but they were good tools for getting the horse to do what she wanted it to do.

She let Nightingale Prancer trot around her for a bit, enjoying the spring in her step. *It's going to be amazing to sit up on her.* Katherine was sure of it already. Together she and Nightingale Prancer would defy all odds.

She heard the gate behind her open and her father walked up next to her.

"She looks beautiful."

"Doesn't she?" Wanting to impress him, Katherine waved the whip again and smacked her lips. To her joy, Nightingale Prancer fell into a canter without a problem. Her form was beautiful and Katherine's heart swelled with pride.

"She's going to be a good horse for you to train on." Her father bumped her shoulder with his. "I'm sorry for being negative when you brought her home."

"It's alright." Katherine didn't take her eyes off her horse. "She did look pitiful. I just had a feeling that she could be something great."

"She has a while to go but I suppose you're right." That was the closest to praise Katherine was going to get right now, gladly accepting it.

*

Nora felt warm inside when she went back to the kitchen. The feeling of Nightingale Prancer's fur was still on the tips of her fingers and Katherine's smile was etched onto the back of her eyelids. *I mean Miss Waterhouse.* Martha called her Miss Waterhouse and Nora was supposed to too. Or so she thought. It was just that Katherine had introduced herself as Katherine in Shireoaks.

"Mrs. Chapman?" Nora said as she entered and saw her boss standing by the counter with a mountain of bread in front of her.

"Yes dear," Mrs. Chapman said without looking up. "Good that you're here. There is a jumping show tomorrow and we have to make sandwiches for all of them."

"All of them?" Nora went up to her and grabbed a pair of bread slices and started buttering them.

"All of them, yes." Mrs. Chapman sounded exacerbated. "Mr. Waterhouse, a couple of stable boys, the veterinarian, and three riders." She seemed to be everywhere at once, cutting bread, cutting cheese, buttering, preparing, and boxing the ready sandwiches. "The problem is that they neglected to tell me. And now I'll have to do twenty ham and cheese sandwiches before even starting dinner."

"Should I start dinner?" Nora felt sorry for her.

"Oh no, no, no." Mrs. Chapman raised her apron and wiped the sweat from her forehead. The action was so crude that Nora almost laughed in shock. Instantly, she liked Mrs. Chapman more.

"Then I'll help you with the sandwiches." She went over to the loaf of bread on the cutting board and cut up the rest of it.

"Thank you, dear," Mrs. Chapman said. "What was it that you wanted to ask me?"

"Oh!" Nora felt herself blushing. "When I met Katherine... Miss Waterhouse... in Shireoaks she introduced herself as Katherine but my sister keeps calling her Miss Waterhouse. It makes me feel odd, I don't know how to address her."

"Stick to Miss Waterhouse." Mrs. Chapman's response disappointed her. "They're kind-hearted, the whole family is, but they like to stand on ceremony. It's important for us to know our place. It doesn't mean that we're less than or that they're worth more than us. It's about the ceremony and acting appropriately."

"I guess." Nora smiled. But it was a forced smile. She looked down on the bread again. She wanted to call Katherine, Katherine. She didn't want the *border* of miss between them. Whatever that meant.

Chapter Fourteen

The next morning found Katherine sitting on a hill in the forest, looking over her home. From the foothill, she could see everything. The buildings, the pastures, the paddocks. She could see Nightingale Prancer's coat shining in the light as she grazed in the field. She could see her father's staff loading the horses that were competing in Edinburgh early the next morning. She didn't want to be there when they did it. She was still too upset that she wasn't allowed to go. Even if her father had given a good reason. It was a test, he said. He was leaving her in charge. She would take the horses in later with just the help of one stable hand. She would make sure that they were fed and calm. Then she was to let them out the next morning. As flattering as it was to have been left in charge, she would have preferred to go with them.

How am I ever going to become a showjumper if I'm not even allowed to go and watch? She sighed and put her arms around her midsection. The wind had picked up. It seemed to be getting colder even though it was just August. Autumn was coming.

When the last of the cars and trucks had left, Katherine got up from her seat and walked back. When she got to the first fence, she crawled underneath it and walked in the field instead of on the path.

Nightingale Prancer neighed in greeting and walked up to her.

"Hello to you too." The horse buffed at her hand, asking for a treat but Katherine didn't have anything.

"You'll have to stick to grass I'm afraid." She started scratching the base of Nightingale Prancer's neck as the horse lowered her head and started grazing.

Katherine turned her face up to the sun and inhaled deeply. This was truly life. She opened her eyes again. The sky wasn't completely blue anymore and there were menacing grey clouds in the distance. Katherine licked her index finger and stuck it up. *Hmm,* she thought, *the wind is going in the other direction.* Hopefully, the storm wouldn't reach them.

"Should we do some training?" She turned her focus to Nightingale Prancer instead. "We could try to put something on your back this time. Maybe not a full saddle yet but a blanket maybe, when you're tied up?" The mare didn't answer but it was not like Katherine was expecting a response. "Or maybe we should just do some more lunging?"

Katherine bit her lip. It would have been nice to have someone to ask for advice.

She grabbed the side of Nightingale Prancer's halter and clucked. She hadn't led the horse without a lead before but hoped that Nightingale Prancer saw her enough of a leader to answer.

When they got up to the stable area, Katherine noticed Nora sitting on one of the benches. Her face was turned up towards the sun and she had pulled up the sleeves of her dress as if she wanted to maximise sun exposure without being indecent.

Katherine cleared her throat. Nora's eyes flew open.

"Oh! Ka... Miss Waterhouse. Hello!" She stood up, a bit unsteadily. She held out her hands to catch her balance on the back of the bench. "For some reason, I thought you had left as well."

"No, I've been left in charge," Katherine said. "Could you get me something in the stable please?"

"Of course," Nora spoke in a hurry. "I don't really know my way in there but if you could tell me where it is and how it looks, I'll do my best."

It was the fastest Katherine had ever heard Nora speak. *I hope it isn't me making her nervous.*

"I need a lead so I can tie Nightingale Prancer up. It's a blue rope. It hangs inside the saddle chamber." Katherine cringed when she thought about the heavy door that Nora would have to open. She wasn't even sure... "You know what. Do you think you can hold Nightingale Prancer? I'll go and fetch it. She won't do anything."

"Oh... I..." Nora looked like she was about to say no. "Yes. Okay. She won't do anything, right?"

"Right," Katherine said. "Just hold right here. I don't think she'll try to get away and I'll only be gone for a minute."

Nora bit her lip but nodded and grabbed the side of the halter, just like Katherine had done. Their hands met for less than a second, making Katherine feel warm inside.

"Thank you." Their gazes met for a moment and Katherine whispered. "Yes, just like that." She cleared her throat and turned to the horse. "I'll be right back, wait here. Be good."

She turned around and entered the stable. She needed to figure out why being near Nora made her feel so bad and so good at the same time. *Maybe it's that she's ill, you're sad for her and feel good for you.* Katherine found the lead she was looking for in the stable chamber. Maybe that was it.

When she got out she found Nora and Nightingale Prancer in the exact same position as to where she had left them. Nora was holding the halter with a death grip and her eyes were on the horse without faltering. Katherine smiled. The vision was entertaining; Nora looking like she was holding a wild beast and Nightingale Prancer, the supposed beast, looking rather bored.

When Katherine took a few steps towards them, Nightingale Prancer put her head up and walked towards her. This made Nora lose her grip with a squeak.

"I'm sorry," she called out.

"It's okay." Katherine patted Nightingale Prancer's neck and connected the lead to her halter. "Thank you for holding her." It was important for her to say it. She needed Nora to know that she was grateful that she was there.

"It's no problem." Nora patted Nightingale Prancer carefully, so careful that Katherine doubted Nightingale Prancer could even feel it. "I was a bit bored, to be honest. With everyone gone, there isn't much for me to do. Even Mrs. Chapman took the day off."

"Oh." Katherine tied the lead to one of the rings on the stable wall. "Well, do you want to help me?" She didn't know why she asked in such a manner. As if they were friends. Nora was one of the kitchen maids. Katherine was supposed to order her around. Not offer her entertainment to stave off boredom.

Nora's face lit up like a Christmas tree and all doubts disappeared from Katherine's mind.

"Yes please." She pressed her flat palm to Nightingale Prancer's shoulder. "But I don't know how much good I'll do. I don't know anything about horses."

Stop being so adorable.

"Oh, I'm sure you know some things." Katherine didn't recognize the tone of her own voice. "I'm sure you know that they bite in the front and kick in the back."

"I couldn't imagine Nightingale Prancer biting anyone." Nora looked with affection at the horse. If Katherine didn't know better, it looked like Nora liked Nightingale Prancer just as much as Katherine did.

"All horses bite, you know," Katherine mumbled. "I'm going to get some brushes. Wait here."

Soon she showed Nora which brushes to use when and how to clean Nightingale Prancer's feet. They brushed her with dandy brushes until Nightingale Prancer shone like rose gold in the sunlight.

"I'm going to try to put a blanket on her," Katherine said. "And tie it with a girdle. She's almost ready for a saddle but not quite yet." She scratched her forehead. "Then we take her for a walk around the paddock. No lunging today."

"Sounds great." Nora scratched the back of Nightingale Prancer's mule. "When can you ride her?"

"I don't know." If it was somebody else, Katherine might have lied or tried to seem more confident but there was no need to pretend with Nora. "I've seen my father and his riders do it before but there doesn't seem to be a pattern to it. Some horses take a few weeks, others a few months." She grinned. "It's a half-ton animal, we are stuck doing it at their pace."

"Probably wise."

Nightingale Prancer didn't complain when Katherine put the blanket on her and soon she was leading her around the paddock. Nora had sat down on the bench to watch. Katherine found, to her surprise, that she missed having Nora next to her. She had hoped that they would walk Nightingale Prancer together, talking. Experiencing it together. *You're losing it, Katherine.* Her behaviour made no sense. She tried to focus on Nightingale Prancer instead. Her mare deserved it.

*

When they were finished and she put Nightingale Prancer out again, Nora came to stand by her.

"Should we worry about those clouds?" Nora pointed far into the distance. The grey mass that Katherine had seen before had gotten closer. Katherine put her hand above her eyes and looked into the distance.

"I don't think so, no." She thought for a while. "We should talk with Arthur." He was the only one of the stable workers who had stayed behind. "If he thinks we should take the horses in, we will."

They walked into the stable, hoping that they would find him mucking out like he was supposed to. He wasn't there, a shovel lying on the floor as if he had left in a hurry.

"Maybe he is in the servants' quarters?" Nora suggested. "He might have fallen ill."

"Maybe."

They walked to the servants' quarters but all they found was Mrs. Chapman, sitting by the main table, smoking a pipe. When they entered she flew to her feet and, not so subtly, hid the pipe behind her back.

"Miss Waterhouse!"

"Don't worry Mrs. Chapman." Katherine grinned. "I don't care that you smoke."

"I know, but I really shouldn't smoke in the kitchen," Mrs. Chapman coughed. "I thought I would get a couple of things done even though it's my day off. A household is never finished, you know. Just now I can think of ten things that need to be done." She looked down on her pipe. "Smoking isn't one of them. A horrible habit it is." She looked down on her pipe and Katherine almost laughed at the fond look she gave it.

"You, if anyone, deserves a break," she said. "But we're looking for Arthur. Do you know where he is?"

"Oh, your mother didn't tell you?" Mrs. Chapman sat down again. "Arthur's wife is in labour. He had to go."

"Oh." Katherine didn't know what to say. "I didn't know he was married."

Mrs. Chapman smiled.

"It's a recent marriage," she said. "Just six months ago." She giggled which turned into another cough. "I guess the baby is coming early." She winked at Katherine.

I don't have time for this. If Arthur wasn't there that meant that Katherine was all alone, caring for all the horses. It made her nervous, even though she didn't dare to voice any complaint. She needed to prove herself. Especially when it came to things that had to do with the horses.

"I will help you." The small voice behind her made her look back. Nora was looking intently at her.

You can't help me, Katherine thought, *you can hardly walk. You had trouble carrying a bag that wasn't even heavy.* She didn't say it though. Nora looked adamant. The need to prove oneself, the need to do the *impossible*, or whatever other people saw as impossible, was important.

I know you. At that moment, Katherine understood Nora. They were the same. Their fights were different, but the same.

"That would be great, thank you," she said.

*

They started by finishing cleaning up the stable, picking up where Arthur had left off. Katherine had given Nora the lightest shovel and pushed her towards the cleanest box, showing her to only put fecal matter in the wheelbarrow. She didn't say it but hoped that Nora would stop if she felt tired or in pain. She didn't want to offend her or hurt her.

She stayed in the box next to Nora's, listening to little groans and whimpers as Nora worked hard. Mucking out could be hard work, even for people who were used to it. Katherine was starting to feel guilty. Maybe it was better to just offend Nora instead of letting her hurt herself.

"I think I need to take a little break." Nora put her head over the box edge and looked at Katherine. Her face was red, puffy and her hair was standing in all ends. It would have been adorable if Katherine wasn't so worried that she was hurting herself.

"No problem." Katherine stretched her back. "Why don't you go out and check on those dark clouds?" As she said the question they heard rumbles in the distance. "When we're done here, we should probably take the horses in."

Nora nodded, exhaling, and inhaling quickly. She yawned as she walked away. Katherine looked down and gripped the shovel in a new grip. She wanted to manage as many boxes as possible so Nora wouldn't feel the need to do more work when she came back.

"Katherine!" It hadn't even been a minute. Nora ran straight in the box and pulled at Katherine's arm. "There is a storm coming. The horses are scared."

Katherine let go of the shovel and they ran outside.

The ambiance had changed. The sun had left, the sky was grey and, on the horizon, it was dark blue. The dark blue was visibly getting closer. A lightning bolt lit the sky up and a rumble followed almost immediately after.

Visions of horses dying after lightning strikes flew through Katherine's head.

"We need to get the horses in!" She yelled. "Can you get the foals?" She pointed at the small enclosure where they kept the younger horses.

"What should I use?"

"A rope, anything. Just put a rope around their neck and pull them into the stable."

Katherine didn't look at Nora and hoped that she would just figure it out. She was looking at the two main pastures. They were lucky several horses were in Scotland with the others. Still, there was Nightingale Prancer, Tampas, Frankie's Dream, and the yearlings... she counted. Twenty horses. There were twenty horses. How they were going to get them all in, she didn't know. She ran back in the stable and got every halter lead she could find.

On the way back, she met Nora coming in, cradling a foal on one side under her arm and a yearling on the other side, a rope around the yearling's neck.

"Good!" Katherine was very out of breath and she was shaking. "Leave them in their boxes and then come back to the pasture. We need to move quickly."

It was raining outside now. The sky had opened and the downpour was making it hard to see. The ground was turning into mud and when Katherine ran from the stable, down to the pasture, she slipped and slid down, on her butt. She was now wet and muddy.

"Damn Arthur's wife." She felt guilty as soon as she said it. "I hope the baby is worth it."

"Katherine?" Nora leaned down and gave her a hand. "Are you hurt?"

"No." Katherine ignored her hand and got up on her own. She handed Nora one of the leads. "You focus on Nightingale Prancer since you know her. I'm going to try to take three horses at a time. We need to move fast."

The horses were running up and down the fence; the air filled with frightened neighs and the sound of thunder. Katherine's heart was beating so hard, she could hear it over the conundrum.

When she entered, several horses ran up to her. They were already wearing halters and Katherine attached the leads to three of them. It hurt her to push away Tampas and Frankie's Dream and some of the others but she didn't dare to take more than three at a time.

She looked up, seeing that Nora had Nightingale Prancer in a grip in front of her. *Thank God.* She made sure to close the gate after them and they took the horses to the stable. Behind them, the remainder of the horses cried. Nora and Katherine shared a look. Nora's eyes were wide. Her hair was wet, her clothes were wet. She looked small and pitiful.

They took the horses inside and headed out again. This time, they walked up to four of the horses. Katherine put the lead on one of them and gave it to Nora. She fixed the other ones. They did that two more times.

"Come on!" She grabbed Nora's hand and they ran outside again. The world was coming down around them. Katherine kept her grip on Nora's hand, almost worried that she would lose her if she let go.

There were only three horses left now. Frankie's Dream, Tampas, and a small pony called Unicorn. Unicorn tended to bite, and Frankie's Dream had already reared twice. It seemed safest to let Nora take Tampas.

"You get him." She pointed at Tampas, who was standing on the side, looking longingly at the stable. She turned around and focused on Frankie's Dream and Unicorn. Unicorn was a stubborn, older pony that Katherine had learned to ride on. "Come on." Unicorn was infamously hard to catch but for once, he came forward and let her catch him.

They left the gate open now. *Let it blow apart for all I care.* Katherine didn't know how she could be sweating when she was so cold and wet.

Nora was ahead of her leading Tampas but he was trotting with his head carried high. He was nervous.

Lightning lit up the sky. Unicorn pulled on the lead and Frankie's dream jumped. Katherine kept her hold on the leads. Everything seemed to happen very slowly. Tampas threw his head back, pulling Nora towards him. He reared. Katherine looked on, unable to do anything, as his hoof hit Nora in the chest.

Nora yelled and fell to the ground.

"No!" Katherine pulled on the leads. "Come on!" She pulled Unicorn and Frankie's Dream forward. Tampas had galloped into the stable. The sight of Nora in the dirt hurt, but Katherine couldn't afford accidentally spooking the horses. *Nora, Nora, Nora, Nora...* All Katherine wanted to do was go and check on Nora but she had to put the horses away first. She put Unicorn and Frankie's Dream away. Tampas had found his box already and was cowering in the corner.

"You fucking idiot." She took the halter lead off, not wanting him to get hurt. She closed the box gate.

She ran outside. Nora was sitting in the dirt; her hand was on her chest and she was breathing in short bursts.

"Nora!" Katherine fell to her side.

"Katherine." Nora looked up at her. "Ouch." She flattened her palm. "Aow, aow, aow."

"Come here." Katherine placed her arm around Nora's back and put her hand in the crook of her arm. "Let's get up."

Katherine led her into the stable, Nora putting most of her body weight on Katherine's arm. She wanted them to get out of the rain. The servant's quarters seemed too far away, as did the main building.

"Let's go into the feed chamber." They walked into the heart of the stable. When they got in there she put Nora on top of a bale of hay. "Let me get you a blanket." It was a horse blanket and full of hair but it was dry and warm.

Nora was looking down at the floor and her breath was still coming out in short bursts. Katherine put the blanket around her shoulders.

"I'm sorry, I need to…" Nora wasn't answering so Katherine went right ahead. Her fingers shook as she opened the buttons of Nora's blouse.

The pale skin was goose-pimpled and her nipples were hard. *Why am I looking at her breasts?* Katherine swallowed. She hadn't expected Nora to be without a brassere. She focused instead on what she was supposed to. Around Nora's sternum, a big bruise was forming. The skin wasn't broken but Katherine didn't feel relieved. What if there was internal bleeding? The thought of Nora dying, here, now, without Katherine being able to do anything was unthinkable.

"Don't die, please." Katherine got up on the bale and pulled Nora into her arms. "I'm sorry. It's my fault. You shouldn't have been helping."

Nora coughed. "I'm not dying. It just knocked the air out of me."

Katherine sighed in relief. Not caring, she held Nora closer and rocked her back and forth. She wanted to comfort both of them and she didn't care how it looked. Instead of pulling away, Nora put her hands on Katherine's arms, keeping them against her.

Okay, Katherine thought to herself as she closed her eyes, *so maybe I like Nora in a way I shouldn't.* She could see it now. What the problem was. She was attracted to Nora. She thought she was cute, adorable, sweet, *lovely.* She didn't know why she hadn't understood it earlier.

Outside, the rain was hitting the ground and roof hard, and the wind turned around. Inside the stable, Katherine could hear the horses crying and occasionally a hoof hitting the wall. Inside the feed chamber, it was silent. The calming smell of hay and feed was lulling Katherine to sleep. She was so tired and her whole body hurt. Nora's grip on her arms had turned loose, signaling that the girl in her arms had fallen asleep.

Katherine closed her eyes too. Falling asleep didn't seem so bad.

Chapter Fifteen

Why does everything hurt? Nora wasn't a stranger to pain but she had never felt this run over before. Her legs were aching, it felt like she had scratches all over her arms and her head was hurting. Her chest felt like she had been shot with a cannon. She tried reaching up but her movement was restricted. *Where am I?* Visions of being kidnapped and tied up flew through her head and panic rose. She opened her eyes. Her fear drained from her and the memories of last night resurfaced.

The storm. Katherine. The horses. Katherine. Helping out. Katherine. Being kicked. *Katherine.* Without looking, Nora knew who was holding her down and who was sleeping underneath her. Katherine's chest was falling and rising evenly. She seemed completely unfazed that Nora was more or less lying on top of her. Katherine still had her arms around Nora. Nora had never been held before.

Is this what Rose and Emily are always talking about? Nora closed her eyes and smiled. She relaxed in Katherine's arms. *Is this how ma feels when pa holds her? Or when Mary is held by her husband?* The realisation that she liked Katherine in such a way should have startled her but it didn't. *I should have known.* She reveled in the warmth of her feelings. It was nice to feel something. Exciting. It didn't matter that Katherine would never reciprocate or that they would ever kiss or… A thrill went through Nora at the thought of kissing Katherine. The thrill turned into goosebumps and she shuddered.

Her surroundings looked warm. Light was flowing through gaps in the wooden roof; the sun hit the hay, making the entire feed chamber shine like gold. The air was cold, however, and Nora was suddenly aware of how wet and cold she still was.

"Katherine." She gently bumped her elbow into Katherine's stomach. Katherine muttered something behind her and shook. She didn't want to wake up. "Katherine, we should wake up."

Katherine's body changed. She went from being completely relaxed to suddenly stiff, releasing her hold on Nora. She stood up without a warning, making Nora fall on the floor.

"Oh, I'm sorry!" Katherine reached down, grabbed a hold of Nora's wrist, and pulled her up. She put both hands on Nora's shoulders to steady her. "There you go."

Nora didn't answer. Words were lost on her as Katherine's gaze transfixed her. They stared at each other. The air seemed to heat up and Nora forgot everything. She forgot that she was cold and stiff. That the wound on her chest had started to pound.

Katherine licked her lips. Her lips were full. Nora had never noticed that about another person before. They looked so soft. Nora wanted to touch them. If not with her own lips then maybe with her fingers. She wanted to touch Katherine's face. The high cheekbones. The dark eyebrows. *Were they suddenly closer?* Nora was close enough to count Katherine's eyelashes. She opened her mouth, ready to say something, ready to be kissed, ready to kiss, ready to—

"Katherine!" Somebody was in the stables. "Katherine? Are you here?" It was a woman and she was yelling. "Katherine, please, darling, tell me that you're here!"

Katherine didn't take her eyes off Nora. "Mother! We're in here."

When the door opened, their eye contact was broken and Katherine walked over to her mother.

"Oh Katherine, I was so worried." Her mother collapsed in her arms. "I didn't dare to go after you when it was stormy. I had hoped you were in here."

"I'm alright." Katherine actually looked guilty. "We took care of the horses and then the storm was too strong. It felt safer to wait here."

"We?" Katherine's mother looked past Katherine's shoulder. "Oh, hello there."

Whatever Nora had imagined Mrs. Waterhouse would look like, that wasn't it. Mrs. Waterhouse looked exactly like Katherine, just older. She had the same high cheekbones, the same eyes, same shade of hair color. Katherine was just much taller and didn't have the singing accent that Mrs. Waterhouse had. Mrs. Waterhouse wasn't British, Nora could tell that much.

"Hello, Mrs. Waterhouse." Nora attempted to curtsy but her body was too stiff.

"Mother, we need to have a doctor look at Nora." Katherine went up to Nora and put an arm around Nora's shoulder. She pushed her forward, towards Mrs. Waterhouse. "She was kicked in the chest yesterday."

Nora blushed when Katherine pulled the front of her dress down, exposing her bruise and upper chest.

"Oh my," Mrs. Waterhouse said. "That is quite a bruise. Of course, we will call for Doctor Tillot."

"That's not—" almost by reflex, Nora started disagreeing, not wanting to be a burden but Katherine cut her off.

"Yes, it is necessary," she said. "We don't know what's going on inside your body." She cleared her throat. "I mean, you are…" She didn't seem to know what to say. She inhaled deeply. "Please? I don't want to worry."

Who was Nora to deny Katherine anything? She nodded mutely.

*

In the end, Nora agreed it was good to see a doctor. She seemed to be getting worse. After having breakfast with Mrs. Chapman, she could hardly move, her limbs were so stiff. Her head and chest were pounding and all she wanted was to lie down and sleep for the rest of the day.

She had hoped to spend more time with Katherine but the elusive Miss Waterhouse had disappeared into the main building and she hadn't been seen since. Arthur had come back with some men that Nora didn't recognize and took care of the horses.

The doctor had come to Nora's room to assess her. He checked her blood pressure and pulse and looked closely at the bruise. In the end he just called it a compression injury and that there was swelling and a lot of bruising around the area. It was of utmost importance that she spent the following week lying down. Even though Nora wanted to work—she wanted to be useful—she was relieved.

I hope that The Waterhouses and Mrs. Chapman won't be too disappointed. I haven't even worked a week and I'm already injured.

In the evening Mr. Waterhouse and his crew arrived back with several medals. Nora didn't see them coming since her window was facing the other way, but she heard them. First the engines, then the happy voices and cheers. Before Nora knew it, Martha had come into the room like a whirlwind, hugging Nora until it hurt, talking about all that she'd seen and experienced. All the people she had met. "He is an actual Olympic Rider, Nora. And he talked to me!"

It was only when Nora kept her hand on her chest that Martha stopped to ask her about what had happened. And Martha became furious. And that's where they were now. Nora lying on the bed, eyes closed, a headache tormenting her, as Martha was walking back and forth in their little room.

"I can't believe Miss Waterhouse put you in danger! You're not even here to work with the horses. You could have died! She's not even feeling guilty, is she? She probably thinks that everyone working here is dispensable."

"You're wrong." It hurt Nora that anyone was talking ill about Katherine. "I offered. You didn't see the state of things. If I hadn't helped, it would have taken Katherine much longer and maybe she would have gotten hurt then."

"And instead you got hurt!" Martha sat down on the bed. "You're not normal, Nora, you can't just do anything you feel like doing. And don't call her Katherine. She doesn't deserve such a pretty name." Martha groaned. "I'm so angry. I hate being angry." She sighed and looked at Nora. "And now you're bedbound for a week. I bet Miss Waterhouse will try to get you fired or something."

"That's unfair!" Nora was shouting too. She couldn't remember the last time she had shouted at anyone. "She wouldn't. You should have seen her!" Nora sat up, as it didn't seem right to lie down and shout. "She was so worried about me. She tried to keep me warm and dry during the night, she…" Nora closed her mouth. The realisation that she didn't want to share details about the night hit her. It belonged to her. To her and Katherine. No one else. "It wasn't her fault."

"I'm going to go and talk to her." Martha took a deep breath. "At least to ask about the salary situation. Since you got injured on the job." She shook her head. "Injured! You're a kitchen maid, not a horse carer." She got up and threw her hands out. "I'm just so angry."

"Please don't be cross." Nora lay down again. Sitting up increased her chest pain too much. "I'm alright, really I am. And all the horses are alright too." *It could have gone much worse.*

"I like horses." Martha looked at her now. "But not more than I like you. I love you Nora. If anything happened to you it would be my fault." Her eyes were large and tears were glistening. "I asked you to come here. I never in my wildest dreams would have imagined that it would be dangerous for you." She sank on the bed now and hung her head.

"Cheer up, Martha." Nora reached for her hand. "It's not dangerous for me. This was a fluke. A freak storm. It's not going to happen again."

"Hmm." Martha grunted in response. "I'm still going to talk to the Waterhouses. I need to check up on your salary situation."

"I don't care—" Nora tried but Martha was already gone.

101

Chapter Sixteen

Katherine was sitting in her room, brushing her hair. She had showered and changed into warm clothes but the chill wouldn't leave her body. She looked at herself in the mirror. She had never seen herself looking quite so pale. Maybe she had caught an illness or something, from that night in the stable.

She put her brush down and got up. Her father was back and she needed to go down for dinner. Something was keeping her back. She felt like a different person and she worried that if she went to face her parents they would notice.

You're being silly. Katherine was never silly. A clear sign that something was wrong. She looked in the mirror again. *So, you like Nora. You like a woman.* "You have feelings for a woman." *Had she said those words out loud?* Katherine clamped a hand over her mouth. She seemed to be having some kind of break down.

"Katherine." Her mother hit the door with three quick knocks. "Dinner is ready, we're waiting for you." She didn't wait for Katherine to reply and instead just opened the door. "Why are you taking so long? You always come down without needing to call you."

"I apologize." Katherine got up from the stool in front of her mirror. "I'm feeling a bit under the weather."

"Oh dear." Her mother came forward and put her hand on Katherine's forehead. "You don't feel warm, you're actually running a bit cold." She took up a shawl that was lying on the bed and put it around Katherine's shoulders. "It's probably from spending the night in the stable. I've already told your father some of what happened but he can't wait for you to fill him in on the details." Her mother leaned down and looked into the mirror too; their gazes met. Her mother looked proud. "He is so impressed with you."

"I couldn't have done it without Nora." The words were a reflex even though Katherine didn't want to bring up Nora. Just thinking of her hurt in a way that Katherine couldn't explain.

"Of course." Her mother squeezed her shoulder. "Such a brave young woman. We should call on her tomorrow after breakfast. Show our concern."

*

Dinner was a bit louder than usual. Her father wanted to hear everything that had happened and Katherine wanted to hear all about the competition and what they had won. It was nice. For once there was no heat on Katherine, no complaints or requests. It was strange to bask in her parents' approval. Katherine liked it.

She cleared her throat, deciding to try something now that her parents were in such a good mood.

"Father, maybe next time I could come with you." He looked at her, a small smile playing on his lips. She decided to continue. "I know you don't want me to just work in the stable or be a horse carer, and I want more than that too. I want to compete. I want to be a show jumper." She couldn't believe she had said it. Of course, that had been her goal the whole time but she didn't think she had ever said it so clearly.

She looked at her mother but Sandrine had her gaze firmly on her husband. Her father chuckled.

"I don't think anything keeping you back, you know that, right?" He sighed. "I'm not saying that I fully approve. As much as I understand your love of horses and riding, I don't think it's appropriate for women to spend so much time on horseback." He leaned back and patted his stomach. "If you would have come with me during this show you would have seen what I mean. Only men ride. The only women there were the occasional stable girl or wives and daughters in the audience."

There was something about the way he said it that rubbed Katherine the wrong way, as if women couldn't be there in their own right but with other people. Wives, daughters, sisters… Katherine felt herself making a fist under the table.

"However," her father continued. "I think it's time you started training for real. Your little protégé Nightingale something isn't ready yet but Frankie's Dream is lacking a regular rider since Tom bought his horse. What do you say?"

Katherine's heart started beating fast. Was her father serious? Was she allowed to train to compete? She opened her mouth, ready to thank her father or squeal in joy when there was a small knock on the door.

"Yes?" Her father said.

All of them turned towards the door. Katherine was expecting Mrs. Chapman since she was the only one who ever disturbed them in the evening. The door opened but it wasn't Mrs. Chapman. It was that talkative stable girl, Nora's sister. Martha was her name, wasn't it?

"Hello?" Katherine's mother said. "Is there a problem?"

"Mrs. Waterhouse," Martha said. "Mr. Waterhouse. Miss Waterhouse." She seemed to focus on Katherine with fire in her eyes. "I'm here to talk about my sister, Nora."

"Oh yes." Katherine's mother nodded. "Is she alright? Do we need to call for the doctor again?"

"Umm…" Her mother's friendliness seemed to throw Martha off. She bounced on the heels of her feet and looked to be struggling for words. "No, I don't think she needs the doctor." She took a deep breath. "But she got injured under reckless leadership if you don't mind me saying so."

Everything inside Katherine turned to ice, causing her to stand up.

"Reckless leadership?" She didn't care that her parents were there. "Nora was brave and volunteered, without her I wouldn't have managed. I assumed that somebody under our employment was capable of deciding to help." She didn't know what offended her most, that Martha was accusing her of putting Nora in danger willfully or the suggestion that Nora couldn't decide for herself.

"Katherine!" Her father stood up as well. "Calm down. Miss…" He looked at Martha.

"Lakes, sir," Martha said. She didn't move her gaze from Katherine.

"Miss Lakes," her father continued, "is just worried about her sister. Now I don't think either of you have a cause for yelling, so please sit down."

Katherine pursed her lips and sat down. Inside her, the ice was melting and fumes of anger tethered around her spine. She didn't stop looking at Martha either.

"What are you worried about, Miss Lakes?" Her father said in a calm tone. "I don't think my daughter did anything on purpose. It was an accident."

Martha looked at him then. Her face had gone slightly pink. "Of course not." She swallowed. "I'm just worried, I apologize." She crossed her hands on the front. "What happens now? The doctor has said that she can't work for a week. Does she have to go home? What about her salary? Since she was injured while—"

Katherine couldn't stay quiet, opening her mouth again. Did Martha suggest they would make Nora leave? Or not pay her? Did Martha think they were monsters?

Katherine's mother was quicker.

"There is no need to worry," she held up her hand. "She can of course stay here while resting, eat with the rest of staff like usual and collect her salary on Saturday morning. Nothing has changed."

"Good." Martha nodded. Katherine hated the look on her face.

"Now," her mother said. "What you did now can never be repeated. Do you understand?" Martha's eyes widened. "You've disturbed our dinner and thrown around accusations. That is not acceptable behaviour. You've been travelling all day and you arrived to find your sister injured, so I can sympathise with that. But this can never happen again. If it does, you and your sister will need to find employment elsewhere. Is that clear?"

The clock in the room struck. Martha fiddled with a small hole at the bottom of her shirt.

"Yes ma'am," she said as soon as the clock had stopped ringing. "I'm sorry ma'am." She bowed her head slowly. "Sir. Goodnight." She bowed her head at Katherine's father too before slipping out again. She hadn't looked at Katherine. *I guess I'm not forgiven.* Katherine couldn't care less even though a nagging thought was worming its way into her head. What if Nora blamed her too?

Chapter Seventeen

"There is a letter for you girls." It was Saturday morning breakfast and Martha and Nora were sitting at the big main table. It was the first day in a long time that Nora was up and walking about, making Martha happy. Happy until Mrs. Chapman handed them an envelope.

"I wonder who is writing to us."

Martha bumped her shoulder. "Who do you think?"

"Ma?" Nora looked so confused, Martha wanted to hug her. For their entire lives, Nora had been plagued by the notion that their entire family didn't care about her. An assumption that wasn't correct but rather a reflection of Nora's non-existent self-esteem.

"Well, of course!" Martha hurried to open the letter and they both leaned over it. Nora was a quicker reader and she leaned back, a hand on her chest, when Martha was only half-way.

Dear Nora and Martha,

I can't believe that you're both working now and I hope this letter finds you both well. We heard about the storm that hit a few days ago. I hope the farm wasn't too damaged? We hardly felt it, we're so protected by the tall houses all around us.

Anne is sick. The doctor thinks it is polio. Your pa is taking her and living at another place for a while. I'm worried about Eunice and the others. Not to mention my health, and the health of your new sister or brother. Please pray.

Martha stopped reading, put the letter down, wrinkling it in her hand. She thought of little Anne. Anne with her freckles, funny commentary and warm hugs. What if she died? What if she got injured like… Martha turned her head and looked at Nora. Her sister's face was completely pale and her gaze was stuck to the table.

"Nora?"

"Huh?" Nora looked up. Their gazes locked. "Oh Martha. What are we going to do?"

Martha took Nora in her arms.

"There is nothing we can do," she said. "I know it's not helpful, I'm sorry." She put her hand in Nora's hair and rocked her on the side. "Maybe she'll be okay. Maybe it's not polio and even if it is, she could survive. None of us died when we had it."

"What if she winds up like me?" The words were whispered in Martha's shoulder.

Martha leaned back, grabbed Nora's shoulders and looked at her intently.

"She'd be lucky to be like you."

Nora produced a smile that didn't reach her eyes. She reached up and wiped a tear from her eye.

"I want to visit her." She picked up the letter and scanned it. "It's not like we can get polio again. I wonder where pa took her."

"Probably to one of Uncle Oliver's fishing cabins in Portsmouth," Martha said. "The sea weather will do her well." She calculated in her head. "Portsmouth is far away. It'll take us a whole day to get there by train."

Nora sighed. "We won't manage."

"Maybe if we work a couple of Sundays, the Waterhouses will let us take a whole weekend off. Then we could go." Martha made a grimace that should have been a smile. The thought of asking the Waterhouses for anything didn't feel right. Not after that night she had stormed in and told them off. She still felt shame at the thought. "You should ask. After your heroism, I doubt they would say no to you." She lowered her voice so none of the people around them could hear. "Plus, I think Miss Waterhouse has a soft spot in her heart for you."

"Stop." Nora shook her head. Martha noticed Nora's blushed cheeks. "I don't want to ask. It wouldn't be appropriate. They've already paid me for a week I haven't worked. I don't want to ask for more."

Martha sighed. "I will ask if I get an opportunity. You want to visit Anne, right?"

Nora looked at her. "More than anything."

"So, we should do it."

*

Martha finished the working day as fast as she could, wanting to minimize the risk of running into Miss Waterhouse. *Katherine.* It was a joke that Nora called her by her first name. Martha hadn't even stayed with the horses as much as she wanted, and there had been no brushing or petting. Just mucking and cleaning tack. That's why, after they had dinner, she had pulled Nora with her and gone to the stable. It was quiet now and Martha didn't think they would be disturbed.

When they entered the stable and closed the door behind them, Nora let go of Martha's hand and walked over to… Martha sighed. Of course, Nora went right up to Miss Waterhouse's horse, Nightingale something.

"Hello girl," Nora cooed. "I missed you. Have you learned any new things lately?" She reached over the box wall and scratched the horse's forehead as if she had never done anything else. "Are you ready for Katherine to ride you soon?"

Irritation rose through Martha.

"Can you for the love of God stop calling her Katherine?" She talked a bit louder than necessary and the horse nearest to her threw his head upwards. "Sorry." She walked up to Nora and talked in a lower voice. "Seriously. She's not your friend. She's not your… anything. You're not supposed to call her Katherine. It's…" she threw her hands out. "Unnatural."

"Unnatural?" Nora raised one of her eyebrows and for the first time in her life she managed to look exactly like their sister Emily. "What are you talking about?" She looked back at Nightingale Prancer. "And she is my friend. I don't understand what problem you have with her."

"She's not friendly." Martha sighed. She understood it sounded strange. "She's downright mean. She acts like she's better than everyone."

"She doesn't to me." Nora didn't even turn around now. She kept her gaze on Nightingale Prancer. "She's nice to me. She's friendly to me."

"Maybe a bit too friendly," Martha muttered. She knew she was close to crossing a line but she didn't care. She had looked forward to Nora coming there but nothing was as she had imagined it would be. They weren't bonding over how horrible Miss Waterhouse was or looking at the horses. Instead Nora had been hurt, bedbound and insisted on *liking* Miss Waterhouse. Everything felt upside down.

"What do you mean a bit too friendly?" Nora turned around now but her hand didn't leave Nightingale Prancer's huge head that was leaning over the box wall, seemingly trying to get as close to Nora as possible.

"She's unfriendly to everyone but you." Martha folded her arms over her chest. "Maybe she…" she lowered her voice even further, "likes you in the wrong way."

Nora's eyes went wide and her mouth fell open.

"How dare…" She fell silent when a strange mewing sound filled the stable. "What's that?"

Martha listened intently. There was a small mewing sound coming from one of the boxes. It sounded like the animal was in pain. Martha and Nora forgot about their fight and started looking inside the boxes, searching for the horse that was hurting.

"Martha!" Nora said after a little while. "Look, I found him."

Martha walked up to Nora. She didn't even look inside before opening the latch on the side of the box and pulling at the door. When it was open, she fell to her knees.

"Hello, baby."

It was one of the recently purchased foals. Martha knew that since the foal was alone without a mother. He was lying down, discharge around his mouth, breathing hard, his eyes open.

"Oh no." Nora sank down to the ground next to Martha and put her hand on his neck. "He feels warm."

"Maybe he has some kind of infection." Martha bit her lip. "Wait here, I'm going to get help."

She got up from the floor and didn't even brush the straw from her trousers before running back to the servants' quarters. It was mainly empty since there was a poker game in Shireoaks tonight but Mrs. Chapman was sitting with her feet up, smoking her pipe.

"What's wrong?" Mrs. Chapman said as soon as Martha entered.

"There seems to be something wrong with one of the foals in the stable." Martha leaned with her hand on one of the chairs, out of breath. "Do we have a veterinarian on the premises?"

"Not after hours." Mrs. Chapman stood up. "Do you think it can wait until morning?"

Martha shook her head.

"You can take a bicycle and get him, I suppose." Mrs. Chapman chewed on the end of her pipe. "Or wake up Mr. Waterhouse."

"I'll take a bicycle." Martha didn't even have to think. "I don't want to wake Mr. Waterhouse unless it's necessary."

Mrs. Chapman didn't seem fully convinced but eventually she nodded.

"Okay, take the bicycle, follow the main road, it will lead you to Shireoaks. He lives in a red house next to the pharmacy. I'm unsure about the address but I was there for tea once. His wife is lovely."

Martha nodded, already regretting her decision to ride a bicycle in the middle of the night. Mrs. Chapman got up, and grabbed a small pale of milk that was standing on the sink. She handed it to Martha.

"Take this, in case something happens. I don't have water to give you but I have some milk. Just in case."

What could happen? Martha was just going to cycle there and then cycle back. Nothing was going to happen. She thanked Mrs. Chapman and then exited the servant's building. She was going to tell Nora what was happening and then she was going to head into the night.

Chapter Eighteen

Katherine was almost relieved when the day of the party came around. As much as she had worried about Nora and wanted to see her, she had stayed clear of the Lakes sisters. It was better this way, she told herself, as she got ready and said goodbye to her parents. She took the car, aiming to make an entrance and drove to Shireoaks. Despite several proposals and an offer to study abroad, Cecilia and Charlotte had remained at home. They were twins turning twenty, and seemed to be enjoying their current life too much to change it.

As Katherine turned onto the pathway surrounded by trees that led to the Smith residence, she smiled. If she had a twin sister maybe she would also have been content to spending her days shopping, throwing parties and… Katherine didn't know what else the twins filled their days with but she knew one thing; their parties were legendary.

The stairs leading to the front door were paved with cressets and the music could be heard from the outside. Katherine parked the car near the others and ignored the look of some people she didn't know when she got out. *Play nice,* resisting the sneer that played on her lips. It wasn't their fault they had never seen a woman drive by herself before.

A man wearing a nice suit opened the front door for her and another, younger man, took her coat when she got inside. The younger one smelled faintly of stable which made Katherine believe that this was a stable boy who had been pulled in when they needed more service. He looked nervous and out of place. The look on his face amused Katherine even though she registered on some level that it was mean of her to think so.

"Katherine!" Her thoughts scattered when Charlotte came up behind her. "I'm so glad you made it." Cecilia wasn't far behind. Their dresses were the same style, one red and the other blue. It was a silly way for grown women to dress but it suited the twins. They hugged and then the twins pulled her into the ballroom.

*

Katherine should have been elated. She had just returned from her friends' party in Shireoaks. Everybody had given her comments on her dress or her hair. A man had asked if he could call on her next week. Katherine had said yes even though she wanted to say no. She could just imagine her mother's happiness when a man, a man of age and good stature nonetheless, called on her. And he wasn't that bad, was he? Katherine entertained the idea of maybe entering a relationship. If she found the right man it had the potential of giving her more freedom, not less.

She sighed and walked into the stable, not caring that she was still wearing her party clothes. She wanted a hug from Nightingale Prancer and she thought she would stop by Frankie's Dream and give him a quick pet too. After all, they were going to start training tomorrow. Training for real this time. Katherine couldn't wait.

She opened the box door and slipped in beside her mare.

"Hello girl."

Nightingale Prancer neighed and blew hot air over Katherine's hands.

"I know, I know." She scratched her forehead. "I know I haven't been here for a while." She had told herself - and others - that she had been busy, or recovering from the cold night in the stable. But the truth was she had stayed away, worried about running into Nora or that insolent sister of hers.

"Katherine?" The small voice made her raise her head. At first, she thought she had imagined it but then she heard a small sniff coming from the box next to Nightingale Prancer's.

She got up and put her head over the other box door, peering down. The foal inside was lying down and his head was resting in Nora's lap. *Nora.*

"Are you okay?" Worry filled Katherine. Maybe Nora was more injured than Doctor Tillot had thought. Then she focused on the foal. "Is he okay?"

"I'm alright, thanks," Nora said. "But something is wrong with him." She pat his little neck. The foal barely twitched. "Martha has cycled to get the veterinarian."

"Now?" The road was treacherous in the night and the veterinarian was at least thirty minutes away. "Are you sure? Why would she do something like that?"

Nora looked at her then. A little giggle escaped her. Perhaps it was a nervous giggle but Katherine didn't care. The sound and look of it sent shivers down her spine.

"I don't think she had any other choice. I doubt she dared to go and disturb your parents again." She looked at Katherine shyly.

Katherine's mouth went dry at the sight. The realisation that Katherine liked Nora the way a man likes a woman hadn't made her feel better. It had ramped them up to overdrive. The sherry Katherine had had earlier didn't help either. *How can one person be so beautiful?* The realisation of Nora's words finally sank in and Katherine coughed.

"She told you about that?" Katherine didn't know how she felt. She wondered what Martha had said. And the biggest question - did Nora feel the same way? Did she think that Katherine didn't care that she got injured?

"She did." Nora looked back on the foal and ran her head over his little body. "I can't believe she went to shout at your parents. It's embarrassing. I'm sorry."

"She was just trying to protect you." *I would have done the same.* "My mother was so angry though. It was almost funny. She doesn't get angry often."

"Do you think her job is in danger?" Nora asked. "I would hate if her position is jeopardized because of me."

"No!" Katherine felt her heart drop. "I wouldn't let that happen." Katherine reached out and touched the soft skin of Nora's forearm. She wanted Nora to look at her. "You were truly a hero the other night." She cleared her throat. *Am I smelling like alcohol?* "You will never know how much I regret you getting hurt."

Nora swallowed and took a deep breath. Katherine could see her chest move.

"I think I know," Nora said, biting her lip. "I can feel it." Her eyes widened. "I mean..."

"Don't worry." Katherine worked against the wish to touch her again. She didn't know exactly what Nora meant but she shared the sentiments of feelings. "You don't think I did it on purpose right?"

"Of course not!" Nora shook her head. "I tried to tell Martha, trust me."

"If you hadn't helped me," Katherine said. "I can't stress this enough. If you didn't help me, maybe some of the horses would have gotten injured." She took a deep breath and swallowed her pride. "Even though I didn't enjoy being yelled at, I'm impressed by your sister's dare."

"She is fearless." Nora's voice was full of pride and something inside Katherine ached. *You're not actually jealous of Nora's sister now, are you?* "She has protected me my whole life. Sure, sometimes it gets over the top but, there is no one else who cares for me the way she does."

"That's not true." *What are you saying, Katherine? Stop talking now.* Katherine's heart started a staccato rhythm. She clutched the end of her dress. *You absolute buffoon. What are you doing?*

"It's not?" Nora looked up at her. Her mouth was making an adorable little 'o'. Her expression was so open and innocent. As if she would believe any word that came out of Katherine's mouth.

"Of course not." Katherine couldn't look away. Nora's gaze drew her in. "When you fell, I was more scared than I have ever been before." There. She had said it.

Nora just looked at her. There was dirt smudged on her cheek. Probably from one of the horses. Katherine was just going to wipe it off with her thumb. That's why she rose her hand. That's why she touched Nora's cheek.

"Katherine." Nora had no business saying her name like that. Half whisper, half prayer.

"Oh no." Katherine leaned in and pressed their lips together.

Curse words flew through her head and she felt like she was dying. Nora's lips were soft and damp and she tasted so sweet it made Katherine's head spin. She needed more. She flicked her tongue against Nora's lips on pure instinct. Nora's mouth opened and produced a wailing sound in the back of her throat when Katherine's tongue entered. Katherine had never kissed anyone else but she

119

couldn't believe anyone else could feel as good as Nora did right then.

She felt Nora's hand on her thigh and she reached forward, taking Nora's face in her hands. The skin under her fingers was so soft. *More. Please. More. Nora.*

The sound of the stable door opening made them fly apart. Katherine swallowed, her chest heaving, completely out of breath. She looked over at Nora who was staring at the foal. Her hair was messy; had Katherine done that? Time seemed to slow down as two sets of feet were walking towards them. Nora looked up. The look on her face was one of absolute terror.

"Did I…?" Katherine didn't know what she wanted to ask. *Did I scare you? Did I hurt you? Did you like kissing me? Did I like kissing you?* The last one was an easy question to answer. Katherine knew, without any need for introspection, that that kiss had been the highlight of her life.

Chapter Nineteen

Nora looked at Katherine. She could hear the footsteps getting closer and she wanted to know what Katherine was going to say. She almost reached forward to grab Katherine's hand. *What were you going to say?* Katherine hadn't hurt her. Katherine hadn't scared her. Nora wanted to kiss her again. She hadn't known it was possible to not be in pain. The only things she could feel were her lips and heart and… the train of her thoughts made her almost choke.

The box door opened and Martha came running with the veterinarian in tow.

"We're back!" She stopped while eyeing both of them. "What are you doing here?"

"That was quick," Katherine said. It was interesting to see all of her body language change. She raised her chin. Nora didn't understand how someone who was so gentle with her could look at her sister with so much disdain. "And I live here. These are my horses. I might as well ask what you're doing here."

"I brought the veterinarian."

Nora felt her face heat up from second-hand embarrassment. It was as if Martha and Katherine had forgotten there were other people there. Not just herself but also the veterinarian.

"He is warm." She decided to do the mature thing and focus on what was at hand. "He has been lying down since we found him." Looking at the foal brought all the worry back. Worry about the foal. Worry about Anne, her sister who now had polio. Nora couldn't believe she had forgotten about Anne. Just because Katherine had kissed her.

The veterinarian looked at them. "If you want me to be able to conduct my examination, we can't be four people in here."

This made them move and they all got out of the box under a chorus of 'of course's' and 'excuse me's'. They got out but stayed in line just outside the foal's box. Nora had ended up between Martha and Katherine. Probably wise since the reconciliation between her friend and sister seemed far away.

They looked on in silence as the veterinarian did his thing. Before long he took a big sigh and got up, stepping out of the box. The look on his face told Nora everything. Her heart sank. The foal was so small. So young. It felt cruel that his life would end so soon.

"There is no hope, is there?" she spoke before either Martha or Katherine. She felt like she needed to know; she couldn't stand not knowing for another second.

"He is displaying all of the symptoms of sepsis." The veterinarian looked right at Katherine. "I think we should put him down."

"Please no." Nora couldn't hold the tears back and she silently let them fall. "He is so little. Can't we save him?"

"There is a wound on his leg, miss." The veterinarian looked at her with kind eyes. "Maybe it was just a scratch from the beginning but it's gone black around it."

"Maybe it happened during the storm," Katherine said. "There were so many things happening, I didn't look at the horses to make sure they were fine. I was distracted." She cleared her throat.

Nora gasped inaudibly. She wondered if the distraction Katherine was talking about was her getting injured. And them falling asleep in each other's arms. The veterinarian talking brought her back to reality.

"An infection on a leg like that is disastrous for a young horse. I'm afraid there is nothing we can do."

Nora sobbed. She didn't know why she was so sad. Martha pulled her into a hug.

"It's okay, little sister." Nora leaned her head on Martha's shoulder. It didn't feel okay.

*

Later the same night, as Nora lay next to Martha in their tiny wooden bed, she forgot about the foal. She forgot about Anne. She forgot about everything other than the feeling of Katherine's lips against her own. Nora reached up and touched a finger to her bottom lip. What did the kiss mean? Nora almost didn't dare to entertain the idea that Katherine shared Nora's… Martha produced a snore and moved to the side, making the whole bed shake. Nora sighed and crossed her arms. It didn't feel right thinking about kisses and feelings when your sister was sleeping next to you. She closed her eyes and willed sleep to come. She wanted to take out her diary and sort this out. She wanted to write about her feelings for Katherine. She wanted to write about everything that had happened.

The next morning brought daylight and Nora was glad to be back at work. Preparing the kettles and frying bacon for the Waterhouses and the rest of the workers gave her a much-needed distraction. She wanted to forget about the foal. She even wanted to forget about Katherine. It didn't feel right to do anything that felt good when little Anne was ill somewhere far away. *I need to talk to Katherine about taking a whole weekend off, I'm sure she will...*

"Ouch!" Nora pulled her hand away from the hot part of the kettle. Apparently even thinking about Katherine in the most innocent of ways caused her hands to shake.

"Are you okay, dear?" asked Mrs. Chapman, appearing behind her.

"Yes, yes." Nora put her finger to her mouth and sucked on it. "I just burnt my finger."

Mrs. Chapman offered to look at it but Nora shook her head.

"Oh well, whatever you say." Mrs. Chapman pointed at a tray with bread, butter, jam, and the newly fried bacon. "Why don't you leave the hot kettles to me and you take that out to the family?"

"I thought you wanted to be the one serving the breakfast?" Nora put her hands on the tray but didn't lift it up right away. What if she dropped it? What if she did something to embarrass her and Martha further? She looked down. Every single plate and piece of china seemed delicate, white with small flowers on them. If she dropped it, they would make a lot of noise.

"I'm sure I can trust you." Mrs. Chapman smiled. "Now go on."

Nora swallowed down any nervous energy she was feeling and picked up the tray. Her hands shook a bit and the china rattled. "Careful!" Mrs. Chapman chimed.

Nora steadied her arms and went through the door, entering the dining hall that was adjoined to the kitchen. It was empty now since the Waterhouses ate in the breakfast nook in the morning. It was the first time Nora had ever been inside the main building and she couldn't help but look at her surroundings as she continued walking with the tray.

She had never been to such a fancy house before. The wallpaper was whole and clean. There was a big bookcase with titles Nora had never even heard of. The big table and matching chairs were made of dark oak. A cozy-looking armchair stood in the corner with a matching fluffy pillow. But it wasn't just the furniture that gave her the fancy impression; it was the little things. Porcelain dogs stood on the window sill, paintings hung on the wall and the tablecloth was of lace. Nora didn't consider herself poor. She had never starved and she and her siblings were never on the street. She knew there were people who were less fortunate. And yet, in this house, she felt shabby in a way she never had before.

She heard voices and walked towards them. *It must be the Waterhouses,* she thought, *waiting for their breakfast.* She wondered what Katherine would think, seeing Nora like this, in a servant way. *She would probably regret kissing me.* Nora frowned. She heard the china rattling again and looked down. *I can't think about Katherine, it makes me lose control over m—.* Before Nora could react she heard steps coming towards her. Around the corner came Katherine, walking right into her.

"Oof." The tray was pressed into Nora's body and she lost one of the sides. Luckily Katherine reached out and grabbed it. All that fell was a small plate. It fell to the hardwood floor and shattered into several big shards. They remained standing there, holding the tray together, staring into each other's eyes.

Katherine looked good. Hair dark hair was up and she was wearing a red lipstick that accentuated the paleness of her skin. Nora swallowed. She could feel herself slowly turning into the color of a tomato, making her feel worse. Why did Katherine have to look so beautiful?

Say something! They couldn't just stand there. Katherine's parents could show up at any minute to see what had happened.

"I'm sorry," she managed to get out. "I didn't mean to break a plate."

Katherine stared at her without saying anything, all the color draining from her face. Even her lips looked pale now. *She isn't going to pass out, is she?*

"Katherine!" Nora was worried now.

Katherine swallowed visibly and shook her head lightly.

"Sorry." Her voice sounded hoarse." Don't worry, it was my fault." She smiled but didn't meet Nora's gaze. "I walked into you." She let go of the tray after making sure Nora had it and she leaned down to pick up the pieces of the broken plate. When she straightened up again she stared intently at the tray.

Nora felt embarrassed. She wasn't used to carrying a tray and her arms had started trembling slightly, something that Katherine could see.

"Let me take it." Katherine held out her hands.

"No," Nora said, holding the edge of the tray harder. This made the trembles worse and when Katherine reached out and took a hold of it, Nora let go. "It's not appropriate." She was whispering, feeling stupid. She couldn't even carry a tray to the breakfast nook. She didn't deserve her job. And to seem stupid and useless in front of Katherine, a person she admired and wanted to impress made it even worse.

"Forget about appropriate." Katherine met her gaze now. "Seriously, you've more than proven yourself. I will tell them that I ran into you and thought that I might as well take it the last few steps. My parents won't think about it, I promise."

What about you? Staring into Katherine's eyes, Nora was transported back to last night. She didn't think she would ever forget that sensation of Katherine's lips, her tongue, the way she tasted. *By God, I want more.* That kiss hadn't been enough. Nora didn't think anything would ever be enough.

Her heart was pounding a little bit faster and she hoped Katherine didn't notice as they awkwardly said goodbye and went separate ways. Nora fled back to the kitchen, both dreading and longing for the next time they would meet again.

Chapter Twenty

Sweat was running down Katherine's back, causing her to clutch her thighs harder around the body underneath her, grabbing a new grip of the reins as she steered the horse towards the jump. Even though she had jumped a couple of times before now, it still created butterflies in her stomach. The promise from her father, the promise that he would sponsor her in a show, drove her forward.

"Come on Frankie." Frankie's Dream shook his head and threw himself over the jump in one big leap. It was a short jump but Katherine felt very proud of both herself and the horse. They cantered around the arena and she held him back, preparing them both for the next and final jump. They sailed over that one too and she gently held the reins in until he fell back into a trot and then a walk.

It's important to let them cool off for at least fifteen minutes, her trainer had said. Since he was sitting on the bench watching her, Katherine wasn't going to ignore his advice. She had been so focused on Frankie's Dream during the past forty minutes she hadn't even noticed that Nora had sat down on the bench too and was watching her with a kitten on her lap.

Their gazes met and she nodded at her; her insides sang when she saw her. *Don't smile too wide,* she told herself. She didn't want to show anyone how happy just seeing Nora made her. She continued walking Frankie's Dream around the arena, doing her best to not look at Nora.

It pleased her, however, that every time she did, Nora was looking at her with a brilliant smile on her face.

The weather was on their side. The sun was shining above them, making every leaf and piece of grass in their vicinity shine. The sand underneath Frankie's hooves was dry, and the sky above them was cloud-free.

Her trainer came up to her and she pulled Frankie's Dream into a halt. He pat the horse's neck and looked up at Katherine, shielding his eyes against the sun.

"You're doing well," he said. "There is a local competition in a few months in London. I'm going to enter you and Frankie's Dream."

Katherine's heart started fluttering the same way it had when she kissed Nora.

"Are you sure?" *Why am I whispering?* She cleared her throat. "Are you sure that I'll be ready?"

"I'm sure." Her trainer smiled. "But I have one more job for you before today is over."

"Oh?"

"There is a show today over at Worksop Livery. I want you to go and look at it. Get familiarised with the praxis at these things."

Katherine agreed. She de-mounted Frankie's Dream and walked with him over to the stable. Nora caught up with her, still carrying the little orange kitten.

"That looked amazing." Nora touched her arm quickly, causing little shivers to travel down Katherine's already wet spine. She shivered. "I don't think I'd ever dare to jump with a horse. I keep thinking you're going to fall." Nora bit her lip. It was adorable. "But you never do."

Katherine chuckled. She took the bridle off Frankie's Dream and put his halter on instead, tying him to the stable wall.

"I have fallen off many times. If you haven't, you aren't riding horses often enough." She put the bridle around her shoulder and undid the girdle as Frankie's Dream put his head down to eat from the bucket of hay she had placed there before they left. "It could be that they're bucking out happiness or maybe they saw something that scared them." She took the saddle off. "Or it could be as simple as them wanting to eat grass." She looked at Nora. She had never talked to anyone who seemed to be listening so intently before. "I was about thirteen at the time, riding Unicorn. Maybe you have seen him, he is a stubborn little biter who both I and my brother learned to ride on." Nora nodded.

"He is that grey one, right?" She pointed at Unicorn who was walking in a nearby pasture, his belly fatter and rounder than ever.

"Yes. Just wait, I'll be back." Katherine walked into the saddle chamber, leaving the saddle, quickly cleaning the bit and then leaving the bridle too. She grabbed a bucket of brushes; Frankie's Dream was sweaty and needed care.

When she got back, Nora had let go of the kitten and instead was standing by Frankie's Dream's head and talking to him in such a soft voice. Katherine couldn't tell what she was saying, as she was cradling his mule in her hand and her other hand was scratching his neck. The sight filled Katherine with warmth. *I've turned her into a proper horse lover, haven't I?*

When Katherine came closer, Nora looked up and took a step back. Her cheeks shone as if Katherine had caught her doing something wrong. *Don't worry, it's not like we were kissing.* Katherine bit her comment back.

"Where was I?" she said instead.

"Unicorn." Nora smiled. She grabbed one of the brushes without Katherine saying anything. They started brushing one side each.

"Oh yes," Katherine said. "The story isn't exactly long. I was going for a hack on Unicorn. We were climbing on a small trail on the hill. Leonard, that's my brother, told me to hold on to Unicorn's mane to not fall off. It's going upwards, so I'm standing up in the stirrups to relieve the weight for Unicorn's back, holding his mane and leaning forward. We get to the apex of the hill," their gazes meeting over Frankie's Dream's back, "and before I know it, Unicorn is trying to eat the grass. His back becomes a slide and I fall forward. To the ground, headfirst."

"No!"

Katherine could see the giggles forcing their way through Nora's body, making her laugh too.

"It was so embarrassing," she said. "And when I turned around, sitting on my behind on the muddy trail, Unicorn wasn't even looking at me. He was busy eating."

Katherine stopped her movement and looked at Nora, biting her lip.

"When do you have to be back at work?" *Are you actually doing this?* Katherine couldn't believe her own guile but the prospect of spending the entire day with Nora was too enticing.

"After dinner," Nora said. "I do the dishes."

"Want to go to a show with me?" Katherine talked very fast, equally scared of what she was saying and that Nora was going to say no.

She didn't dare to look at her now and looked down on Frankie's Dream instead. He had been sweaty when they had finished but his coat was shining now and he was standing still with his head lowered. He seemed to be so relaxed he was sleeping.

"Do you really want me to come?"

Are you joking? Katherine wondered if Nora was thinking about their kiss as much as she was.

"Yes." *Please.*

*

Katherine showered, changed into a white shirt, grey skirt and panty-hose plus, brushed her hair, and met Nora by the parking lot. Nora had changed out of her working clothes too and was wearing the same dress as she had when they had met in Shireoaks. She looked just as pretty now as then but there was life in her eyes and color in her face that hadn't been there then. She looked healthy. Katherine couldn't help herself when she walked around the car and opened the door, hoping that no one could see her from the window.

She started the car and quickly put it in drive, wanting to get away from there. When they had gotten out on the road, lush fields on both sides, the sun above them, the future in front of them, Katherine felt unsure. Nora and she hadn't been fully alone since the night with the foal and both of them knew what had happened then. Fighting against the urge to touch a finger to her lips, Katherine glanced at Nora without moving her head, hoping that she wouldn't notice that Katherine was looking. Nora was looking out of the window and humming in a small voice.

She seems relaxed enough, Katherine thought, almost feeling offended that Nora seemed so comfortable in her presence. Did she not think about their kiss as Katherine did? Did she not wonder when they could kiss again as

Katherine did? Did Nora not wonder what their kiss meant as Katherine did?

"Katherine?" For a second Katherine worried that she had said any of her thoughts out loud.

"Huh?" They passed a hole in the road that made the car bump; usually, Katherine was more careful. "Oh sorry."

"Don't worry," Nora said. "I was just asking what kind of show we're going to but you seemed to not be listening."

"No, no, I was listening, I just…" Katherine blinked a couple of times, telling herself to focus. "Sorry, I guess I was just dreaming. We are going to a jumping show. My trainer wants me to pay attention to how it's done and learn. Have you ever been to a show before?"

"No," Nora said.

Chapter Twenty-One

Nora felt silly to admit such a thing, never having been at a horse show before. There seemed to be a cleft between them. They had grown up in such different places and had such different experiences. They might as well have grown up on different planets. Nora could tell, just from the few weeks she had stayed at Waterhouse Acre Stables, that Katherine's planet was better.

There was so much she wanted to tell Katherine, so much she wanted to ask her and talk about but she didn't dare, so she just looked out of the window. Katherine seemed terribly distracted anyway and Nora wasn't sure Katherine was even able to respond. She wanted to ask her about permission for Martha and her to go to Portsmouth and visit Anne, who was recently diagnosed with polio. She wanted to talk about their kiss. More than anything she wanted to talk about Katherine. What her childhood was like. If she was close with her brother. Why she wanted to work with horses. What scared her. What made her happy. Nora wanted to know everything.

She focused on the world outside instead. Everything was so beautiful, Nora couldn't be in a bad mood. Instead, she kept her gaze on the horizon and hummed one of her favorite songs. It was hours before they would go back to Waterhouse Acre Stables. There was time to ask her later.

Within the hour they arrived and Katherine parked the car next to the others. Before Katherine had turned off the engine, Nora hurried to open her door. She had never gone in Katherine's car without Katherine opening the door for her. It made Nora feel strange and she wasn't entirely sure if it was in a good or a bad way. Nora soon forgot to overthink things, instead of focusing on the surroundings. She noted the cars and the wooden stands with the riding arena behind them. There was a stable on the side, smaller than the one at Waterhouse Acre Stables, with chipped wood and a small field with a white picket fence.

The air was crisp outside, smelling of leather, horses, and manure. It was a smell Nora was learning to love. It didn't just remind her of her new home, her new life, her new independence. It was a scent that reminded Nora of Katherine and that made it so much sweeter.

A loud male voice was shouting information from the speakers, asking the first contestant to get ready and for the spectators to sit down on the wooden stands around the arena. The courtyard was full of people. Trainers and riders, sponsors in black or grey suits. Families. Women in beautiful hats or furs. Children in expensive clothing, with pigtails and smiling faces. Everyone seemed to be moving a different way. Nora felt like she was stuck on a small rock on a lake that couldn't decide on the current direction. The sights, the smells, the sounds. She swallowed. What if she was lost in all of this? What if she fell? What if everyone trampled her? *Okay, now you're being silly. Just enjoy.*

"Come on." All of a sudden Katherine was by her side, grabbing her arm and guiding her through the crowd. "Don't worry, I'll make sure you find somewhere to sit."

Most of the seats were already taken. Katherine elbowed her way through the crowd with Nora behind her, throwing herself over two seats on the left side. The bench was wooden and a piece of wood underneath cut into her calves but Nora didn't care. She couldn't believe she was out with Katherine to watch a horse show of all frivolous things. She could have stood for the entire show if necessary. She was too busy drinking it all in to notice if she was uncomfortable.

"Wait for a second, hold my seat." Katherine got up and Nora put her hands on Katherine's seat, almost falling forward, hoping that no one would try to sit there. She followed Katherine's back, smiling when she saw what her friend was doing. Before long, Katherine came back carrying two caramel apples on sticks.

She handed one to Nora then sat down with a thump on the other seat. She stretched her back, put one hand behind her head, and leaned backward. The sigh she expelled was one of relaxation. It helped Nora release her stress too.

"Let's see then," Katherine said. "My trainer wanted me to pay extra attention to a woman called Patricia Roberts Smith, one of the biggest women in show jumping right now. Her father was one of the founding members of The British Jumping Association."

"I didn't even know there was such a thing." Nora had her eyes glued to the arena.

"It's good that they exist," Katherine said quickly. "There used to be so much bad information out there. At first, it was just the military jumping, leaning backward instead of forwards as we do now. That's worse for the horse. And the rider."

The first equipage was coming onto the arena now. The large horse had a shiny black coat. "A thoroughbred," Katherine whispered close to Nora's ear. The small puff of air-filled Nora with a million small butterflies and she suppressed a giggle. She zoned in on the horse instead. It really was beautiful and she understood Katherine's breathlessness.

The man on top held the reins short as they trotted around the arena. At halfway they broke into a gallop. The crowd calmed down as if they collectively held their breath as the rider steered his horse towards the first jump, a red gate. They flew over it in a fluid movement, reminding Nora of something out of a fairytale.

Nora leaned forward so that Katherine could hear her.

"That's so beautiful. I understand why you like it."

At Nora's words, Katherine turned around. Their faces were so close, Katherine's smile so pretty, half-way between happy and surprised.

"Thank you," she said. *Did she just look at my lips?* "It means a lot that you understand."

"Of course," Nora whispered. She licked her lips and if she didn't know better, she thought Katherine was looking at them. *There are people all around,* Nora's mind said when her soul was screaming at her to kiss her again. Their faces drifted closer to one another. Katherine's eyes widened and her complexion changed. *Not here,* she mouthed.

That moment the crowd cheered and Katherine turned towards the arena, as did Nora. The rider on the black horse had finished, waving at the spectators as he exited.

Nora hoped that Katherine wasn't upset that Nora had distracted her while he jumped, but Katherine looked relaxed. She leaned back in her seat, keeping her gaze on the arena. She didn't even look distracted. Nora however, couldn't forget what Katherine had said before turning back to the arena. *Not here.* Nora sighed and wiggled her toes inside her shoes. *Not now.* Surely *not now* meant later. *Not now* didn't mean never. *Not now* meant that Katherine was planning to kiss her again.

*

The rest of the show continued but Nora couldn't pay attention anymore. The horses were beautiful and at first, it was exciting to see man after man making their way around the arena. But after a while, it got a bit boring. Since Katherine had brought her, Nora was fighting not to show it. She didn't want to be anywhere else, she just couldn't focus properly on what was happening. Instead, she was paying attention to Katherine or looking at the people sitting near them. It was interesting to see what kind of people went to horse shows. It seemed to be single men or families, no single women other than Katherine and Nora.

It's a man's world, Nora thought and stretched her back. She had known so already of course but she hadn't thought about it being a problem before seeing Katherine trying to make her own way.

"It's her." Katherine gently tapped Nora's arm with her elbow. "Patricia Roberts Smith."

Nora looked with interest at the equipage that came trotting into the arena. At first, it wasn't even clear that it was a woman riding. Ms. Smith looked and moved like any man on top of the horse, except her body was smaller and softer and Nora could see that she had a chest. Otherwise, there was no difference. Her horse was white, with a small head and a long flowy tail. Its mane was braided and it looked like a unicorn without a horn.

Nora and Katherine stayed quiet while Ms. Smith made her way around the arena, over the gates, and bounce jumps. She looked to be completely in control, steering her horse with small movements. Nora had moved to the edge of her seat and held her breath. She wanted Ms. Smith to not just do as well as the men but better. She wanted Ms. Smith to win. To win all of it.

When Ms. Smith and her unicorn cantered across the finish line, the crowd roared and Nora applauded until her palms were burning. Without thinking she wrapped herself around Katherine's arm and leaned in close.

"That was amazing!" She laughed. "Do you think she will win?"

Katherine didn't pull her arm from Nora's grip. Just that was a win.

"The judges are going to calculate the points," she said. "In just a few minutes, we'll know."

When Ms. Smith was awarded second place, Katherine and Nora cheered. The winners came back into the arena and the judges came in to put ribbons on the horses' bridles. Nora didn't care about the others but kept her gaze fixed on Ms. Smith. Her horse got a red and silver ribbon. She looked up at the crowd and smiled widely.

"She is so brave," Nora said to Katherine. "I'd never dare to compete with so many men like that."

Katherine snorted and opened her mouth. She closed it again and chuckled. "I was about to say something that I can't say here."

"In the car then." Nora bit her lip.

Katherine looked at her. "If I remember." Her eyes twinkled.

The winners galloped around the arena and then it was finished. The crowd started dispersing. The sellers of apples and popcorn and chips disappeared. Nora got up on wobbly legs, as sitting for so long had made her stiff. She toppled, thinking that she was going to fall over but Katherine lent her a hand. When they were down on the ground again, they let go of each other, and Nora walked behind Katherine, making their way back to the car.

Katherine opened the door for her like usual and Nora sighed as she sat down. The car seat was much more comfortable than the wooden bench. As soon as Katherine had sat down and started the engine, Nora couldn't wait anymore.

"What were you going to say before?" Nora asked. "When we were talking about Ms. Smith."

Katherine's mouth fell open and then she produced a loud laugh that Nora had never heard from Katherine before. It was contagious and she snickered, hoping that Katherine would soon say whatever it was that was on her mind.

"Oh, it's just that." Katherine chuckled again. "There is nothing in the penis that makes you a better rider."

"Oh." Nora's face went red. What was Katherine saying? That didn't sound like something a young lady from a rich family should say. That sounded more like a comment from Martha's mouth or perhaps one of Nora's other sisters. "Oh, I see."

Katherine glanced at her and chuckled again.

"I've made you all embarrassed, I'm sorry." She didn't look sorry at all.

"It's okay," Nora said. "I'm from London, remember? I'm used to the rough language, I just…" she coughed. "I didn't expect it from you."

"No but seriously." Katherine nodded her head. "If you think about it. Why are most riders men? You saw Patricia Roberts Smith come in second place. If she had just been a few seconds faster, she would have been in first place. If she can do it, I can do it. Anybody that wants to can do it."

"I suppose." Nora couldn't find any reason to disagree. "It just seems a bit strange." She looked for proper words. "Most girls or women I know aren't interested in anything other than finding a man and having children." She thought about the people in her own family. "Except for Martha I suppose, but even she's had a boyfriend. My older sister is married with a child. My two younger sisters talk about nothing but boys." Talking about her siblings reminded Nora about Anne. *I need to ask Katherine about going to Portsmouth.*

"And what about you?"

"What about me?" They passed a field that held several cows. Nora looked at a little calf following its mother with a smile.

"What do you dream about?" Katherine didn't look at her. "Husband? Children? A home of your own?"

"Oh." Nora touched a hand to her chest. No one had ever asked her that before. "I don't actually know."

Katherine puffed.

"What do you mean you don't know?"

Nora sighed. "Because… because…" she could hear the annoyance in her own voice but couldn't stop it. "Because I don't have a future."

"Of course, you have a future. What kind of talk is that?" Katherine's tone of voice was very dismissive and it lit a fire in Nora.

"You don't understand what it's like! My whole childhood was just everyone waiting for me to die. The very week before I was offered the job I have, my ma told me that no one would ever want to hire me. Why would a man want me? Can I become a mother? We don't even know how long I'll live." Nora swallowed back tears. "What's the point?" She sobbed and turned away from Katherine. She was making a fool of herself. *Well, now Katherine is never going to ask me to go anywhere again.*

Katherine violently turned the wheel to the left and drove into a small groove. She stopped the car and turned off the engine.

"Nora." Her voice was gentle and soft like honey. "Please look at me."

I don't want to. There was dust on the car door and Nora wiped it with her finger. Katherine reached over, grabbed a hold of her chin, and forced her to turn.

There were many things Nora expected to see in Katherine's face. Disgust, pity, discomfort. She didn't see any of that. Her heart sped up when Katherine leaned in. She puckered her lips, closed her eyes, getting ready. But Katherine didn't kiss her lips, instead she pressed a kiss to each of Nora's cheeks. Light as butterflies and just as sweet.

"There." Katherine beamed. "Now calm down and listen to me." She kept her hand on Nora's chin.

Nora nodded, wordlessly. Her heart was pounding and sweat was running between her breasts. She didn't know whether if it was the August heat or Katherine's gaze that was making her perspire.

"Now first of all," Katherine said, speaking in a calm tone, "I didn't mean to upset you with my question. You're right. I don't know what it's like to be you. I don't know what it's like to not know the limits of my own body. I don't know what it's like to fear death." She let go of Nora's chin and put her hands in her lap. Nora immediately missed her touch. "With that said, I think you're allowed to have dreams." Katherine bit her lip. "If you want a man, you will find one that wants you. Not all couples have children. And my parents have a couple of friends who actually adopted a child from another country. If that's what you want to do, that's what you should do. No excuses." She touched her hand to Nora's. "As for me, I'm going to be a world-renowned horse rider." She grinned and stretched her back, looking so proud that it made Nora chuckle. She reached up and wiped her tears. Katherine handed her a handkerchief.

"Thank you." She dried her cheek and tried to hand it back but Katherine just waved her hand and Nora put it on her lap. It had lace on the side and it was embroidered, sporting a *K* and a *W*. Nora ran her hand over the letters. *Katherine Waterhouse,* that must be what the letters stood for. Katherine. Katherine who tried so hard to understand her.

Nora cleared her throat. It was now or never.

"Katherine?" Another tear fell and she wiped it up right away.

"What is it?"

"My little sister Anne, she's got polio as well. My pa has gone away with her to not put the rest of the family in danger. They're staying at my uncle's house in Portsmouth. Martha and I want to go and visit but we need more time than just Sunday. We were wondering if we could work a few Sundays to make up for taking a few extra days off around a weekend maybe next week."

Katherine raised her eyebrows. "Are you asking me because neither you nor your sister dares to ask my father?"

Nora felt her cheeks redden and nodded.

"My sister has, as you know, already made quite a fool of herself."

Katherine smiled. "I'm sorry your sister is ill." She touched her hand to Nora's again. "Of course, you can go to Portsmouth. My parents are nice people. My mother is big on charity and they wouldn't say no."

Nora didn't hear the end of that sentence, all she heard was 'Portsmouth' and 'you can go' and she was filled with so much relief and happiness. Giddy emotions filled her and gave her the bravery she needed. Tears forgotten, her past forgotten, their roles forgotten; Nora moved forward, put a hand on the back of Katherine's neck, and kissed her.

Chapter Twenty-Two

Something is going on. Martha couldn't put her finger on it but she knew that something was wrong. It had started almost immediately after Nora had moved to Waterhouse Acre Stables and grown a bit every day since then. Nora had stayed there for over a month and by now, Martha's gut was telling her that something bad was about to happen.

It wasn't like her to be overly suspicious but ever since Nora had come back from an excursion with *Katherine,* giddy with stars in her eyes, Martha's suspicions were growing. The smile she had on her mouth when telling Martha that they could go and visit Anne should have been a sign enough. A sign that Nora was… what? Infatuated? In love?

Martha kicked the hay bale, anger rising through her. It had been a week since the Portsmouth trip and she was still angry. Angry at Anne being ill. Angry at her mother having lost the baby. Angry at Nora and how she didn't feel like she was able to protect her.

"How I was I supposed to know that I was bringing my defenseless little sister to a place with a… with a… with a lecher?" Martha muttered under her lips. The stable was empty save for Unicorn who had eaten too much grass and needed to stay inside for the day. Plenty of room for Martha to growl at herself.

Of course, she hadn't had confirmation that something going on between them. *I'm not stupid.* Martha dumped straw in one of the empty boxes. She could see it in

Nora's eyes. That was the look of someone in love. And Katherine… Martha spat on the ground… was the only one Nora had been spending time with.

Something must be wrong with her. Martha went back to get more straw. *Taking advantage of a cripple like Nora.* Martha's insides hurt when she thought of Nora. Her poor sister! Nora always thought of herself more capable than she was. Katherine had to be a monster, showing interest in someone like that. Giving Nora the hope that she would find love, only to let her down later.

Having finished the boxes, Martha left the stable, walking over to the courtyard with her thoughts still running. She wanted to clean up before dinner. There was straw and hay in her hair and dirt under her fingernails. Mrs. Chapman would be cross with her if she showed up like that at the dinner table and that was the last thing Martha needed.

Maybe it's that time of the month, Martha thought when she entered the bathroom. She decided to run a bath and reached for the two faucets above the tub. They were rusty and hard to turn like usual but Martha knew it would be worth it. There was a rumbling pain starting in her lower abdomen. *Ugh.* Martha always became stressed out during her period but usually she directed that aggression towards herself, not Nora, and not someone outside the family.

She undressed with a sigh and sank into the warm water of her bath. She leaned with her back towards the tub wall and closed her eyes. Maybe she was taking the Nora thing too personally. It was only because it reminded her of Gwendolyn. Martha scoffed. Yeah, Gwendolyn, right. She meant Mrs. Allen.

Mrs. Allen was just a distant memory now. A memory from almost three years ago. A memory of hugs, kisses, fluttering feelings and hope. In the end, of course Mrs. Allen hadn't left her husband, but dropped Martha like a hot potato as soon as her husband came back from the war. Their kisses hadn't mattered. Martha's feelings hadn't mattered.

Martha sank deeper and let her face emerge fully in the water. She held her breath. Mrs. Allen. She hadn't thought about her for at least a year. She had buried it deep inside her memory, too painful to think about.

The soap was slippery and she almost dropped it; halfway disgusted that it had recently been used, she washed herself quickly. *Boys, I mean men, are just as nice anyway.* Martha didn't know if everyone could be attracted to the same sex. She knew, however, that men were just as interesting to her as women were. And she would rather choose a normal life than the one of a—

The water was turning cold and Martha didn't want to waste any time. At other times she had offered Nora to share the water before pulling the plug but Nora was helping Mrs. Chapman. Martha didn't feel like talking to Nora anyway.

"She's being stupid," Martha muttered to herself as she dried off. "Even if she happens to like women too, doesn't mean she has to act on it." *Maybe I should find a nice man for her. So, she can see.* Deep down, something ached inside Martha when she thought those words. But Nora was her little sister, Martha was supposed to look after her. Especially since it was Martha's fault. She was the one who had introduced her to a sexual predator. Anger flared up inside her when she thought of Katherine. Martha had to do something. And soon.

Chapter Twenty-Three

The wood on the bench was cold and damp; Nora could feel it through her dress. She pulled the shawl her mother had sent her closer around her shoulder. Sir Phil, one of the stable cats, came and stroked himself on her legs. Nora mindlessly put her hand down and scratched his head. It was enough to make him purr. She hardly registered it as her eyes were fixed on Katherine and Nightingale Prancer, who was walking around the paddock. Arthur, one of the stable boys, was walking next to the equipage, leading the horse.

Nora's insides were a tangled mess of happiness and nerves. It was the first time Katherine was sitting up on Nightingale Prancer. Everything was going well and Nora stayed seated even though she knew she had to leave any minute to go and help Mrs. Chapman prepare dinner. She just wanted to stay there for a little while longer, breathing in the cold air, smelling the comforting scent of horses and manure, keeping her gaze fixed on her favorite horse and person.

Nightingale Prancer threw her head and increased speed, tripping like a ballet dancer going forward. Katherine stilled her movement and straightened her back. Nightingale Prancer was a young horse and Katherine had explained to Nora that a young horse was especially skittish. Nora crossed her fingers under the shawl, hoping that everything would work out.

When Nightingale Prancer and Katherine walked by on the side closest to Nora, their gazes met and Katherine threw her a winning smile. *She's so pretty.* Nora returned the smile. She couldn't help but think back to the last time they had been in a car together. The kisses that they shared. How soft Katherine's arms felt when they were around her. Nora felt her face heat up and almost hoped that Katherine would see it. She wanted Katherine to know what she was thinking about.

*

This is the best day I had ever had, Katherine thought as Frankie's Dream threw himself over another box jump. She was on a roll. First, she had ridden Nightingale Prancer for the first time and it had been successful - then had eaten a lunch that Nora had prepared for her - now she was training on Frankie's Dream and she was finally feeling like a future within horse jumping was possible. She finished the rest of the jumps and slowed Frankie's Dream into a walk. She let him cool off and her thoughts drift, relaxing. A wind came through the paddock, making some leaves rustle, but Frankie's Dream just flicked his ears and Katherine pat his neck. She walked him to the middle and climbed off, taking him into the stable to brush him inside the box. Usually she preferred brushing them outside but the wind was picking up and autumn rain hung in the air like a silent promise.

Frankie's Dream seemed to enjoy being inside too. There was hay on the box floor and he started eating as soon as she released him. When Katherine closed the box to go and get the brushes, Nora was walking towards her, carrying the bucket with the brushes. At the sight of her, Katherine's heart did a happy dance. Nora smiled shyly at her.

"I saw you come in with Frankie's Dream. I thought I would help you."

I Love you, Nora Whispered

Just the sight of you helps me more than anything else. Katherine's mouth went dry and she couldn't stop her actions. Completely oblivious to her surroundings, she walked up to Nora, put an arm around her waist and pulled her closer. She leaned down and kissed her. A small noise of surprise escaped Nora but it quickly turned into a gentle humming sound. Katherine had been right, this was one of the best days she had ever—

"What are you doing?" Martha's voice rang inside the stable.

Nora stiffened and pulled away but Katherine didn't let go of her waist. She didn't care that Martha had seen them.

"Martha…" she started but Martha was quicker. She walked towards them with her fist raised. She pointed a finger in Katherine's face.

"What do you think you're doing?" Her face was red, all her freckles standing out in sharp contrast.

"Martha, we weren't…"

Martha ignored Nora completely and looked only at Katherine.

"Have you no shame? Taking advantage of Nora like that."

Katherine's insides turned into ice. Any fire or happiness she had had disappeared and she went numb. She let go of Nora and crossed her arms.

"Do you have such low thoughts of your sister?" She didn't take a single step back even though Martha was still inching her way closer. Katherine wasn't one to be intimidated.

"You know she isn't like other people."

"Hey—" Nora's voice came from behind Katherine.

"My sister," Martha continued, "my sister doesn't know what's good or bad for her." Martha sighed. "She needs care. Not to have someone take advantage of her."

"Take advantage of her?" Katherine felt like growling. "You think I'm taking advantage of her? I want nothing but—"

"Enough!" It was the loudest Katherine had ever heard Nora's voice sound. It echoed through the stable and Frankie's Dream jumped in his box.

"How dare you!" Nora got in front of Katherine, looking at Martha. "Is that what you think of me? As some helpless little girl? As an... invalid?" Nora's voice was breaking and her whole body was trembling. Katherine reached out and touched her shoulder. Nora turned around fast. "And you? Standing in front of me like I need you to protect me." Her eyes were shining with unshed tears. She closed her mouth, her grimace one of disgust. "I expected more from the both of you." She sobbed once. Then she turned around and ran out of the stable leaving Martha and Katherine behind.

"I've always known there is something wrong with you."

Katherine couldn't believe Martha dared to talk with her like that. *I should get her fired,* she thought, but decided against it. What would Nora think of her then? Would Nora even keep her job if Katherine got Martha fired? And what reason should she give to her father for wanting to fire Martha?

"I'm not the one who just hurt Nora." Katherine was tired and her tone conveyed it. "I have to brush Frankie's Dream, please leave."

Martha crossed her arms. "I think it's time for Nora and I to find a new place to work."

Anger made Katherine's nostrils flare. She dropped the brush she had just picked up.

"Are you seriously going to cost Nora her job as well?" She stared Martha down. "You really have such little faith in her?"

Martha's eyes shifted but she didn't say anything else. She just made a small *hnf* and left the stable. Katherine's heart was pounding hard. She picked up the brush and went back into the box to brush Frankie's Dream. Katherine wasn't one for being melodramatic. *So why do I feel like this is the beginning of the end?*

Chapter Twenty-Four

Angry tears were flowing down Nora's cheeks, hitting the hay bale she was sitting on. In her anger she had run to the back of the stable and climbed the gnarly ladder up to the hay loft. She must have climbed it on raging adrenaline because now her body was hurting as bad as her heart and she had no idea how she was going to get down again.

"Serves them damn right," crossing her arms, "if I never see them again." She sighed. If she died up on the hayloft, it would probably just prove them right. That she couldn't take care of herself. That she needed them taking care of her. Nora didn't need them, she wasn't as weak and helpless as they thought.

She clenched her fists and worked against the wish to hit her own chest in anger. More tears pressed themselves out. *Oh, if I could just stop crying.* When you wanted to be angry it was embarrassing to cry instead. She lifted her foot to kick the wall but lost her balance and fell backwards with a yelp instead.

Not a moment later somebody was climbing the ladder and Martha peeked her head over the edge.

"So, this is where you're hiding." She got up and sat next to Nora.

"I'm not hiding," Nora said. "I want to be alone. Please leave."

"Can we talk?" Martha reached out but Nora moved out of her reach. "Please, I didn't mean to hurt you."

"You embarrassed me." Nora kept her gaze on the horizon. She couldn't look at Martha right now. "All my life I thought you were the one who treated me like normal. The one who didn't just see somebody sickly and *useless*." Goodness, she was going to cry again. "Katherine likes me! For me! She wants to kiss me and hold me and she listens to me."

Martha didn't answer. Nora didn't look at her but when Martha had continued being silent for quite a while, Nora glanced at her. Her sister was biting her lip as if there was something she wanted to say but knew she shouldn't. She was looking at the horizon, not at Nora.

"What?" Nora's heart was pounding again. So hard it hurt. *Please don't say it, Martha, don't say it, please, I trust you.*

"Well." Martha talked slowly. "Why does she like you?"

Nora felt like she had been slapped. She brought her hand up to her chest. In one way she was surprised she was still breathing, that Martha's cruel words hadn't killed her right then and there.

"I know it sounds harsh, but Nora." Martha reached for her and Nora didn't move away. There was no point. She couldn't feel Martha's hand on her shoulder anyway. She didn't think she would be able to feel anything ever again. "Nora, my darling, she's a lady of society. Older than you. More experienced than you. She comes from a nice family and goes to parties where they serve champagne. She is served dinner every night in that beautiful dining room. Do you think she has ever heard her parents fight over money? Or assisted her mother in childbirth like you and I did once when the doctor wasn't fast enough?" Martha sighed. The grip on Nora's shoulder became harder.

"You are my best friend. There is no one on this earth I love more than you. You are my sister. I couldn't bear to see that sexual deviant take advantage of you."

The words hung between them. Nora didn't know what to say or do. She kept her gaze on the horizon. On the pastures. The horses. She could see Unicorn grazing in the field, next to Tampas, Frankie's Dream, and other horses she hadn't learned the names of but had hoped to.

"I need to leave." She sighed. "I can't stay here. I need to go back to London. Right now." She couldn't imagine staying there another night. Another day. Another hour. Another minute. She stood up. "I think I should go and speak to Mrs. Chapman."

"Wait a second." Martha reached for her again but this time Nora stepped out of her reach. She was getting closer to the edge. Her joints were hurting but maybe she would manage the climb down without injuring herself too badly. "Let's leave it a few days at least. We have a new paycheck coming in a few days. It also gives me some time to inquire about new jobs for us."

Nora nodded. She didn't want to talk to Martha anymore. She had gone numb. She didn't know if she agreed with Martha or not. She peeked over the edge, half expecting, half wishing, Katherine to be down there, looking up at her. Nora didn't even know what she would have done if Katherine would have been there. How it would feel to see her.

"How could I have been so stupid?" Nora didn't know how she hadn't seen it before. Why would a woman like Katherine be interested in someone like Nora? It had been for nefarious purposes. A breeze came by, rustling her clothes and her hair. Goosebumps stood up on the back of her neck.

"You weren't stupid." Martha came up to stand next to her. "And you are lovely, you know that. Adorable. Pretty. Kind. There is a man out there for you. That I promise you. But someone of our standing and background. Someone back in London. Someone who can socialize with our family without our poor ma having a heart attack."

"I suppose you're right." But something inside Nora was whispering that Martha was very, very wrong. She felt anger still moseying somewhere deep in her core.

Martha went down the ladder first just so that she could catch Nora if she fell. Nora's joints felt like they were made of tin. She held on until her hands turned white but she managed down the ladder without falling or getting help. They walked across the courtyard and into the servants' quarters. As soon as they entered, Mrs. Chapman announced that Mrs. Waterhouse was looking for them.

Nora went up to the main house, insisting that Martha stayed behind. If Mrs. Waterhouse was going to fire her or embarrass her in some other way, Nora wanted to be alone. There was no other reason why Mrs. Waterhouse could want to talk with her. That much was clear; Katherine must have said something. The timing was too perfect.

The stones leading up to the main building were wet as it started to rain. Nora felt like she was walking to her execution. Whatever Mrs. Waterhouse was going to tell her, she deserved. She should have never begun a relationship with Katherine.

The door was opened by a man Nora had never seen before. His outfit screamed butler, but surely if he was a butler, Nora would have seen him before.

"I'm here to see Mrs. Waterhouse," Nora said.

The man nodded and stepped aside, letting her in. He led her to the sitting room that Nora remembered from carrying the breakfast tray almost every morning for the past week. Mrs. Waterhouse was sitting on one of the chairs, a book on her lap. She was wearing a dark green dress of a fabric Nora didn't recognize. It certainly wasn't cotton.

When Nora came in, Mrs. Waterhouse stood up and walked towards her in quick strides.

What is happening? Mrs. Waterhouse's smile was scaring Nora. Was Mrs. Waterhouse happy that Nora had done a bad thing? Maybe she liked firing people.

"Dear girl, I have some great news!"

Dear girl? Nora stood still as Mrs. Waterhouse grasped a hold of her shoulders.

"Do you remember Doctor Tillot who gave you a check-up after that horrible storm?"

Nora nodded, not daring to say anything.

"He contacted us wondering if you would consider being part of a new study."

Nora swallowed, her head swimming. She had been so sure of what Mrs. Waterhouse was going to say that she couldn't fully understand what was happening.

"A new study?" She blinked a couple of times and was happy that Mrs. Waterhouse's hands were still on her shoulders. She was about to fall. "Can I sit down please?" She didn't care if it was proper or not. Her knees were trembling.

"Of course, of course." Mrs. Waterhouse put her down on the sofa and sat down next to her, cradling her hand like a concerned mother. Nora didn't think that anyone had looked at her with such a mixture of pity and sympathy. Nora didn't know if she liked it or not.

Grateful that Mrs. Waterhouse seemed to give her a few minutes, Nora took a few deep breaths, steadying her thoughts.

"You said Doctor Tillot is offering me a study?"

"He is offering a place in a study being conducted in London." Mrs. Waterhouse opened her mouth, showing a row of very white teeth. "It's an experiment testing a new medication that you're supposed to take once a week and then go there once a month to test your physical capabilities."

Physical capabilities. Medication.

"Will they cure me?" Nora had to ask.

"No, dear girl." Mrs. Waterhouse's eyebrows knotted. "But they hope to make you better. Help you build back muscle you lost. Have more energy."

So, Katherine hadn't told Mrs. Waterhouse anything at all. Not that Katherine would have said anything, implicating them both.

"Okay." Nora nodded. "Tell him thank you for the opportunity. I want to do it."

Mrs. Waterhouse clapped her hands together, looking very pleased with herself.

"That's great. I'll send word to him at once and alert Katherine."

Nora's insides went cold. "Ka… Katherine?"

"Well yes," Mrs. Waterhouse said. "I know she treasures you as a friend and since it was Doctor Tillot's idea, and mine, I couldn't bear it if you sat on the train to London by yourself. No, no, no. Of course, Katherine will take the car and drive you there and back. She needs to pay a call to my sister anyway."

"No." Nora held up her hands. "Please, you've already done so much."

"I won't take no for an answer." Mrs. Waterhouse grabbed her hand again and squeezed it.

Even if she was grateful for the opportunity to go to the study she was starting to feel a bit uncomfortable because Mrs. Waterhouse's behaviour. *I'm not a charity.*

She exhaled and nodded.

"Okay, thank you, ma'am."

*

The clock struck four and Nora excused herself. She needed to go and help Mrs. Chapman in the kitchen even though she had rather gone to speak to Martha about what had happened. *No,* she thought to herself, *I don't want to tell Martha anything.* Nora wasn't sure why but she didn't feel like sharing this with her sister just yet. Her insides were a mess and she didn't know what to think. She didn't know if she feared or longed for spending more time with Katherine. She knew what Martha would think about it.

She greeted Mrs. Chapman with a mute curtsy and went over to the counter to start chopping the carrots right away, ignoring any looks. *Katherine.* She took up a carrot and cut it in half. *Katherine would answer.* She put the carrot in a pot of water and took another carrot. She chopped it quickly. *Katherine would tell her the truth.* Nora understood now that she needed to talk to Katherine. Put her back against the wall. She couldn't just rely on Martha's understanding of the situation. Two more carrots; chop, chop. *Katherine.* Nora grimaced. The line between love and hate was very thin.

"Nora!" Mrs. Chapman came up next to her. "What is wrong with you?"

Nora stopped the knife. She looked at Mrs. Chapman hoping that the pain in her eyes didn't show.

"I apologize," she said, hoping that Mrs. Chapman would leave it at that. "I find myself in a bad mood."

Mrs. Chapman nodded curtly. "Okay then. We will finish here, serve dinner. Then I will light my pipe and we'll talk." She looked at Nora over the rim of her glasses. Her brown eyes had more honey in them than Nora had realised. *What's with everyone today?* It seemed as if everyone wanted to talk to Nora. There was no way for her to disagree so Nora just nodded and then they got on with dinner preparations.

Once dinner was served and the Worker's Stew was bubbling away on the stove, Mrs. Chapman poured them both a cup of coffee and pointed at one of the wooden chairs in the corner. "Sit," she said.

Nora sat down and took the coffee, mumbling a word of thanks. Her head was aching and there was a stiffness in her bones she didn't recognize. Maybe she was regressing. The doctor had said there was a possibility that she would get worse. Maybe it was happening.

Mrs. Chapman sat down with a groan and rubbed one of her knees.

"I have arthritis in my knees," she said. "Will you get me my pipe?" She pointed to a shelf over the stove and Nora went to get it. Her limbs were aching too but she gritted her teeth, not wanting to show Mrs. Chapman that she was in pain.

"Helen, the one who worked in the kitchen before you, had asthma." Nora looked up with an eyebrow raised. "The one before that, Josephine, had some kind of menstrual ailment." Mrs. Chapman chuckled. "It seems like Mrs. Waterhouse likes hiring kitchen aids with ailments.

She has always been like that, I'm afraid. You shouldn't be offended if she puts focus on that. She didn't even know of your condition when she hired you, she must have felt like she hit the jackpot…"

"That's not it." Nora sighed. She picked on a thread that had come undone on her skirt. "I mean, I don't like that she acts as if I'm charity."

"She told me about the study," Mrs. Chapman said. "And of course, I think you should do it. Even if she doesn't have the right intentions it could help you, it could—"

"That's not it." Nora realised what she had done. "I'm sorry for interrupting you." Mrs. Chapman nodded. "It's not about the study, or even about Mrs. Waterhouse. It's about something my sister said."

"Martha?"

"Yes." Nora pursed her lips. "Martha." She sighed. She had pulled the thread loose and there was now a hole in her skirt. She would need to mend it before sleeping. "She said something that upset me. I always thought she saw me for who I am. And now I realise she just sees me as the rest of the world sees me, as an invalid. A cripple." Nora hadn't even known she could express what was bothering her that well.

"You're being silly." Mrs. Chapman took a puff of her pipe and the sweet-smelling smoke worked its way into Nora's nostrils.

"Am I?" Nora pursed her lips, getting ready for being angry with Mrs. Chapman too.

"Yes." Her voice was calm as she puffed on the pipe. "She got you a job. If she only saw you as an invalid I doubt she would have. Most big sisters are overprotective, you know that, right? Mine certainly was. Still is, although we don't see each other as much anymore. She lives in Cardiff with her daughter and three grandchildren." They locked eyes. "I think you could be the most capable woman in the world, but if you have a big sister, she would still act like everything you do is a mistake or that every man you meet would be out to corrupt you."

Nora stayed quiet while digesting what Mrs. Chapman had said. Maybe she had overreacted a bit. If Martha had said something to her six months ago she doubted she would have even reacted. Martha always saw things for the way they were and she spoke her mind. Nora wanted to remember that Martha had said something similar many years ago. *Why would she be friends with you?* It had hurt but Martha had been right. The popular girls had just been friends with her to humiliate her. To shame her.

"A year ago, I probably wouldn't have reacted this way," Nora said finally. "I wouldn't have cared, I would have been grateful for her protection and that she was looking out for me."

Mrs. Chapman nodded but said nothing.

"I'm not the same person anymore." Nora let go of the thread and leaned backwards. "I don't know why I'm just not the same. I have changed. I want to make decisions for myself now." She sucked in air through her mouth; she could feel the need to cry again and refused to. "Anything other than that feels wrong. I don't need her anymore." One tear fell. "She is my sister, and I love her. She's my best friend. But I don't want her to take care of me anymore."

"You want to be independent."

Nora looked at Mrs. Chapman.

"I suppose so."

"So, tell her." Mrs. Chapman shrugged. She seemed to think that it was that simple. "And just be. You have a job here, whether or not Martha works here. You lead separate lives. Be friends. Fight like sisters do, then make up. It doesn't need to be more serious than that."

"I think I want to go and talk to her now." Nora stood up. "Thank you for this."

"I didn't do much." Mrs. Chapman put the pipe in her mouth again, pushed it to the corner and kept talking. "Go ahead. I'll wait for the stew a little while longer before bringing it over. Just put out some plates and spoons after talking to Martha."

Nora agreed and left. The sky was darkening outside. It was almost September now and Nora could feel the cold from the ground through her shoes. In the corner of her eye she thought she saw a shadow and turned around, thinking that it was Katherine. One of the stable cats jumped into her vision from somewhere and disappeared back into the shadows. Nora shook her head and went into the servants' quarters.

She found Martha in their room, lying on their bed and throwing a marble up, only to catch it and throw it up again. She sat up as soon as Nora came in.

"What did Mrs. Waterhouse want? I have been waiting for hours."

"Oh." Nora had almost forgotten about that. "It wasn't about Ka... Miss Waterhouse or anything like that. But there is something more important I want to talk about. Can I sit down?"

Martha scrambled up and sat to the side with her legs criss-crossed, her trousers giving her the ability to do so. Still in skirt, Nora sat with her legs down on the floor even though it wasn't as comfortable. She almost wished she was wearing trousers too. There was something very titillating about the thought of sitting with your legs in any way you wanted.

"I'm not a little girl anymore." Nora forced herself to look straight at Martha. "I appreciate you looking out for me but it's not nice to tell me that I'm unlovable." She held up her hand to silence Martha. "I know that wasn't your intention but when you tell me that I can't trust my view of people, my perspective and gut, you're telling me I can't trust myself." That's when Nora realised she had to not just confront Martha but Katherine too. She let her hand down. "I think I'm done."

Martha nodded. "I don't think I have much to add," she said, looking tired. "Are you angry?"

Nora reached over and grabbed her hand.

"I was. Very." She giggled. "But I talked with Mrs. Chapman and realised that no matter how old I am, you will always want to protect me. In the same way you do everything. Bluntly." Their gazes met. "I'm not angry anymore, no."

Martha nodded. She didn't say anything but just held Nora's hand.

"So, what did Mrs. Waterhouse want?" The room was getting dark and neither of them had left. Somewhere in the back of Nora's mind she knew she should go and set the table. Soon the others would come in and Mrs. Chapman would come with the food. She told Martha, in short terms, what Mrs. Waterhouse had said. About the doctor. The study. She didn't at first mention that Katherine was going to drive her but when Martha asked if she was getting money for train fare, she couldn't bear to lie.

"So, Katherine is going to drive you?"

Nora nodded. She didn't care about Martha's opinion in this matter anymore.

"Will you kiss her?"

Nora stayed silent for a moment, unsure. She wanted to talk with Katherine before kissing her again. Her gut told her that there was no uncertainty.

"I don't know." But that was a lie.

Chapter Twenty-Five

It felt strange to sit next to Nora in the small confinement of the car. For once she hadn't opened the door and they hadn't properly greeted each other. Katherine felt wrong, cold and strange. It wasn't that she wanted to be cold and indifferent to Nora; she didn't want to be unpleasant to her. *She's going to think I don't love her anymore...* Katherine's heart skipped a beat. Not that she had loved her in the first place. Katherine didn't know what their kisses or her feelings meant, but surely it wasn't love?

She started the car and they drove away from Waterhouse Acre Stables. The further away they got from there, the more Katherine relaxed. She grabbed the wheel with just one hand and pulled her other through her hair, scratching her forehead a bit. It had been a week since the incident and she had been ignoring both the sisters since then. Martha and Nora had talked like normal, laughed like normal, seemed like normal. Katherine's insides ached at the thought that Nora had taken Martha's side in the whole thing. *Even though I probably deserve it.* Katherine should have looked for Nora that first day and not just disappeared into her own life of riding and being the Waterhouse daughter. By now it would probably not mean as much; Katherine had let too much time pass by. She still hadn't been able to say no when her mother had told her; if there was even a slight chance that Nora could get better, Katherine would do anything. She also hoped that the long ride to London would give them time to talk. Even if Katherine herself didn't know how to start the conversation.

It's not fair to wait for Nora to start the conversation.
Katherine chewed on the inside of her cheek.

Nora looked well. There was a small smile playing
on her lips, and her face had color. Her hair was getting
longer and she had made a small braid. Katherine wanted to
undo the braid and run her fingers— the car touched the
plants on the side and Katherine looked to the road again.
She couldn't believe Nora had distracted her so much she
had almost drifted off the road. She glanced at Nora who
was now looking at her rather than the road with a raised
eyebrow.

"Are you alright?" she asked at the same time
Katherine said, "So how have you been?"

Fuck. Katherine cleared her throat.

"So how have you been?" She repeated since Nora
stayed silent.

"Surprisingly well." It was the first time Katherine
had heard Nora sound confident. "Mrs. Chapman is giving
me more and more responsibility. I just love working for
her."

"Good, good." *By God Katherine stop sounding like
you're your father talking pleasantries before turning to
business.* "How is your sister?" Katherine wanted to slap
herself and held onto the wheel even harder.

Nora laughed, an easy pearly sound that Katherine
wanted to hear more of.

"She is well except she doesn't want to work at
Waterhouse Acre Stables anymore."

Katherine's eyes went wide and she unintentionally
stepped quicker on the gas for a moment.

"What?!" She coughed. "Sorry, I mean, why?
What?"

Nora laughed even more.

"She wants to protect me from you. Can you imagine?"

Katherine was starting to sweat. Anger, confusion and sadness whirled around her in a mess. She was turning carsick, which has never happened while driving before.

"We fought," Nora continued. "I was so angry with her. How dare she?" Her voice had taken a sharp tone. "Like I can't protect myself or I can't use my judgement of the people around me." She sighed. "Mrs. Chapman made me understand that it's the nature of big sisters. They just can't help themselves."

"You talked to Mrs. Chapman about... this?" A rabbit ran in the road and Katherine steered the car out of the way.

"Not about us or anything," Nora said quickly. "I just told her about the fight I had with Martha." She took a big sigh. "It might not make much sense for you, but the fight we had wasn't about you. Martha and I are allowed to have different opinions on people. It doesn't matter if she hates you and I li... don't hate you. The problem was that she doesn't trust my judgement and some things she says tell me I shouldn't trust my judgement either."

Katherine's heart was pounding in a nervous rhythm and she stayed quiet. This wasn't the same shy girl she had found in Shireoaks just a couple of months ago. This was a woman who spoke with confidence.

"What did she tell you?" Katherine's mouth felt dry when she tried to swallow. "That made you not trust your judgement?"

Nora stayed quiet for a moment. Just breathing. They were driving through Shireoaks now, past the store where they had met.

"Just don't be angry with Martha if I tell you," Nora said. "She means well and she has her reasons for saying it."

Katherine was already angry with Martha but she hummed in agreement.

"She doesn't even focus on the fact that you're a woman," Nora said. "Although I assume that isn't great either that she asked me why you would like me. She said that you're a lady of society, older than me, more experienced than me. She said that we are from different worlds." She took another deep breath. "I don't think you realise who I am sometimes. How many times I have heard my parents fight over money. I have nine living siblings. I have never worn a piece of clothing that isn't a hand-me-down. We had less money when I was younger, less to the point where I have gone to bed without supper. I call my parents ma and pa because mother and father are for richer folk." She stopped her monologue. "She also said that she couldn't bear to see a sexual deviant take advantage of me. So perhaps the woman thing isn't so great either."

Katherine felt like she had been punched and had so many thoughts running through her head. She didn't know what part was more offending to her. Or if anything were. Well, the sexual deviant wasn't great but… was Katherine a sexual deviant? Was it abnormal and wrong to like women? What…

"Do you agree with what she said?" *I have to know.*

"Well," Nora spoke slowly. "I agree with some of it. We do come from different worlds. Very different worlds. I don't know how well we can relate to one another. It works while we're here, away from everything and everyone but it's an illusion. I'm still Nora Lakes from the Lakes family from London."

Katherine could feel Nora looking at her. She tried to not look back. She was distracted enough. She needed to keep looking at the road. They had to get there in one piece.

"What about the sexual deviant part?" *What about the taking advantage part?* Katherine was so scared to ask because she was scared of the answer.

"I don't know," Nora said. "It doesn't feel wrong to kiss you. It doesn't feel wrong to like you. I want to be your sweetheart in every sense of the word. I want you to be mine." Katherine was amazed by how casually Nora was talking about their feelings. "But Martha did bring up questions in me."

Uh oh.

"Well, why do you like me?" The question seemed to etch itself into the atmosphere of the car. "What do you see in me? Martha was right about some things. I'm an invalid. A poor invalid no doubt. What do I have to offer you? Not money. Not even physical capability. We don't even know how long I'll live."

"Don't say that." Katherine's insides ached. "You're healthy enough. Surely you will live for a long time. And the doctor…"

"Your mother was very clear on the premise of the study," Nora interrupted her. "It's experimental; it's not made for curing me. It's testing to see if there is any way we can make the symptoms better." She sighed. "And the rest still stands. I'm a poor invalid. Why are you interested in my kisses at all?"

In her twenty-five years, Katherine had never imagined she would ever have to talk about her feelings in such a manner. She hadn't been taught to put words on things like that. Talking about attraction, wanting and what she saw in someone, it seemed to be more taboo, than kissing a woman. She ran her thoughts over and over, thinking of a good enough answer.

"You have nothing to say?" Nora sounded sad now, her voice empty and flat. "There is not a single word you can say to me?"

"You're pretty." Katherine's heart was beating fast. She would have done anything just to stop the car and run screaming away from there. But she couldn't. She had to stay and fight. Fight for Nora. "I find you interesting. I want to hear your opinions on things. See the world through your eyes." Katherine didn't know where the words were coming from but she continued. "I find you brave. I think if I had your illness I'd just lie on my bed all day, not wanting to do anything or experience anything. You fight." Her voice broke. And when had her eyes filled with tears? What was this? Katherine didn't cry. "You are fearless. If somebody told me you were trying to be the first to climb Mt Everest I would believe them. I would think you're insane of course because like Martha, all I want is for you to be safe. But I also believe you need to set your own limit. I want to see how far you can go. I just… I believe in you." *And I want to kiss you. So, so, so much.* "I don't think your illness makes you weak. In fact, far from it."

When Nora hadn't said anything still, Katherine glanced at the side. Nora was looking straight ahead, tears glistening on her cheeks.

"Please say something," Katherine begged. Had she offended Nora? Made her sad? Or had Katherine said too much? Perhaps it was Nora who was just experimenting with their kisses. *Please don't break my heart.*

"I don't know what to say." Nora wiped her cheeks with her sleeves. "Please stop the car."

"Why?" Katherine glanced at her again. They were out in the country, at least an hour to the nearest town. "Are you going to be sick?"

"Please just stop the car."

Katherine did as she was asked, pulled to the side, and stopped the engine. She turned to Nora to ask her what it was when Nora put both hands on her cheeks and pulled Katherine into a sloppy kiss that tasted of sunshine and tears.

Chapter Twenty-Six

Kissing Katherine was like reaching the surface after swimming for a long time. Nora tilted her head to deepen their kiss and smiled against Katherine's lips. Her insides were like molten lava in a confusing mess of love, gratitude, and desire. She couldn't believe the things Katherine had said about her. The thought that somebody like Katherine thought she was brave and strong was dizzying.

They didn't stop kissing until Nora's lungs were aching. She pulled away with the last nibble on Katherine's bottom lip. She felt flushed and alive and giddy. She reached up with one hand and touched her own lips. They felt warm and swollen. The sensation excited her.

"I still don't know what to say after such a speech." She laughed, a burst of strange laughter born from joy instead of humor. She looked at Katherine who was looking just as confused and breathless as she was. "I have only been described as kind and meek before. Sweet spirited maybe." Another chuckle escaped her. "You describe me as powerful. I like it."

"I would describe you as powerful every day for a kiss like that."

Nora's insides lurched at Katherine's words and she wanted to pull her in for another kiss. But they had to keep driving if they were going to make it in time.

Katherine's words had changed something in her. Now she couldn't wait to go to the doctor. Katherine and her mother were right. If there was any chance that Nora could get better, she had to try. Her goal wasn't to climb Mt Everest, of course, but there were things she wanted to try. *I want to ride horses,* she just realised. *I want to learn to ride.*

"Let's drive to London." She reached out and gently patted Katherine's cheek. Katherine pressed a kiss to the palm of her hand, causing shivers and goosebumps to travel from Nora's hand to her shoulder. "I want to go to that doctor. You are right, maybe I can get better. It would be nice to be able to carry stuff or walk without pain."

Katherine smiled at her and nodded.

"I have my hopes up." She placed her hand around the key and turned it. The engine sputtered but didn't start. "What?" Katherine looked down at the dashboard and tried again. The engine went silent with a small pop.

"Katherine?" Nora said. "What is wrong with the car?"

"I don't know. Just wait." Katherine opened her door, got out, and walked to the front. She opened the hood of the car.

Nora had never seen the insides of a car and scrambled to get out of the car too. She was curious.

The weather was still nice outside and there were birds singing. Katherine was leaning over the engine, soot on one of her cheeks. She must have touched it after touching the car hood. Nora wanted to wipe the smudge away but didn't disturb Katherine. Instead, she just looked down at the engine. Warmth was radiating from it and it was smelling faintly of smoke.

"My big sister Mary worked at a car shop during the war," she said instead. "She didn't teach me much though and she stopped as soon as the war was over."

"Maybe it overheated?" Katherine muttered. "I know embarrassingly little about cars for being able to drive."

"What should we do?" Nora bit her lip. "We're in the middle of nowhere." She looked all around them but only saw field after field.

"Nottingham is that way." Katherine pointed in front of them. "I could walk there, see if we could get some help."

Nora squinted her eyes but still saw nothing. She didn't want Katherine to just leave her there.

"How long will it take us to walk there?"
Katherine looked up at the word 'us'.

"Maybe thirty minutes at a healthy pace." She seemed to think for a moment. "You know, you could wait by the car." She looked at Nora. "And rest. I don't mind walking by myself."

"You're the one who said that you wouldn't be surprised if I decided to climb Mt Everest." Nora smiled widely. "Surely I can manage a brisk walk to Nottingham."

She could see in Katherine's face that she wouldn't deny her. Katherine grabbed their bags, locked the car, and they both set off.

Walking was easier than usual. It felt as if Nora could run on the thought that Katherine believed in her alone. She felt like skipping and jumping for joy but resolved to just walking. She needed to conserve energy. Instead, she relished in the sunlight, enjoying the smells and sounds of the British countryside. She delighted in Katherine being next to her. Martha had been wrong. Katherine wasn't above them, or more than them, better than them. Katherine was just a woman and Nora felt more than equal to her.

It took them almost an hour to get to Nottingham and Nora had to rest several times to get there. When they had reached the first couple of houses, Nora was sweating like a hog, her legs felt like spaghetti and her heart was doing a strange staccato rhythm that was scaring her. If they had to walk all the way back, Nora wasn't sure if she would make it. None of this she said to Katherine, not wanting to worry her.

They reached an auto shop and Nora sat down on a bench outside while Katherine went in to talk to the people who worked there. Nora scrambled in her bag for anything flat she could fan herself with. Disappointed at not finding anything, she just waved her own hand in front of her face. Clouds were gathering in the distance but it was still very hot. Maybe a storm was coming? Instead of worrying, the thought made Nora smile. The last storm they had suffered through had led to something good. She saw it as the first time Katherine and she had ever gotten close. *Even if it was just hugging and sleeping.* It was actually crazy that Nora had ever listened to Martha's words about Katherine. That night in the storm had proven to Nora how Katherine cared for her and believed in her. Even if they hadn't even kissed yet.

Katherine came out of the garage with a disappointed look on her face. She still had soot on her cheek. Her hair was messy and she was sweaty and flushed. Her black skirt looked fine but her white shirt looked crumbled with the sleeves rolled up. She was a picture of a mess but Nora didn't think she had ever looked more beautiful. The look on her face was worrying her though.

"What's wrong?"

Katherine sat down on the bench next to her, leaned forward, and put her head in her hands. Nora fought against the wish to scratch her neck for her. Her mouth watered. The more she looked at Katherine's neck, visible under her short bob, the more she wanted to kiss or bite Katherine there. *Maybe I'm suffering from heat stroke.*

Katherine straightened her back, making Nora's stray thoughts go away.

"They are busy now. I offered them five pounds just to drive out to our car to take a look at it but they declined. They said to come back tomorrow morning."

"My doctor visit," Nora said. "The study. My appointment is this afternoon."

"I know." Katherine looked at Nora. "I am so sorry, I did all that I could." She looked so sad, Nora's insides ached.

"Don't worry." She patted Katherine's shoulder. "Of course, it isn't your fault." She bit her lip. "If anything, it's my fault. I asked you to stop the car."

Katherine smiled then, a tired but genuine smile. "And I'm happy you did. It was for a good reason." She got up and offered her hand to Nora, pulling her up. "The man inside told me about a bed and breakfast just down the road. We can stay there tonight and I'll ask to use the phone. I will call my mother for Doctor Tillot's phone number."

"I have his number." They picked up their bags. "Your mother gave me a note with all the information she thought I would need before I left this morning. The address to the place, his number. The other doctor's number." Nora did feel worried that she was going to miss her appointment but there was also something so exciting about checking in to a bed and breakfast with Katherine. She almost felt happy that the car had broken down.

As they got closer and Nora saw the rates for a room on the sign outside, she stopped and took hold of Katherine's arm, stopping her too.

"I want to pay for half."

Katherine squinted her eyes.

"Why? I have enough."

Nora nodded. "I know you do and I know you don't mind but I do. I can't just let you pay for everything for me. It doesn't feel right. I make an earning wage and I have enough to pay for half of one night." It would make a dent in the money she had stored in her bag but she didn't care. It wasn't like she stayed at a bed and breakfast often. She could afford to splurge. And she wanted Katherine and herself to be on common ground.

"If you want." Katherine nodded and they entered the house. Getting a room was easy since it wasn't peak season. They called Dr. Tillot who, while disappointed, understood their trouble. He told them to be at his office tomorrow afternoon instead.

*

Dinner was eaten an hour later at a nearby pub where Nora let Katherine pay. She couldn't afford it and Katherine insisted. Nora wanted to be independent but she also recognized that she needed to eat. As they walked back to the bed and breakfast, anticipation rose between them and Nora was dying to reach out and grab Katherine's hand. She didn't want to raise any suspicion from the people on the streets so she settled for just walking next to her. Neither of them said anything. A nearby jasmine bush grew and made the air sweet-smelling and dense. Nora yawned even though she didn't feel tired.

"Remember the night of the storm?" she asked.

If Katherine smiled Nora couldn't see it, since Katherine was that much taller and still looking in the front. But when she spoke, her voice was full of joy.

"Yes." She looked down, her eyes sparkling. "I can't believe you let me hold you. It doesn't feel like we knew each other then."

"You were keeping me warm."

"I'm still so sorry about you being kicked," Katherine said. "If I knew that was going to happen, I never would have…"

"Hush." Nora grabbed her hand then, not caring who saw. They had arrived at their destination. "Come on."

Their room was small with twin beds that could be pushed apart or together. They were currently pushed together and neither Nora nor Katherine had made any move to push them apart.

Nora didn't know what she was hoping for. She sat down on one of the chairs by the window and watched as Katherine locked the door. When Katherine turned around and looked at her, her facial expression was unreadable.

"Are you tired?" She took a step towards Nora.

Nora shook her head. She didn't think she had ever felt so awake in her entire life; for once she didn't pay attention to her knees or joints or hurting head. *Wait a minute,* Nora smiled at Katherine, *nothing is hurting.*

"That makes me happy." Only Katherine's reply told Nora that she had said her thought out loud and her cheeks heated.

Katherine was standing right in front of her now; she towered above her since Nora was still sitting. Tingles were traveling up and down her arms, heat was pooling in her center, and butterflies traveled up to her throat. *I'm either going to die or be sick,* Nora thought, praying that she hadn't said that out loud. She didn't want to deter Katherine from doing whatever it was that she was planning to do.

Their hands met, Katherine reaching down, her hands cold in Nora's. Their fingers entangled. And there Katherine stopped. Her smile went from sultry to mild to confused, her eyes widening.

"What's wrong?" Nora stood up and let go of Katherine's hand to squeeze her shoulder.

Their faces were close and their breaths mingled. Katherine was smelling sweet with a slight undertone of horse, but not in a bad way. Katherine looked deep into Nora's eyes. It felt as if she was staring into her soul.

"I have no idea what to do." Katherine was usually a pale person but now her face turned redder than the shade of her lipstick. "Oh god." She turned away from Nora, fell down on the bed, and clutched her face in her hands. "What am I saying?"

"What do you mean?" Nora looked at the figure on the bed. "What is it that you want to do?" Realisation hit her and she felt like her whole body turned pink. She was melting on the inside. Katherine was adorable. "Oh."

Katherine sat up and stared at her. Her make-up was a little bit smudged and Nora longed to go over it with a wet cloth. Katherine's face was nicer naked anyway.

"I thought we would be together." She bit her lip, and it almost looked painful. She sighed. "I haven't... I have never. I don't know what to do with a woman."

Nora sat down on the bed, but not right beside her. It felt safer to have a bit of distance between them.

"You are the first person I have ever kissed." Nora didn't know whether to laugh or cry. She longed for their dinner when the conversation had flowed easily and they weren't sitting in this room. Alone, awkward, unsure. "I don't know what to do either. Maybe—"

"I want to have sex with you." Katherine pursed her lips and reached forward, placing a hand on Nora's knee. "Just so there is no confusion." There was a determined look in her eyes, similar to when she was about to go jumping. Or during the storm when they had realised to brave the outside together. Similar to the first time they had kissed.

Nora licked her lips. *Me too.* She could say that. Or perhaps *let's just kiss and see what happens.* There were no words that could describe what she felt. There were no more words to be said. It was time to forget about everything and just do what needed to be done. Needed to be done for both of them.

Nora got up to her knees and edged closer to Katherine. When she reached her she put her hands on Katherine's shoulders and pushed. In one fluid motion Katherine was on her back, Nora on top of her, Katherine's hands on her waist. Katherine's eyes had gone black and her lipstick was smudged even though they hadn't kissed yet. She could feel Katherine's heartbeat through her ribs and wondered if Katherine could feel her nipples hardening. Her clothes felt restricting and harsh on her skin and she moved her legs, wanting to be free. When she moved, Katherine closed her eyes and her mouth fell open. A low groan started in her chest and it spurred Nora on. She wanted to hear more. See more. Feel more. More of everything. More of Katherine.

Katherine's eyes were still closed but Nora kept her eyes open as she moved her leg to be between Katherine's thighs; she pressed down as hard as she could without being restricted by their skirts.

"Mmm, Nora." Katherine pulled Nora's shirt out of her skirt and moved her hands over Nora's bare skin, the sensation dizzying. The swell of her breasts was pressed against Nora's breasts.

"I want to be naked," Nora whispered, unsure where her daring came from. She rolled over to the other side and got up to a sitting position. She fumbled with the small buttons, hurrying to get her own clothes off. She didn't look at Katherine but she could hear movement behind her.

Her shirt ended up on the floor. Then her bra. Then she stood up and pulled her skirt down her hips, the whole time looking at Katherine. Katherine was staring at her, still lying down, with her mouth slightly open. Her face was flushed, her lips swollen. Their eyes locked as Nora pulled her skirt fully down. Soon all she was wearing were panties and her fanciest stockings. Her skin was burning everywhere Katherine's gaze hit.

Did Katherine like what she saw? Nora looked down. She hadn't judged her own body before except in relation to her illness. She looked down at her modest chest, flat stomach, and tiny thighs. Katherine looked so much healthier and curvier. She had muscles. Nora felt more like skin and bone.

"Do you like what you're seeing?" She stroked her hands down her hips.

Katherine sat up and licked her lips.

"You make me hungry." Her voice was dark. "Come here."

Before Nora could react, Katherine had reached forward; she tugged on her arm, and Nora fell with a thump on the bed. Katherine attacked her mouth, kissing her deeply, devouring her. Katherine flicked her tongue across Nora's bottom lip, making Nora produce a feminine sound low in her throat.

Not stopping to kiss her, Katherine turned them around so that Nora was on her back. She left her mouth and started nibbling her way down Nora's throat. *Oh, my goodness.* Nora kicked out with her legs, no longer in charge of what her body was doing. If Katherine kissed her breast or touched her nipple in any way, Nora thought she was going to die.

"I can't wait anymore." Nora didn't know if she had thought the words or said them. Or maybe Katherine had said them. She touched Katherine's shirt and tried to undo the buttons, ripping some of them in the process. It was as if she was possessed. When she couldn't get Katherine's shirt from her skirt, Katherine sat up and proceeded to rip all her clothes off.

When she was just in panties and stockings too, she dove in for more kisses and they rolled together on top of the bed, fighting for the chance to be on top. Nora laughed loudly, feeling free as she pushed Katherine down and sat on top of her. It felt almost indecent to sit half-naked with her legs spread on either side of Katherine's hips. She could feel Katherine's warmth underneath and she rocked her hips gently, unable to sit still.

She had assumed that Katherine had been spending time in the sun but now it was clear that Katherine was just naturally tan. Her mother was from Italy after all, but Nora had never reflected on it until she was taking in the soft tan skin of her belly and chest, places that had never seen the sun. Or the brown nipples that filled Nora's mouth with saliva. She understood what Katherine had meant with the word hungry.

"You are the most beautiful person I have ever laid my eyes on." She put her hands on Katherine's shoulders, not yet daring to touch her breasts. Fireworks set off behind her eyelids when Katherine took hold of Nora's hips and pressed her down while angling her own hips upwards. Moving back and forth, Nora found a rhythm over Katherine's mound that made her feel things she had never felt before. She closed her eyes, her head falling backward, her hips going faster and faster. Heat was spreading on the insides of her thighs. Nora had come before of course, in the bath, in her bed, in her sleep but always on her own and it had never felt as complete as this. It felt as if something hollow inside her was finally being filled. Filled with Katherine. Nora opened her eyes and looked down. Katherine had a raw look on her face, flushed and full, and was biting her lip. She hadn't given up the grip on Nora's shoulders.

"You're making me wet." It was true. Nora was very wet by now and it was starting to leak through her underwear and onto Katherine. For some reason, it only spurred her on and the movement of her hips grew. Her muscles were starting to ache, not used to the workout; but she couldn't, wouldn't stop.

"Katherine." She didn't recognize her own voice. "Katherine, something... something... oh no. Not... so... soon."

"Shhh." Katherine put a finger to Nora's lips, chuckling. "You don't want to let the whole hotel know what we're doing, right?"

At that moment Nora didn't care but she tried her hardest to stay silent as pleasure fell over her in waves. It grew from the core of her and out in every limb, down her legs, up her abdomen, in her arms. When it reached her heart and mind, she fell forward. Her eyes filled with tears and her chest ached. She put her head on Katherine's naked shoulders and stretched her legs along the length of Katherine's legs. Everything between them was sweaty and sticky and Nora's tears fell against Katherine's neck. Katherine held her and let her cry.

Nora wanted to tell her all. How she didn't hurt anymore. How Katherine was everything. How she wanted to give Katherine as much as she had been given. How this night had changed everything. But Nora said nothing. She cried in Katherine's arms. And Katherine held her and let her cry. As Nora wept the world floated away and before she knew it she was asleep and dreamt of nothing.

Chapter Twenty-Seven

A ray of sunshine had worked its way through the curtains; Katherine had followed it as it had traveled over Nora's naked back and had now landed in her hair, making the otherwise dark strands shine like gold. Katherine didn't think she had slept much but she didn't care. After Nora had fallen asleep, Katherine had, with gentle hands, taken off her underwear and stockings with limited help from her lover. Katherine chuckled as she remembered Nora's almost drunken behaviour. Nora hadn't woken up during the entire night but Katherine couldn't stop watching her. Even when little snores and grunts exited her. Katherine wondered what Nora had been dreaming and hoped it was a good dream.

It was strange to be completely naked, even in bed. Katherine couldn't remember if she had ever been naked before, except for taking a bath. The sheets were cool on the skin of her legs and it was freeing. Realizing that an equally naked Nora was within an arm's length was dizzying. Katherine reached out. She didn't want to wake Nora up, exactly, although if she did it wouldn't be bad. She started stroking her hand up and down over Nora's back. To her delight, Nora stretched and started making a strange purring sound.

"My goodness." Katherine laughed. "You're like a cat."

"A stable cat." Nora turned her head with a brilliant smile, sleepy look, and messy hair.

Stop making me love you. Katherine choked on the words she wanted to say but couldn't. Instead, she leaned forward and pressed their lips together.

"Do we have to go yet?" Nora whispered in her ear.

Katherine shook her head, lost for words. Nora had lifted the duvet that had shifted to lie between them and the lengths of their bodies lined up. Katherine didn't know what time it was and didn't care.

Nora placed her arm around Katherine's waist and pulled her close, making a humming noise. She leaned forward and whispered in Katherine's ears, causing goosebumps down Katherine's neck.

"You made me feel so good yesterday." Nora pressed a kiss to Katherine's cheek, a kiss that might as well have been between her legs considering the visceral reaction in Katherine's body. "I can't believe I fell asleep before I was able to... umm." Nora's ears went pink.

She leaned back and looked into Katherine's eyes.

"Lie down on your back please."

Katherine did as she was told. Nora leaned over her, holding her own head up on her left hand and placing her right hand high up on Katherine's chest. She started tracing the line of Katherine's collarbones.

"Can I..." she bit her lip.

"Whatever it is-" Katherine's voice was husky. "-you can do it. Anything. Everything." *I am yours.*

Nora nodded as a blush spread over her face and down her chest. The tip of her tongue peaked out in the corner of her mouth as if she was concentrating deeply. She pressed her whole palm down on Katherine's collarbone and then she lightly, lightly, went lower until she was cupping Katherine's breast.

"Hngh." The touch was like a feather and Katherine, in a desperate move, put her hand on top of Nora and pushed it harder against herself. Her nipple tightened and her insides clenched too. "Nora." She was growing hard and wet so fast it was almost painful.

"What is it?" Nora sounded worried. "Am I hurting you?" She tried to move her hand but Katherine didn't let her.

Katherine shook her head violently, her corresponding even though Nora had barely touched her. The reaction of Katherine's body was almost scary. *When Nora touches me, I feel like I'm going to die…*

"I'm just so swollen," she croaked. "I think all the blood is rushing there. It hurts a bit."

"Oh." Nora glanced downwards. "Maybe I should…" She squeezed Katherine's breast gently and then stroked downwards. Katherine left her own hand on her breast, needing the pressure there. Her nipple was so hard Katherine almost wondered if she was cold.

She sucked in air through her lips when Nora ran her fingers through the curly hair at the base of her stomach. *Please, please, please, lower.* Nora's touch was too light, in the wrong place, not in the right rhythm. Instead of the pain receding, Katherine was being teased to the point where she forgot her own name. She dug her heels into the mattress and groaned.

"You're teasing me." She said through gritted teeth. "To… the… right."

Nora moved her fingers but Katherine was so wet, so slippery, Nora quickly disappeared from where Katherine needed her the most. Katherine was about to push away Nora's hand and do it herself when Nora made a groaning noise.

"Just wait." Nora pressed a quick kiss to Katherine's left nipple and then moved downwards to the bed.

Katherine lifted her head, dizzy. Every single part of her was aching, itching, needing, wanting.

"What are you doing?"

"Just wait." Nora lay down between Katherine's spread legs and looked right at her. Katherine lifted her head but dropped it again. The sight of Nora between her legs was too arousing and she was already in such a bad state.

"Here, right?" Nora pressed a single finger to where Katherine needed it most. Stars exploded behind Katherine's eyelashes and all she managed was to hum in reply. She was so wet and even with full vision of what she was doing, Nora sometimes went too much to the right or too much to the left. The pain was only increasing. Katherine needed to release badly.

"Never mind." Nora removed her hand, moved forward, and tentatively flicked her tongue on Katherine's most private part.

"Oh my…" Fire licked at her core, turning into water that hit her in waves. Nora licked again and again and the sweet agony continued. Nothing could have prepared Katherine for what this was like, for how this felt. *I love you, I love you, I love you, I love you.*

Katherine fell into her body, a new person. Her skin was covered in a slight sheen of sweat and she had never been in more need of a bath.

"The best thing that has ever happened to me was this. Just now." Katherine sighed contently. "This moment right here. I will never be happier."

Nora laughed against Katherine's thigh.

"That sounds so sad." She peeked up at Katherine. "I hope to make you happy many more times." She looked shy, the lower part of her face wet. Katherine chuckled at the sight.

"I'm sure you can." She reached down and scratched Nora's scalp. "I think we both deserve a bath now, don't you think?"

*

After a nice chilled bath where they had gotten clean and kissed quite a bit more, they found themselves checking out of the bed and breakfast. They walked over to the auto shop and one of the mechanics drove them back to their car and fixed it. It turned out that there was dirt in the carburetor and the mechanic took it out and cleaned it. They had to throw away a bit of gasoline which Katherine didn't like but soon the car was running.

They paid the men, thanked them and they were soon on their way.

The sun seemed lighter, the sky clearer, the grass greener. Katherine had rolled the windows down all the way and was whistling a tune she had heard on the radio earlier the same week. Occasionally she looked over at Nora who was sometimes looking outside, was sometimes sleeping. They stopped halfway to fill the tank. On the side of the road, violets were blooming and Katherine picked them up to give to Nora.

They got into London around noon with four hours to spare before they had to meet Doctor Tillot.

"Could we go and see my family?" Nora asked.

"Yes but…" Katherine grimaced. "What should we tell them? It's strange enough for the daughter of your employer driving you all the way to London without following you in there. Are you sure it's appropriate?"

Nora snorted.

"Let's see if they notice first," she said. "And let's just tell the truth."

"Huh?" Katherine's heart skipped a beat.

She felt a hand on her leg. Nora squeezed.

"That we're friends. And that you were coming to see your friends here in London anyway."

"My aunt."

"Your aunt." Nora nodded. "Then that's what we will tell them."

*

Nora couldn't put a finger on why she wanted to show Katherine the place where she had grown up. She wanted to have Katherine in her room, show her their kitchen, their sitting room, her belongings. It would make Katherine more real to her. To push the two parts of her life together. And if Katherine was real, so was Nora. And everything that had happened to Nora would be real too. Anne and their father were still in Portsmouth and it was during school hours; Nora hoped that at least someone would be home. It would feel sneaky if she just came home and left again without anyone knowing.

They parked the car close to a nearby church and walked the rest of the way. The gnarly rose bush that rose in front of the house had started to rot when Martha wasn't there to take care of it. Nora tried the front door and pushed it open.

*

Katherine didn't know what she had been expecting. She knew, in theory, that Nora didn't come from an affluent family. She knew that they lived in a bad part of London. Nothing, however, had prepared her for the little semi-detached house in a row of semi-detached houses. The air stank of smoke, urine, and something Katherine couldn't quite place. The house was grey but patches of the color were missing as if somebody had tried to paint it. There was a small patch of grass in front of the door but it was yellow and gravel was spread on top of it. A plastic toy lay in the corner.

Nora opened the door, got inside, and shouted a hello. Katherine followed her inside. The front room was dark and the floor looked dirty. An array of shoes was on one side and there was a set of stairs, leading to the second floor.

"Nora?" A voice came from what Katherine assumed was the kitchen. "Is that you?"

A stodgy woman wearing a flowery apron showed up in the doorway. She was as short as Nora with Martha's eyes and coloring.

"Ma!" Nora walked forward and fell into her mother's arms. "I'm so sorry about the baby."

The baby? Katherine cringed inwardly. Was Nora's mother still having children?

"Don't worry, cookie." The woman leaned back and pinched Nora's cheek. "I'm just glad nothing happened to me and I have all of you. And I'm more excited to hear about the appointment. Mrs. Waterhouse is so nice to make something like this happen." She looked to the side and eyed Katherine. "Oh, we have company!"

"Yes, ma." Nora walked over to Katherine and placed a hand on Katherine's back, pushing her forward. Nora's mother smelled like food. Sausages. Potatoes. Oil. Katherine swallowed and shook the hand that was offered.

"This is Katherine Waterhouse, daughter of my employer."

"I'm Mrs. Lakes." Her hand was calloused and rough. "Nora didn't tell me we were expecting company, otherwise I would have made sure to clean up a bit." She smoothed down her hair, making absolutely no difference.

Katherine smiled and hoped it wasn't as strained as it felt.

"Don't worry," she said. She looked at the surroundings. "It looks… lovely." She choked on the word and Nora glanced at her.

I'm so sorry. Katherine knew that she was being horrible. She knew that she was being judgmental and unpleasant and she just couldn't help herself.

"The rest should come home within an hour," Mrs. Lakes said. She grabbed Nora's hand and gaped at Katherine. Her mouth was smiling but Katherine knew. Mrs. Lakes didn't like her. "I shall go and make some tea and you can tell me all about the treatment. Did you hear about the washhouse over on Queensway? It's automatic! Can you imagine? The government is going to put me out of business, I swear."

Her sister doesn't like me. Her mother doesn't like me. Katherine sighed and plastered the smile on her face, hoping it would stick through this whole visit.

The Lakes kitchen was cream-colored with a rug on the floor. There were dishes in the sink and the cup Mrs. Lakes put in front of Nora wasn't clean. Nora was starting to look increasingly uncomfortable too and she wasn't meeting Katherine's gaze. *I'm sorry.* Katherine didn't want to hurt her. She didn't want to offend her. But Nora had to know that this wasn't... good. This wasn't nice. Katherine wanted to get out of there.

They drank tea which tasted surprisingly normal to Katherine but when she asked for milk and sugar, Mrs. Lakes laughed.

"There is no milk left from breakfast Miss Waterhouse," she said. "And Nora's pa is bringing us sugar when he comes back, right now I have none."

Mortified, Katherine just nodded. She looked down at the cup, feeling Nora's gaze on the top of her head. After a while, the door slammed and the kitchen was flooded with Nora's siblings.

Katherine had thought that Martha was a handful but she was nothing compared to the five Lakes children that stormed the kitchen. Nora pointed at the different people and all of them shook her hand. Emily, Rose, John, Eunice? Katherine's head spun and she couldn't keep them apart. They were all talking on top of each other and none of them seemed very interested in Nora or Katherine although the oldest girl, Emily looked at her with curiosity in her eyes. She sat down next to Katherine and opened her mouth.

Katherine stood up from her chair.

"Nora, I think we should go."

Nora looked at the clock on the wall.

"But it's only..."

"There might be a lot of traffic," Katherine said. She looked at the door. Her escape to freedom was so close.

"So, leave the car and take the tube." Mrs. Lakes said. "It's quicker anyway."

Nora met Katherine's gaze and it was as if she knew, knew everything. *Please help me.* A strange smell was settling in Katherine's nostrils and she felt like she was going to throw up. The walls were closing in on her. Heart pounding. Throat closing.

"I think we should go, Ma." Nora looked at her mother. "Katherine is right and we can't take the tube. We need to head back to Waterhouse Acre Stables again after my appointment so we need the car."

Mrs. Lakes pursed her lips but said nothing, just nodded. She didn't look at Katherine. Which was kind of rude. The whole family came with them to the door. The girls curtsied to Katherine as if she had been a gentleman and everyone hugged and kissed Nora. They said their goodbyes and opened the door. Nora promised to write a letter as soon as possible, telling them about how the appointment had gone.

Katherine sucked in air greedily as soon as she got outside. She couldn't smell urine anymore.

"Come on." Nora locked their arms together as they walked to the car.

Is she planning on saying anything? Katherine was aware that she hadn't behaved well. She knew that she was being a stuck-up snob who couldn't wait to run back to her comfortable life. And it was true. Katherine wanted to go home. She wanted to take Nora with her and her feelings for Nora hadn't changed, but she wanted to go home now.

They drove in silence to the doctor. Nora seemed to only want to look out the window and Katherine kept her eyes upfront, her knuckles whitening from the grip on the wheel. She was waiting for the words. The words of disappointment from Nora.

I Love you, Nora Whispered

Doctor Tillot's study was run in a building near South Kensington. As they drove by rows of pretty streets, parks, and buildings, Katherine wondered what Nora thought about her world. Was she as disgusted and shocked by her family as Katherine was by hers? She pulled the car into the parking lot and turned it off. She kept her eyes on the dashboard. It was amazing to think about how fast they had gone from ecstasy to agony. Here they were.

"Here we are." Nora touched her hand and Katherine looked up. *Had she read my thoughts?* Katherine was feeling strange.

"Do you want me to go with you?"

"No." Nora shook her head. "This is something I have to do by myself."

Okay. Katherine ran her fingers over the palm of Nora's hand. Part of her wished they were still in bed. That today hadn't happened. Something had changed yet again and Katherine didn't know yet what it meant. The uncertainty was killing her. Not caring who saw, she put Nora's hand to her lips in a featherlight kiss. Their gazes met, and Nora's eyes were like honey.

"I will be back to pick you up in an hour. If you need me earlier," letting go of Nora's hand, "have Doctor Tillot's secretary call Mrs. Oswald in Richmond."

Nora nodded. She took a deep breath, seemingly gathering courage. She gave Katherine one last look, opened the door, and left. *There goes my girl.*

196

Chapter Twenty-Eight

Sweat was running down her back, her cheeks wet and itchy from shed tears. When she glanced at herself in the waiting room mirror, Nora could see that she looked like a downright mess. The session with the doctor had been hard. Over and over, he had forced her to walk, and move, bending her joints, holding on to bars, jumping. He had also given her a small plastic bottle of pills that she had to take every day. Nora wasn't sure what was in the pills but she had gladly signed the waiver saying that she understood that it was experimental. If Nora going through this could help even one person to not suffer, it would be worth it. And perhaps she could get better in the process.

She took her jacket and walked down to the street. Katherine's car was parked on the corner. Nora saw it and walked slowly towards it. Taking Katherine to her family had been a mistake. She had known it as soon as they had walked through the door. The smells and sounds and sights that were familiar and comforting to Nora had seemed different. She could imagine what it all seemed like through Katherine's eyes.

Her steps faltered and she slowed down. *I'm proud of where I come from.* Katherine looked through the window but didn't smile or wave. *I love my family.* Katherine waved but the look in her face was unsure. *If Katherine can't deal with where I come from, we have no future.* Nora raised her hand and responded. When she had almost reached the car, Katherine got out.

"Hello." Katherine took a step forward; she looked so much like a lost puppy that Nora had to give her a hug. Holding her felt right even though it didn't feel normal between them.

Katherine walked around, opened her door, and watched Nora sink into the seat gratefully. She had been in Katherine's car so often it felt like home. Her feet belonged on this floor, her butt on the seat, Katherine by her side. The car started.

"How did it go?"

"It was hard," Nora said. "At first, we talked for a while. He wanted to know everything about the time I had polio, and what things are hard for me; if I have trouble breathing or swallowing." Before Katherine managed to ask, Nora answered. "No, I don't. I get out of breath faster than normal people of course but he wasn't concerned about that." She swallowed. "Maybe he should have been. He gave me pills. And then we had a session of physical therapy." *Now came the difficult part.* "He wants me to come back once a week." Katherine gulped. "Not to see him. He wants to find me a physical therapist that I can train with regularly, here in London. To keep up with mobility and to monitor if there is any regression or repression."

Nora looked at Katherine's hands. She didn't know if Katherine knew that it was so obvious when she was stressed with how she was holding the wheel. Nora couldn't take it anymore, she reached out and touched her fingers to Katherine's hands.

"Please relax, darling," she said. They were stuck in traffic and cars were all around them. "I didn't say I'm about to move here, I just..." She bit her lip.

"What?" Katherine looked at her. *Were those tears in her eyes?*

"Martha is looking for jobs for us here, closer to home." Nora hadn't planned to say anything but after the fiasco with her family, she wanted to test Katherine a little. "Maybe it would be good for us." And it would be nice to be here when Anne came home too, but Nora didn't say that.

"What?" Katherine's voice was shrill. "Are you serious? What about... what about us?"

Nora chewed on her bottom lip, searching for the good words. The traffic lessened and they had almost left London now. *I don't want to break her heart.*

"You didn't like my family." *What?* "Sorry, that's not what I meant to say, I just..."

"I didn't mind them." Katherine's voice was still shrill, sounding nervous. "I'm sure they're lovely."

Nora sucked in air through her mouth. She had never been angry with Katherine before, not like this.

"It doesn't feel nice knowing that you hate where I come from," she said.

"But I hate everything!" Katherine snapped. "I hate everyone; why should your family be any different?" She stepped on the brakes so fast, Nora was thrown forward. The car stopped with a groan. Katherine hit her fist on the wheel. She opened the door and got out, slamming it shut.

What just happened? Nora stared, wide-eyed, following the angry figure on the other side. Katherine was walking down the nearby field, looking as if she wasn't planning to come back. Her back was jumping as if she was sobbing hard. *Don't go.* Nora fumbled with the lock on the door, forced it open, and ran after her.

"Katherine!" The field was bumpy and a rock caught Nora's foot. She fell forward with a yelp. Tears were running down her cheeks now. She didn't want to fight. She didn't want to make Katherine angry. It had just hurt her to see how Katherine had acted and to know that Martha and the others would never accept Katherine. Not even as Nora's friend.

"Nora." Katherine kneeled beside her where she was still lying on the ground. "Are you injured?"

She put a hand on Nora's arm and pulled her up. As soon as Nora was on her feet, she grabbed hold of Katherine's hand, not letting her go again.

"I'm sorry I got angry." Katherine's face looked destroyed, wet, red, and still somehow beautiful to Nora. "I don't know what happened when we visited your family today." She sighed and then did something that Nora never thought she would get to see. Classy, rich, beautiful Katherine, sat down on the ground and crossed her arms. It made her look like a grumpy little girl.

Not seeing there was anything else to do, Nora sat down next to Katherine. She picked three pieces of grass and started braiding them. They weren't in a hurry; she could wait for Katherine.

Nora had started to feel cold when Katherine started to talk.

"You don't know who I am," she said. "I feel like a fraud when I'm with you." The sigh Katherine produced was the saddest sound Nora had ever heard. "I'm not a nice person. Whatever that sister of yours had said about me is probably true. I'm a rich brat who only cares about horses. I didn't like the house you grew up in. It smelled. It was dirty."

Nora winced.

"I didn't like your mother. I didn't like your siblings. I don't even like my parents." Katherine shrugged. "I hated my brother growing up. Sure, I don't tell anyone that." She sobbed and Nora reached for her hand. She didn't know if Katherine would accept her touch or want it but she wanted to provide comfort. Whatever Katherine was telling her, it was clear that it was important. "I'm not a pleasant person like you. You smile at things, genuinely. You laugh. You love things."

"So, do you," Nora interjected.

"I smile at you," Katherine dug her fingers into the ground. "I smile at you. I like you. I…" She reached over and put a finger under Nora's chin. She cupped Nora's jaw and pulled her into a cold, salty kiss. "I love you. I hate everything, but not you." She chuckled mirthlessly. "And perhaps Nightingale Prancer. And Frankie's Dream."

"And Tampas and Unicorn." Nora stared into her eyes. "Or any of the other horses." *She loves me.* Nora's heart was beating fast. *She loves me.* Do I love her back?

"Anyway." Katherine let go of Nora's chin and touched her own lip. "I realise now that maybe we're too different." *What?* "You are so sweet and nice and I only have friends because my mother made me." Nora's mouth dropped open. "When I'm with you I forget everything. I forget that I've been angry my whole life. I forget that I don't enjoy my life. I forget…" She sucked in air through her mouth. "I forget to hate everything. I forget to dislike things."

"I love you too." If anyone could relate to Katherine hating things and keeping her anger a secret, Nora could.

Katherine looked up, color draining from her face. "You do?"

Nora took her hand and leaned her head against Katherine's shoulder. They were still sitting on the ground in a random field in the British countryside but somehow it was perfect.

"I do." She pressed a kiss to Katherine's shoulder. "If anybody can understand the hatred towards family members or hatred against oneself, it's me." She bit her lip. "I have a book you see. A book of secrets. I don't know if I will ever show it to you but if I do, it's mainly spiteful thoughts about my family. I'm not proud of it, but it got me through life. It made me survive until I could meet you." She had to continue. "But you can't hate my family. You can't hate Martha. I can't allow it. If you truly love me, I need you to be able to visit my home without looking like you're constipated." Katherine snorted at Nora's words and Nora laughed. It felt good to release the pressure that had been building between them. Maybe everything could work out.

"What kind of relationship do you think I should have with your family?" Katherine asked. "As a daughter of your employer? I'm Miss Waterhouse to them. What reason can we give for me to come with you even one more time?"

"You're my friend," Nora said. "And we're not the first women to ever be together, you know? Martha had a *friend* once. She thinks I don't know but I do. It was one of the army wives who did her washing at ma's place. Ma knew too." Nora tangled their fingers together. "She didn't seem horrified. Not happy, but not horrified." She could feel Katherine stiffen next to her. "I'm not saying we should tell a single soul. Not even Martha. I'm saying that if they found out it wouldn't be the end of the world either."

Katherine relaxed again.

"I have no idea how my parents would react."

202

Nora kissed her shoulder again. She didn't want to worry about the future.

"Can you make me one promise though?" Nora didn't want to push the issue, not when Katherine was still distraught. Katherine seemed to have calmed down, however, and Nora couldn't leave it alone.

"Anything." That one word meant almost more than any *I love you*'s that Katherine had shouted out during their previous love-making.

"You can't be rude to my family. They mean the world to me, even if I dislike them sometimes. It hasn't been easy for them either, having an invalid—"

"You're not an invalid." Katherine stood up and gently helped Nora to her feet too. "You're far from an invalid. But okay, I will do my best to like them."

"That's all I can ask for." Nora looked around them to see that no one was watching, then she stood on tiptoe and pressed a quick kiss to Katherine's lips. "Let's go home."

Chapter Twenty-Nine

Martha had finished her duties early and was now pacing back and forth. Residual tension was still in her shoulder. First one of the younger horses had developed colic late last night and Martha and one of the other stable hands had taken turns all night walking him to make sure he didn't get volvulus. It was only when the sun was up and the horse was out of danger that Martha realised that Nora hadn't come home.

After the horrible night, she had yelled at the entire Waterhouse family, Martha didn't dare to ask them if they had heard from Katherine, so she was stuck asking Mrs. Chapman as soon as breakfast was over. Mrs. Chapman didn't know.

Since then Martha had waited. And waited. And waited. She had eaten dinner with the others— bangers and mash, her favorite—but then she had gone out again. The sky was darkening and the shadows were getting longer. She leaned her back against the cool wooden wall of the stable and tried to relax. From her position, she had a full view of where Katherine usually parked her car. When they arrived— and they would—Martha would see them. If they didn't Martha would just have to seek out Mr. and Mrs. Waterhouse in spite of her better judgement.

The sound of an engine was getting closer and Martha's heart skipped a beat. When Katherine's car came to a halt, Martha almost ran forward but at the last minute stopped still. She remained in the shadows, watching.

It took a while for them to exit the car but there was no light inside and it was so dark, Martha had to squint. *Are they kissing?* They wouldn't kiss in such a way that everyone could see them, right? Martha squinted even harder and leaned forward as much as she dared, without taking her back off of the wall. *Okay,* she thought, *it's not actually possible to see them.*

A door opened and she put herself flat against the wall with a gasp. Katherine and Nora hugged for a long time. *Go up there and say something.* They let go of each other and Katherine picked up Nora's bag and walked her to the servants' quarters. They were too far away for Martha to hear what they were saying but they seemed to be talking. Their hands met.

Martha sighed. It didn't matter if she thought that Katherine was the most horrible person in the world, it was clear that she cared for Nora. If she didn't she wouldn't carry Nora's bag to the door. Nora was staff after all. Martha found herself once more thinking about Mrs. Allen and their summer fling. She still remembered their break-up as if it was yesterday. The way a cold hand had taken her heart in a grip and squeezed. The way she thought she could read Mrs. Allen's eyes. *You don't want to break up with me. You don't. You don't.* Mrs. Allen had said that she did. When Martha had come home that night her mother had held her when she cried as if she knew.

Nora went inside and Katherine closed the door behind her. Martha expected her to leave right away but Katherine kept a hand on the door. *Is she smiling? Is she pining?* Her behaviour was bizarre.

Katherine left the door, went over to the car, and got her own bag out. Before she started walking towards the main building, Martha set off.

"Wait!" She ran over to Katherine.

"Where did you come from?" Katherine looked around as if expecting more people in the shadows.

"Never mind that." Martha's heart was beating fast. "I'm sorry! Okay, I'm sorry for talking bad about you to Nora. I don't think you deserved it. Even if…" she stretched her neck… "you're not the most pleasant person." She smiled sheepishly, unsure if it could be seen in the dim light or not.

Katherine dropped her bag and folded her arms over her chest.

"What do you want?"

"What do I want?" Martha wanted to touch her hand to Katherine's arm, being used to communicating by touch. She didn't think touching Katherine was a good idea. "I want a good life. I want to earn enough to be able to send money back to our family in London. I want Nora to be happy. I want her to be loved. I want for her what I want for myself and all my siblings. A good relationship." Katherine stayed silent. *How is she seeming taller?* Martha pursed her lips. She wasn't to be intimidated. "Do you like her? *Like her?* Are you fond of her? Do you—"

"Can you keep your voice down please?" Katherine waved her hands in front of Martha's face. "With every word you've talked louder and louder, do you want to wake everyone up?"

"Sorry," Martha hissed. "I'm just saying…" she bit her lip, unsure what it was that she was saying. "I'm just saying… what I wanted to say is that it's Nora's birthday tomorrow." That wasn't what she wanted to say at all but once the words had crossed her lips it felt important. "It's her birthday and I think you should do something for her."

"Do you now?" Katherine hadn't moved. She inhaled slowly. "Thank you for telling me. I wouldn't have wanted to miss it."

"You really like her then." It was said as a statement this time, not as a question.

"I don't know who should be more offended that you seem unsure, Nora or I," Katherine said curtly.

The words made Martha ashamed. Did she really think so little of Nora that she didn't believe it when someone liked her? An owl cried in the woods, making goosebumps stand up on the back of Martha's neck. Autumn truly was coming.

"I'm not perfect," she said, making Katherine snort. "I'm just a protective sister. Is there nothing about that that you can recognize?"

"Being a protective sister?" Katherine shook her head no. "But I can understand being protective of Nora." Martha would have given anything to see Katherine's facial expression and not just her statue stance. "She is wonderful."

"That she is." Martha reached out then and touched her arm. "Let's be friends then." She felt the forearm under her hand tense but she dug her fingers in. "For Nora."

The arm was still tense but Katherine nodded. A door opening on the main building made them both look up. Martha removed her hand. It was late.

"You should go," she said. *Come on, Martha, be nice.* "Thank you for… ahem… listening to me."

Katherine nodded again.

"You too I suppose." Katherine picked up her bag again. "Well, goodnight."

Martha stayed, watching Katherine walk up to the main building. She was unsure how she felt, if she was alright with Katherine and Nora being sweethearts or if there was still something about the whole situation that bugged her.

She shivered as the wind picked up. Nora was going to wonder where she was and Martha wanted to hear everything about their trip, what the doctor had said and done; if Katherine had the ability to be sweet and romantic. Martha turned around and walked towards the servant's quarters. The lights were already off.

She opened the door with minimal creaks and tip-toed across the communal area. She found her room, opened the door, and was accosted by Nora. Nora beat her fist into Martha's chest and then pulled her into a hug.

"You idiot! Do you know how worried I was when I arrived and you weren't here!" The hug was so perfect and Martha felt herself relax when she rested her head on Nora's shoulder. Nora had both arms around Martha's waist. The scent was comforting with an underlying scent of something that Martha didn't recognize. *Nora didn't smell like Katherine, did she?* The thought was slightly nauseating. They let go.

"Now tell me." Nora tapped her violently, but not painfully, on the shoulder. "Where were you?"

"I was in the stable," Martha said. "Then I talked with Katherine for a while."

"What?" Nora's eyes widened. It was evident what she was thinking and Martha held her hands up.

"Don't worry, I didn't say anything bad. I promise."

Nora chewed on the insides of her cheeks and Martha recognized the nervous action. She placed her arm around Nora's shoulder and led her into the room. They sat down on the bed. The room was dark except for a small kerosene lamp on the desk. Martha took Nora's hand in hers.

"We decided to be friends, believe it or not." Martha squeezed Nora's hand.

"Really?" Nora seemed to not believe her.

"Well, I said let's be friends." Martha chuckled. "And Katherine didn't say let's not."

"That's something at least." Nora's shoulders dropped from the tense state they had been in. She leaned herself back. "Was she nice to you?"

"She was herself," Martha said. It was nice to hear that Nora cared. "But she wasn't unpleasant either. She listened to me and we called a truce. For you." She reached up and took Nora's chin in her hand. "She called you wonderful."

Nora's blush was evident even in the dark room.

"Did she really?"

Martha nodded.

Chapter Thirty

Katherine's eyes opened, her lips were parted and her heart was beating fast. Between her thighs, a remaining pounding was still going even though her hand was nowhere near the spot. She closed her eyes again, wishing the dream would come back. The dream that had made her come so hard it had woken her up. She licked her dry lips. *Nora.* No other person had ever made her feel so much, so fast, so intensely.

She sat up. *Nora!* Everything came back from last night, even the latest events. The talk with Martha. Katherine had gone upstairs, popped into her parents' bedroom to let them know she was there and retreated to her room. Not to sleep but to prepare for the next day. Nora's birthday. The birthday of her sweetheart. It was a very important day. Katherine had never celebrated a sweetheart's birthday before. She wanted the day to be perfect.

She had made a birthday card out of paper she had found in a drawer, written with the most beautiful calligraphy she could manage. Smiling at herself, she had gone through the house looking for everything she would need. A map of the nearby area, her photo album, writing paper, pens, a red silk band, and an old silver locket she found among her childhood things. With her loot she sat at her desk under lamplight, preparing until birds had started singing. She must have gone to bed. She must have fallen asleep. Otherwise, she wouldn't have suddenly woken up.

A smile played on her lips and she laughed from the joy coursing through her chest. She couldn't remember the last time she had felt so happy. She pushed her duvet out of the way and jumped out of bed. A glimpse outside told her that it still wasn't so late.

On her desk, a small green package lay together with the map and a bunch of scribbled notes. She took a bag from under her bed and put all the contents inside. Her riding clothes were lying on the floor next to her closet; she gave them a quick sniff and then put them on. She was planning to spend her day around horses so it didn't matter how she smelled. She did make sure to apply her make-up carefully and fix her hair. She wanted to feel beautiful.

"It's Nora's birthday," she told herself in the mirror. The smile made her face look strange, she wasn't used to smiling so widely.

Exiting her room, she headed to her parents first. She knocked and went inside without even waiting for the reply. Her mother was still sleeping but her father was sitting up; smoking a pipe and reading the paper. A tray with two teacups stood next to the bed. Katherine grabbed one and drank the tea. *Good, Mrs. Chapman is up.*

"Good morning, Katherine." Her father looked at her above his glasses.

"Good morning, father." She cleared her throat and filled her mother's teacup again. "I'm going to be borrowing Martha and Nora Lakes today, is that alright? Is there anything special planned?" She crossed her fingers behind her back.

"We have nothing planned," her father said. "But isn't Martha that loud stable girl? We need her for mucking out." *Please.* Katherine looked at him, waiting for him to finish. "But I suppose we can spare her for a couple of hours. How long do you need her?" He was assuming that she needed the Lakes sisters for something worthwhile and not a birthday adventure. Katherine wasn't going to correct him.

"Until five in the afternoon." Maybe they would be home later than that, maybe earlier, but she wanted to give them all enough time to truly enjoy themselves.

"Fine." Her father looked back at his paper.

*

Katherine couldn't control her movement but ran down the stairs. The door of the kitchen swung open with the power that Katherine hit it with. She went inside like a whirlwind.

"Mrs. Chapman can…" She stopped, silent, smacking her mouth closed. She had come face to face with Nora. Her sweetheart had an amused look on her face.

"Mrs. Chapman has gone to the restroom," Nora said. The bacon was sizzling in the pan, making the whole kitchen smell divine. Nora was holding a spatula. She was wearing a black dress with a white apron.

"Katherine." Nora laughed and took hold of Katherine's arm. "Are you listening?" Her lips were red, moist, ready.

Not able to wait anymore, Katherine put a hand around Nora's waist and pulled her into a morning kiss. Nora made a surprised noise but reciprocated the kiss, putting her hands on Katherine's shoulders. When they pulled apart, Nora looked even happier. Steps outside the kitchen door made them move away from each other, but Nora's smile never wavered.

"Good mo—"

"Happy birthday."

Nora's mouth dropped open. "Martha told you?"

Katherine nodded.

"I'm sorry for this, I was going to ask Mrs. Chapman," she said. "But can you make three bacon sandwiches?" It felt wrong to ask Nora to do it, maybe Katherine should…

"Sure, anything else?" Nora didn't seem to think it was strange.

"Can you put some coffee in a thermos? And do we have any fruit?" Katherine's heart was beating a strange rhythm she didn't recognize. "Let's say you were packing for a picnic, what would you bring?"

Nora giggled. She put her hand up to her mouth.

"I've never seen you like this before," she said. "I guess bacon sandwiches, a coffee thermos, and fruit salad should be good. How does that sound?"

"That sounds perfect." Katherine couldn't help but pull her in for another kiss. "Here." She took out a pair of riding trousers from her bag. "I've gotten you excused for the entire day. Can you pack up the picnic, put these on, and meet me at the paddock in thirty minutes or so?"

Nora accepted the trousers with a raised eyebrow. She looked at them carefully.

"Are these yours?" She said eventually. "They won't fit me."

"They're from when I was a teenager." Katherine bit her lip. *Just do as you're told,* she wanted to say. Not to be mean but because she honestly couldn't wait to execute her plan. *You're going to have so much fun, just trust me.* "I think they should fit you, and if they don't just put on tights and a very loose skirt." At the word 'loose' she turned pink and scratched the back of her head. "Or come and find me in the paddock and tell me that it doesn't fit you, alright?"

"Alright." Nora nodded. Her smile was so earnest it made Katherine ache. *I've done nothing to have her looking at me that way.* "Off you go then, see you in a bit."

Katherine pressed another kiss to Nora's cheek and left the kitchen through the other door, heading right outside. She continued walking in quick strides, on her way to the stables. The sun was shining above and the morning birds were singing. The only sign that autumn was coming and that summer was waning was her mother's hollyhocks and rambling roses. Just a week or so ago, Katherine could have sworn they still had color. Now the flowers had dropped and the leaves were turning grey. Something about the sight caused shivers to travel down Katherine's spine but she shook her head, trying to forget and continued down the garden path. She needed to find Martha.

*

Nora could almost not hold her excitement as she prepared the sandwiches, put the fruit salad in a container, and filled a thermos. Mrs. Chapman came back but didn't raise a brow when Nora told her she had been excused for the day. "Maybe they need you down with the horses," she just said and that was that. When everything was packed into a bag, Nora took the trousers and left the kitchen. It was getting warmer outside. *Maybe today is the last day of summer,* she thought. The outside was beckoning and Nora couldn't wait to see what Katherine had in store for her. She put the bag outside the servants' quarters and wobbled into her room - the excitement was making her unsteady - and got dressed in the trousers and a shirt from her own wardrobe. She only owned one pair of shoes, so they would have to do. Ready and dressed, she headed outside, grabbing the bag and walking as fast as she could towards the paddock.

Already before she went around the corner, she could hear Martha and Katherine talking.

"But you have ridden before?"

"Yes, yes, it's just been a while since —"

Neither of them looked up as Nora reached the paddock. They were standing with a small black horse, fully tacked, between them.

"Hello?" Nora opened the paddock gate and went inside.

At her words, the women in her life both looked up.

"Happy birthday!" they said in unison, immediately looking annoyed at each other. Nora didn't know whether to be touched or amused.

"Thank you," she laughed. "What have you two gone and done?"

Her eyes were drawn to the horse and she walked up to it, touching its silken mule. It had the kindest pair of eyes she had ever seen.

"This is Catleya of Gallus," Katherine said. "She's one of the mares we use for breeding."

"Oh?" Nora was transfixed by Catleya. "She is pretty."

"That she is." Katherine gave Catleya's neck a pat. "She is getting older though and hasn't kept anything since the last filly."

"You're losing your babies?" Nora looked at the horse again. She remembered how sad her ma had been after the miscarriage and it was nothing she wished on anyone. Not even a horse.

"During the last year, we have just let her walk in the fields and let my father's nephews ride her when they come to visit." Katherine made a grimace. "They're just above ten, both of them. Little monsters they are but Catleya never seems to mind." She bumped Nora's shoulder with her own. "And that's why she's perfect."

"Perfect?" The cogwheels in Nora's head were turning but she didn't dare to hope. "Perfect for what?"

"Today is the day you ride, little sister." Martha grabbed her hand. "Katherine planned all of it."

"Really?" Nora moved her head between both of them, unsure what to think.

"Yes." Katherine put both her hands on Catleya's fur. "We're going to lead you around the paddock first, making sure you can walk and perhaps trot a bit. And if that feels okay, we will saddle Unicorn for Martha and Frankie's Dream for me and we'll ride out for a little excursion."

"A picnic." Nora didn't think she had ever felt so happy before.

"A picnic." Katherine nodded. "But first riding. The clothes fit well, I trust."

Nora nodded, unable to get any words out. She looked at Catleya again. *Soon I'll sit on top of you.*

"Hang on, I'll get a stepstool." Martha disappeared to the side.

"Let's try to lead her first," Katherine said. She gave Nora the reins. "Hold these, stand next to Catleya's head and walk."

Katherine placed herself on the other side, not holding the horse at all, with Nora between them. They started walking. For once, Nora was very aware of her limp so she talked, trying to trick herself into forgetting.

"I can't believe you did this for me."

"Don't be silly, I'm enjoying this too." Katherine let her fingers briefly touch Nora's. "Now, I know you know this, but it's important to pay attention. After the storm and all. But even during good weather a horse can suddenly get scared of something. It's good to always be aware of your surroundings. Hold the reins with both hands. You can walk next to your horse or a bit in front since it's supposed to look at you as a leader."

"I love you," Nora whispered as a response. She was dying to kiss Katherine and wished they were inside somewhere.

Katherine looked like she wanted to say something but Martha chose that very moment to come back with a small wooden stool.

"Here!" She was a bit out of breath. "I found it in the stable chamber."

"Good." Katherine nodded. "Then let's lead Catleya to the middle of the paddock."

Nora did as she was told. Her heart was pounding hard now. Not just excitement but nerves and fear. What if Catleya ran away with her? What if Nora fell off and broke all her bones? What if she embarrassed herself or hurt Catleya or… It was time. Catleya was standing in the middle of the paddock. Katherine was holding her and Martha was standing by the stool, waiting to give Nora a hand.

"Are you ready?"

There was no other answer than yes. Nora nodded, pushed her teeth together, and got up on the stool. When she was there, Catleya's back was at her waist level and didn't seem so tall. Martha showed her to put one foot in the stirrup in front of her, then she swung her leg over

Catleya's back. And there. She was on top of a horse. She released a breath she had been holding and bubbly laughter rose through her stomach. Even though Catleya hadn't taken a single step forward, Nora already knew this was the most fun she would ever know.

"Are you okay?" Katherine came to stand on her other side. She helped Nora's foot into the other stirrup. Nora had already gathered the reins and Katherine showed her to place them between her thumb and her little finger to get the best grip. "Feeling safe?"

"Very." Nora smiled widely. "This is the best thing I have ever done."

"Really?" Something naughty flashed in Katherine's eyes but disappeared almost completely. She looked down, picking at something on Catleya's saddle. "The first time I sat in the saddle, I was horrified. It was the scariest thing I had ever done."

"Really?" Martha was on the other side, looking at Katherine over Catleya's back.

"I was five." Katherine grinned. "It took me several years before I dared to ride again."

Martha opened her mouth as to answer but Nora hurried to talk before her.

"This is fun and all, but I want to ride now." Nora didn't even wait for Katherine or Martha to tell her what to do; she had been watching Katherine and the other riders for weeks. She had seen them walk on and how they had gently squeezed the middle or kicked them in the stomach. Nora didn't want to kick Catleya but she put her heels firmly to Catleya's side and to her delight, Catleya started walking forward.

Nora understood that Catleya was an exceptionally kind horse who eagerly did what she was told but she couldn't help but feel very proud. Nothing in her body hurt and the slight swaying of Catleya's walk felt natural. *I want it to go faster.* Nora bit her lips. She felt like a teenager, wanting speed and to throw caution to the wind. Being on horseback freed her from her own body, freed her from her worrying soul. She touched her hand to Catleya's soft fur.

"You are so sweet," she said. "I hope you know that."

When Catleya had walked her around the whole paddock, Katherine met up with her. Martha had gone to sit down on the bench.

"Are you sure you haven't ridden before?"

Nora laughed.

"I'm sure." She couldn't stop smiling. "I want to try to trot."

"Alright." Katherine nodded. "I'm going to hold Catleya's head just in case this first time. Trotting is very bumpy and..." she stopped talking as if gathering her thoughts.

"You're worried how I'll do," Nora filled in. She touched her hand to Katherine's shoulder. "Don't worry, I'm not offended or anything. I'm sure it will be fine, let's go."

"Okay, push with your ankles now."

"What?" Nora's eyebrows knotted. A fly came to sit on Catleya's back and she waved it off.

"That's what it's called when you press your heels into her side to make her go faster."

Nora did as she was told, at the same time Katherine smacked her lips together. Catleya raised her head slightly and started trotting.

The body underneath her became bumpy and Nora struggled to hold her balance. She grabbed hold of the top of the saddle and felt all her confidence run off her. She wanted to tell Katherine to stop, for Catleya to go back to walking. She wanted to go back to the feeling she had had before. Something made her not say anything though. She tried to sit deeply and just feel the movement. The saddle hit her tailbone but the pain wasn't acute and after a few minutes, it didn't hurt at all. When they had trotted all around the paddock, Katherine slowed down. Sweat was running down Nora's back and she felt her arms aching.

"How was that?"

"Bumpy," she said, swallowing.

"It is," Katherine said. "I wanted to have you feel it even though I'm planning for us all just to walk when we're out." She touched a hand to Nora's knee; a touch that might have been innocent but it shot tingles down her leg. "Now we're going to try something different, it's something that makes the trot less bumpy. Even with good knees, it's tough so we'll see how you feel."

She lets me set my own limit. The thought was enough to make Nora feel confident again. She pressed her lips together and nodded. She was determined to manage this lesson.

"Good girl." Katherine grinned and something dark swirled in her eyes again as she looked up at Nora. *Oh lord, we are in trouble.* Nora's gaze fell on Katherine's lips. Did Martha have to be with them the entire day? Would they have a chance to sneak away for at least a quick kiss?

"What do I need to do?" she asked, trying to clear her mind. Catleya neighed, making her chest rumble. It was such a strange sensation and Nora loved it.

"Every other step she takes you sit down, and every other step she takes you stand up."

What? Katherine must have gone insane.

"Stand up?"

"Oh yes." Katherine nodded. "You've seen me jump, right? When the horse jumps, I stand up in the saddle." She took a hold of Nora's ankle. "Let's try it. Let go of the reins, I got her. Just stand up."

It felt strange but Nora stretched her legs and stood up. It worked as her butt came off the saddle, but oh my, it was hard to keep her balance. Within what felt like less than two seconds, her thighs were quivering from the effort.

"Sit down again," Katherine said. "I know it's a hard job to keep up all the time, but when trotting you will feel, hopefully, that you're almost pushed up. When you get the rhythm, it's no effort on your part."

"Are you sure?" Nora couldn't see how she would ever be able to manage the feet of trotting.

"Of course," Katherine laughed. "Want me to run next to you?"

Nora nodded and off they went.

*

After about twenty more minutes, Nora got off to head to the restroom while Katherine and Martha prepared horses for themselves. She couldn't say she had mastered the rising trot exactly but perhaps it hadn't been quite as bumpy as the first time. *Either way,* she thought as she wobbled towards the servants' quarters, *we're not planning to trot during the outing and I'm a natural at walking.* She tripped over a rock and almost fell; instead of cursing under her breath or feeling ashamed, it made her miss Catleya. When Catleya walked for her, it was no problem. Nora hurried on, she couldn't wait to be back on horseback.

When she got back to the stable, three horses were tied up to the stable wall, tacked and ready. Catleya, Unicorn, and Frankie's Dream.

"I can't believe I have to go on this fat pony," Martha said but with a big smile on her face.

Nora chuckled. Unicorn did look very fat, not having been ridden for a while. She was happy that she had Catleya to ride on.

"There you are," Katherine said. "We have packed saddlebags with the food for us and some hay for the horses. There is a stream in the woods they can drink from. Are you ready?"

Their gazes met and Nora nodded. Happiness spread like wildfire through her body. Was it allowed to be this happy? Was it allowed for life to be this good?

Katherine helped Nora up on Catleya before getting up on Frankie's Dream. Martha sat up on Unicorn and then they were on their way. Katherine in the lead, Nora second, Martha last. They rode past the paddocks filled with happy, well-fed horses, past the small playpen with the foals, eating, and playing. They left Waterhouse Acre Stables behind them and walked into the forest.

There was silence in the woods, silence, and peace. The trees seemed to envelop them from behind and the only things they could hear were the sounds of the hooves hitting the ground. Occasionally Martha made a grunt or curse word when Unicorn tried to stray from the path to snag himself a delicious branch or piece of grass.

Katherine held her horse back so Nora could ride up next to her.

"Having fun?"

"This is the best day of my life," Nora said without thinking. "Well, maybe the second best."

Katherine smiled at Nora's words. She bit her lip and looked upwards. *Oh, what I wouldn't give to be able to read her thoughts right now.*

"Good," Katherine said eventually. "I'm glad. We will ride for another forty minutes or so, then we'll reach a stream. There we will stop, water the horses, and have a picnic."

"Sounds lovely."

"No!" They heard behind them. "Noooooo."

Nora held Catleya back and turned her head around. Laughter bubbled in her throat and she didn't manage to hold it back. Unicorn was grazing next to the path and in front of him, on the ground, sat Martha with a big patch of dirt on her cheek. She looked up at Katherine.

"Your stupid fat pony keeps wanting to eat grass. He put his head down so fast I rolled down it." Her mouth was a thin line but there was laughter in her eyes. When both Nora and Katherine chuckled, Martha laughed too. "Okay, fine, fine." She got up on Unicorn again.

The stream Katherine had mentioned ran through a picturesque clearing with flowers growing between the trees. The women took the bridles off the horses and tied them up with halters instead. Katherine also showed the others how to release the girdle just a little bit in case the horses wanted to graze.

When that was done, Nora took it upon herself to prepare a picnic for them. She took out a blanket Katherine had packed and spread it out on the ground. She took the food out; the bacon sandwiches, the fruit salad, the coffee. The sun was shining through the trees and she turned her face towards it, feeling the rays on her skin. She felt so alive it hurt.

"I didn't even know I was hungry," Martha said, devouring the bacon sandwich in three quick bites.

Katherine chuckled. "And you complained about the way Unicorn was eating."

Nora smacked her hand over her mouth, unable to believe Katherine had just said that.

"Pfft," Martha didn't reply and instead grabbed the thermos with coffee. "Everyone knows that riding makes you hungry."

Nora's stomach rumbled and she couldn't help but agree. She handed Katherine a sandwich and grabbed one for herself.

Once they had eaten, Katherine stroked her hand over her trousers, cleaning it.

"I think it's present time."

"Present time?" Nora said. "No, you've already done enough. Both of you. The picnic, the riding... You don't need to."

"Don't be silly," Martha said. "You know rich people get both a party *and* presents and your sweetheart is rich, so..."

"Martha!" Nora threw a look at Katherine but she didn't look offended at all.

"Well." Katherine took out a small box from one of the saddlebags. "She isn't wrong."

"No, me first." Martha pulled the saddlebag to her and rummaged through it. "Here!"

She placed the package in Nora's lap. It was wrapped in brown paper, the same type of paper the sandwiches had been wrapped in and about as big as Nora's palm. Nora took the paper off slowly, wanting to savour the moment. It was a book.

"It's 'The Little Prince' by French author Antoine de Saint-Exupéry. It's supposed to be for children but it's supposed to be lovely and I thought it would suit you."

"Thanks." Nora ran her fingers over the cover. She didn't own many books so this was a gift she treasured. "I love it."

She looked up, locking eyes with Katherine. *What was Katherine going to give her?*

"Here." Katherine evaded Nora's gaze and placed the small box in her hands. It was a proper jewelry box. Wooden and red with little white flowers painted on it. Around it, Katherine had tied a red silk band.

"You've given me a jewelry box?" Nora traced it with her thumb. It was already the prettiest thing she owned. She didn't even need to look through her other belongings. "Thank you so—"

"No!" Katherine cleared her throat. "I mean, no. I mean, yes." She fell silent and licked her lips. Her face was bright red. Nora and Martha locked eyes. Nora felt like giggling at Katherine's strange behaviour but held it back. *It's for me. Her stumbling behaviour was prettier than the box. What a gift.* "Your present is inside. The box is yours too of course but the thing inside is the real gift."

"Oh." Nora turned her focus to the box. She undid the ribbon, moved the little metal hatch, and pried the box open. "Oh." She didn't know what else to say.

Inside the box was a little locket made of silver, attached to a silver chain. The locket was engraved with lines and little flowers. Nora picked it up, speechless and breathless. It was cool against her heated skin.

"Open it." Katherine sounded equally breathless.

Nora stuck her fingernail into the locket, finding the locking mechanism and prying it open. It had room for two photos and Katherine had already put two photos there. Nora's heart pounded fast as she took in the sights. On one side there was a photo of Katherine, staring into the camera with a smile on her face. On the other side, there was a photo of Nightingale Prancer and Nora was damned if the horse wasn't smiling too.

She looked up at Katherine, unsure what to say. All color had drained from Katherine's face. They stared at each other, neither of them saying anything until Martha cleared her throat behind them.

"I only had one photo of Nightingale Prancer," Katherine said. "I wanted you to have it."

Without thinking about what she was doing, Nora closed her fingers around the locket, put both hands on the ground, and leaned forward to reach Katherine's lips. Katherine's lips were tense and Nora wondered why at first until she realised she was kissing her in front of Martha. She leaned back with a small noise, feeling her face grow very hot.

"Sorry," she mumbled at Katherine and turned to look at Martha.

Martha was looking down, fingering a lint piece from the blanket.

"I'm glad you like it," Katherine said. She was blushing a bit too but her eyes were sparkling. Nora didn't think she had ever seen Katherine look that young. "It felt silly at first but I wanted to give you something you would like, really like." She bit her lip. Nora wanted to kiss her again but the thought of embarrassing Martha and Katherine wasn't quite as tantalizing.

"I do really like it," she said. "I wish there was something else that I could say that conveys just how much I like it."

"Girls!" Martha rolled her eyes and laid down on her back. She put both hands behind her head and put one foot on top of the other knee. "Wake me up when it's time to head back."

Nora and Katherine locked eyes and both fell into laughter.

"Thank you so much," Nora said. "I'll never take it off."

Chapter Thirty-One

Sweat was running down her back and the horse's pelt was glistening. Even though they had only walked, the sun was hitting them hard. Even though Katherine had enjoyed the whole of their outing she was looking forward to getting out of the saddle, getting into the cool stable, maybe drinking some water. *Maybe Mrs. Chapman can make some lemonade.*

Katherine twisted around in the saddle to take a look at the people behind. Nora's arms were visibly shaking and her face was sunburnt. Katherine had never seen a woman with dark hair get freckles before but the sun had painted cute little spots all over Nora's nose and cheeks. She even had a couple on her chin and forehead. She looked tired though and Katherine was happy that their outing was over.

They rode over the yard, toward the stable and Katherine hurried to jump off. She threw the reins over to Martha who seemed to be reading her mind. Nora had let go of the stirrups and looked like she was thinking of jumping off without aid. If she said it out loud, Katherine would let her but both of them knew that Nora was tired now. Katherine walked over to her, reached up, and put her hands on Nora's waist. Their gaze locked and the air between them ignited. Katherine's heart started pounding hard and she struggled to keep her facial expression.

"Just slide down." *Stop sounding so breathless.* "I'll catch you."

Without letting go of the eye contact, Nora put her right leg over the horse's neck and then slid right into

Katherine's arms. Katherine couldn't stop herself from hugging her just a bit but let go so Nora could take Catleya's reins.

The horses were sweaty and they spent a long time brushing them, before releasing them into the pasture. Nora even gave Catleya a small hug which Katherine found adorable.

Martha had to run to the restroom so Nora and Katherine gathered up the brushes and walked into the stable together. Neither of them said anything. The air between them was thick and Katherine wondered if Nora could feel the anticipation just like she could.

Katherine walked into the stable chamber, placing the brush where it was supposed to go. She regarded Nora's back as Nora did the same. When Nora straightened up again and turned around, Katherine couldn't wait anymore.

Nora made a surprised noise when Katherine grabbed her shoulders against the wall, leaned down, and started kissing her. Nora's arm came to rest on the back of her neck and Katherine thought she would die, as nothing would ever feel this good. She pressed their bodies together, hoping she wasn't squishing Nora against the wall in the process. She could feel Nora's heartbeat against her own. *I love you so much. I love kissing you so much. Where have you been all my life?*

Somebody cleared their throat behind them, making them jump apart. Katherine had to blink a couple of times as if she couldn't focus. Her father was standing in the doorway. The expression on his face was unreadable.

"Miss Lakes, I think you should go pack your bags. And you should tell your sister to do the same."

Nora didn't leave, instead, she intertwined her fingers with Katherine's. They were big and wide and questioning. She would listen to Katherine even though Katherine's father was her boss. Katherine loved Nora for her bravery. She wanted nothing more for Nora to stay there but she needed to face her father alone.

"Go," she whispered, giving Nora's hand a final squeeze.

Her soul fell to the ground as Nora nodded, walking past Katherine's father and out of the stable chamber. Katherine didn't know what was going to happen now but braced herself for the worst.

*

Martha was leaving the restroom. Her bladder had been aching since they had reached the clearing over an hour earlier but she didn't think that Katherine would have approved of her going in the forest. Now she felt light as a bird and was ready to get on with her real job. She was sure that there were things for her to do. In a stable, there was always stuff to be done. She had enjoyed the day though. *I was so wrong about Katherine,* she thought. Even if she was a bit of a bitch, it was clear that she liked Nora a lot.

The door swung open and Nora came in. Her face was red and her eyes were filled with unshed tears.

"What's wrong?" Martha reached out but Nora backed away.

"I'm sorry," she mumbled and took off, running to their room.

What has happened? If it was Katherine, Martha was going to wring her neck. Everything had been going well, what could have happened that had destroyed the lovely day they had been having? Instead of heading outside, Martha headed straight for their room. She went inside and took care to both close and lock the door.

Nora was lying on the bed, crying into her pillow. Martha had seen this before. *I guess I was right.* She sat down and started making circles on Nora's back with the palm of her hand. *I didn't want to be right.*

"I'm sure Katherine didn't mean it, whatever it is she said," Martha said. "She cares for you, that much is clear."

Nora stopped sobbing and put her hands on the mattress and pushed herself up. Her face was puffy to the point of looking like someone else.

"She didn't say anything." Her voice was low and dark. "Her father, however…" she burst into tears again. "Oh, Martha, I have ruined everything." She leaned her head on the wall and looked up. The next sob sounded more like a wail and Martha worried that somebody would hear them and come looking.

The bed creaked under her when Martha sat down and put her arm around Nora. She pushed their heads together.

"Shhh," she said gently. "Shhh. Just cry, you don't need to tell me what happened right now. Just calm down first." She pulled Nora onto her lap and rocked her as if Nora was a child.

*

A knock on the door woke Nora up. At first, she couldn't tell where she was. Her limbs were aching and the leg she was hammering her fist against must have gone completely numb because she couldn't feel a thing.

"Stop hitting me." *Oh.* Her limbs were tangled with Martha's. They must have both fallen asleep because the room had gone dark.

Somebody knocked again, more carefully this time. "Girls? It's Mrs. Chapman."

Martha pushed off the bed, making herself free from Nora. She walked up to the door and opened it. As soon as the door swung open and Nora could see Mrs. Chapman's face she remembered. She remembered everything. The happiness. The kiss. Katherine's father. Agony pierced her chest so hard she felt like she couldn't breathe.

"Now I don't know what has happened," Mrs. Chapman said, putting her hands up. "But I've been asked to make sure you have left." She crossed her arms and looked at them both.

If Martha was surprised, she didn't show it. She crossed her arms too, throwing a quick look at Nora and then back at Mrs. Chapman.

"Alright." She nodded. "We will go right away."

She took up her bag and Nora's from under the bed.

"Come on." She offered a hand to Nora who was still sitting on the bed. Nora took it gently while looking at Martha's face, looking for any sign that Martha was angry, disappointed, distraught. Martha's face had become a statue.

They quickly packed up their things under Mrs. Chapman's eye. They shook hands with her, thanked her for this time, and then walked into the night. The sun had almost completely fallen and the ground underneath them was dark.

Nora's insides had gone as cold as the ground, and she couldn't tell if she was tired or not. There was a lump of tears in her throat, growing bigger by the minute. Fear was gripping her soul.

"We're going to have to walk to Shireoaks," Martha said. "I hope you will manage."

"Of course, I'll manage," Nora snapped but felt guilt right away over her tone. "Sorry."

"It's okay."

Of course, it isn't okay, Nora almost tripped on a bigger piece of gravel. She swore under her breath. *I lost both of us our jobs. I ruined everything. It's not okay.*

A car was coming closer behind them, the engine sounding louder and louder. Unsure if the car would be able to see them in the dark, Nora grabbed the hem of Martha's shirt and pulled her to the side.

As the car turned up next to them, Nora's heart did a double-take. She didn't even wait for the door to open before pulling it open herself. Katherine got out and threw her arms around Nora.

"I'm so sorry!" Nora sobbed loudly into Katherine's shirt. "I'm so sorry!"

"Shhh." Katherine pressed a kiss on the top of Nora's head. "It's not your fault."

Nora lifted her chin and looked into Katherine's eyes. She needed to know if Katherine was okay, anything else was unbearable.

Katherine's mouth opened a bit as if she was going to say something. Her eyes were dark, and in the ambience, Nora couldn't read anything in them. Instead of saying something, Katherine leaned down and kissed her. It was a soft kiss, a sad kiss, a kiss tasting of tears, despair and strangely, hope. Nora found that the kiss grounded her. *Everything would be okay.* They had found each other.

They knew that they existed. As long as they were both alive there was hope.

"I'm so sorry," Katherine said when they came apart. She lifted her gaze from Nora to Martha. She was still waiting for her usual anger. Instead, she felt empty. She didn't even feel worried. "I didn't know how my father would react. I am so sorry that you're out of a job because of Nora's and my... indiscretion." The word felt wrong.

"Don't think about it." Martha shook her head. "And don't call your feelings for my sister an indiscretion."

Katherine looked down at Nora again.

"No," she said. "I shouldn't."

"Are you okay?" Nora reached up and touched her fingers to Katherine's cheeks. "He isn't hitting you, is he?"

Katherine shook her head. "Don't worry about me. I can take my father's anger."

A lamp was lit all the way over on Waterhouse Acre Stables, like a beacon in the darkness.

"I have to go back." She let go of Nora, but not before kissing her one last time, and got into the car again. "Everything will be good." Her eyes were only on Nora. "I will fix it. I promise."

What she was going to fix, Nora didn't know. Katherine didn't say, she just closed the door and drove off into the night.

Chapter Thirty-Two

"Could you pass me the carrots, please?" Her mother's hand was very pale, something that Katherine hadn't reflected on before. Her own hands didn't look like that, even if they had the same shape. She spent too much time outside, doing manual labour. Her hands were tan and calloused. Like her father's.

"Of course." She picked up the plate and put it in her mother's hand. She then turned back to her own plate of vegetables, Sunday roast, mashed potatoes, and Yorkshire pudding. She had poured so much gravy on the whole feast that Mrs. Chapman had offered her a soup dish as a joke.

She sighed as she pushed a pea around the plate. This was her favorite meal every week and she couldn't find her appetite. The whole day had been a disaster.

"I saw Mr. Porter was here today." Her father's voice echoed in Katherine's head. It had been a week since Nora and Martha had left and even though he tried to be normal with her, Katherine wasn't having it. Mr. Porter was Katherine's trainer.

"Yes, father." She didn't look at him. Instead, she gathered some mashed potatoes and gravy on her fork and popped it in her mouth. She didn't care that she was using the fork as a spoon, one of her mother's pet peeves. Who cared about table manners anyway? Nora always used the fork that way, and in the wrong hand, it seemed easier to eat that way.

"How did it go?" It was the most her father had dared to talk with her all week. All the other nights, the days Katherine had actually attended dinner with them, the conversation had all been about the weather.

"How did what go?" Katherine put a piece of roast in her mouth and chewed it slowly.

"The training." Her father's gaze was burning on the side of her face. *I will not look at him. I will not look at him.*

The training hadn't gone well. It was as if Katherine couldn't focus. Frankie's Dream had fought with her the entire way. When Mr. Porter had told her to trot in big circles to open him up, make them both more flexible, their circles had become forced triangles. Frankie's Dream had picked up on her negative energy and when she kicked him into a walk he had just irritably waved with his ears and ignored her. There had been no jumping.

"Fine." If her father had seen part of the session and knew Katherine was lying, he didn't show. He just made a humming sound and continued eating.

Katherine was relieved her father didn't prod more. She was embarrassed at her performance during the lesson. Usually, Frankie's Dream and her worked together and didn't fight. She had felt so bad she had snuck him several carrots after the lesson. Mrs. Chapman wouldn't miss them.

"Katherine." Her mother lifted a wine glass and took a sip. By the time she put it down, Katherine was looking right at her. "Your father and I have been talking…" *Oh.* Katherine looked down at her plate again. It felt like this meal would never finish.

Her mother cleared her throat. What was she going to say that was so difficult? Katherine didn't know if she should feel worried or curious so she landed somewhere in between.

"Your father and I have been talking to the Johnsons." Her mother's fingers were circling her wine

236

glass. If Katherine hadn't known better she would have thought her mother was nervous. "Their youngest, George, has now moved away from home and branched out on his own."

They're not suggesting....? Katherine put her fork down and leaned back in her chair, staring at her mother.

"He has his own stable now, only because of his love of horses." Her mother smiled. "He works with… well, something with politics, down in London but when he is home he rides a lot." She took a quick sip of wine. *Here we go.* "We think he would be a perfect match for you."

The words landed between them. Katherine's eyes went wide and then she closed them, gathering strength. How could she make them understand? Understand that she was carving out her future as they spoke. She had already looked through her finances and sent away for access to an inheritance from her father's sister she had received a few years ago. She wasn't going to tell her parents that, however. Not until everything was finalised.

"It would be a great match," her father added. "He loves horses just like you. He is a few years older than you without a wife. He comes from a good family. I met him once and he is very kind and polite. He, if anyone, wouldn't mind a wife who rides."

Ha, I wouldn't mind a wife who rides either. Katherine smirked at her thoughts. Maybe she had had too much wine and not enough food. She quickly popped more mashed potatoes in her mouth before she said anything she would regret.

"Of course, you decide who you marry yourself." Her mother glanced at her father. Katherine wanted to know what was said behind closed doors. How disappointed were they with her? How stressed were they to get her married off? "You're an adult now, Katherine. We don't decide for you."

"However," her father spoke now. "That doesn't mean that we can support anything you do."

She looked at him then. She was an adult and avoiding him this way was childish. He looked like he had aged several years in a week. Against her will, a pang of guilt shot through her. His skin was a bit greyer, his hair a bit whiter.

"It is time to find a husband and form a household of your own," her father continued.

Katherine had plans. She just couldn't tell them yet. They weren't finalised yet. If she told them now they might be able to stop her somehow.

"I was thinking of opening a stable of my own." *Oh crap.*

Chapter Thirty-Three

"Ouch!" The steam from the brick copper rose quickly when Nora lifted the lid, causing her to drop it. Her hands were already red and itchy and she had only been working at the washhouse for a week. *If Katherine saw me now she wouldn't recognize me.* Nora hardly recognized herself either. She couldn't see her reflection in the steamy window but she knew. She knew her cheeks were red and she knew her hair was plastered against her scalp, wet and sweaty. Her clothes were powdered with water stains and her stomach was completely wet. She knew that underneath the white material her skin was irritated and blotchy. It was almost nice to be in London when she looked this way; there was no chance that she would run into Katherine. Even on purpose.

Oh Katherine. Nora started ringing the clothes by hand before mangling them. At first both her mother and Nora herself had been so sure that the wet clothes and linen would be too heavy for her. But it was manageable, heavy but manageable. She had built her muscles while being on the farm, even if she hadn't worked directly with the horses. She wasn't as weak anymore. Her hands were stronger, her arms were stronger, her legs more stable. It might be the doctor's treatments too; she had been in for a second treatment last week. She preferred to think that it was because of Katherine. And Nightingale Prancer. And the whole of Waterhouse Acre Stables.

When she had rung the laundry, it was time to start mangling. She wanted it to be done before her mother came back. The first couple of days she had been in charge of lunch and making sure Anne had food. Soon as they both realised that Nora could do the majority of the work, they had agreed that mother would work fewer hours.

As she started mangling, Nora chuckled at herself. The palms of her hands were stinging from the hard labour but there was joy forming in her heart. *I wonder if I've always been capable,* she thought and wiped sweat from her forehead. *I don't know why I didn't believe in myself.* It was hard work and her body hurt. But her body was so much more capable of anything and everything that she could ever have guessed. And it was getting stronger. *If I keep going,* she took a deep breath, *things will just get easier.* If she kept at it.

The door swung open.

"I'm back."

Her mother looked healthier since cutting down the hours at the washhouse, but it wasn't hard to realise that she was getting older. In the past the realisation would have caused Nora to panic, but it didn't anymore. She loved her family but not because she needed them to survive. Loving was the end goal now. If she had to deal on her own, she could.

"How is Anne?" Nora asked. Anne and their pa had been back in London for a couple of days.

"I don't know." Her mother sighed. "I know the doctor said she isn't in danger anymore but she is still so tired. I had to spoon feed her." Their gazes met. "I don't like leaving her."

"So, don't ma." Nora touched her hand. "I'll finish up here."

Biting her lip, her mother looked hesitant. "Are you sure? Mrs. Waterstone is coming at four o'clock to pick up her laundry and she likes it to be perfectly pressed. Did you use bleach? I don't know how but the linen from the Waterstone household is always yellow. I think her husband must be very sweaty or—"

"—or it's Mrs. Waterstone who is going through the change," Nora filled in. She laughed. Before meeting Katherine and being outside her family she had never noticed how her sisters talked and how they had gotten it from their ma. *No wonder stoic and silent Katherine felt like a fish out of water when meeting them.* Thinking about Katherine made her laughter stop. It hurt to think about her. Nora missed her too much.

"Are you sure you can handle it?"

Nora nodded. "I do. I'm about to start another load." She was going to let it hang dry during the night to save physical labor. "But Mrs. Waterstone will have her laundry on time."

"Remember to…"

"I'll remember to collect payment." Nora wasn't offended at her ma's fussing. She felt like laughing again. She felt free. Her mother wasn't used to relying on Nora, so of course she was going to be worried.

"I'm so proud of you." Her mother nodded and touched her hand to Nora's cheek. "Finally, a daughter to take over after me here at the washhouse."

Nora's smile strained on her face as her mother left a sandwich, said bye and left. Her words rang inside Nora's head. *Finally, a daughter to take over after me here at the washhouse.* She wished she didn't have time to ponder her ma's words but she was waiting for the water to boil and her sandwich to eat. Every bite turned to paper in her mouth. *A daughter to take over after me.* Was Nora that daughter? *Here at the washhouse.* Nora looked around the room. The dark, grey walls, the dingy wooden floor. The sheets and shirts hanging from the ceiling, every shade of white different. The stinging smell of bleach and soap. Was this her fate? To gather strength and energy and happiness only to drown it in water mixed with laundry soap? Was this it?

The last bite of her sandwich was swallowed and she stood up again, ready to get going. She would do her duty. She would collect Mrs. Waterstone's payment and deliver the clean laundry and she would start two more loads and she would go home and laugh with Martha. She would eat dinner and enjoy her newly found appreciation for her crazy family. But no way was her future found within these four walls. This couldn't be it.

*

"You smell," Martha said as she sat down next to Nora at the dinner table.

"At least she looks better than you," Emily said, not looking up from staring at her reflection in the knife.

"Well." Martha grinned and shared a look with Nora. "I can't argue with that."

Neither can I. Nora felt rough after a whole day in the washhouse but it was nothing compared to Martha. Martha's cheeks and arms were covered in soot and her hair was several shades darker than usual.

"But what do you expect when I've been cleaning chimney brushes all day." Martha had taken whatever job she could find and was working for one of the master sweeps in town, cleaning the instruments that the chimney sweeps used.

"At least you're not inside the chimneys." Their mother chuddered. "I'll never forget when old Mrs. Quentin signed over both her sons as climbing boys. One died and the other has been walking funny lately. And can you imagine that they employ girls too? Could you imagine? Me signing over Emily or—"

"Ma!" Emily dropped the knife on the table. "I'm almost fifteen. If anybody is being signed over it should be Rose." She grimaced towards her little sister.

"Nu-uh." Rose made a face. "I'm also too big. It'll have to be Anne."

Anne looked up from her place at the bottom of the table, her face scrunched and the sides of her mouth dropped.

"What are we talking about?" Her voice was small.

"Nothing." Martha shook her head. She looked at Rose. "No one is being signed over. Don't scare Anne."

Rose rolled her eyes and looked down at her plate, picking at the peas that were there. Nora and Martha shared a look. Martha shook her head but looked like she wanted to laugh.

"John has gotten a job," their pa said.

John's face turned red and looked like he wanted to sink through the floor. Nora understood him, and didn't like when everyone's attention was on her either. And yet she couldn't resist jumping from her seat and hugging him.

When all the congratulations were over and everyone had sat their butts down as her pa said, her pa explained that John was going to start work next Monday in a factory. Nora didn't think she had ever seen her pa so proud. He was always prouder when his sons did something than when Nora or her sisters did something. It didn't upset Nora though, she figured that since boys were underrepresented among her siblings, her pa felt that his sons were extra precious.

Precious. That's how Nora felt too. Her family was precious. Utterly precious even. As she looked around the table, she saw Emily and Rose bicker, her ma and pa share a loving look, and John still looking down at his plate with Eunice trying to get his attention. Rose had stopped pouting and was helping Anne cut up her meat. It was easy to feel the presence of the siblings that weren't there too. Thomas and Mary who were probably sitting down to eat with their own families at this very moment. Edward who they would never meet again but somehow was always with them too. This was home. And there was no place like home.

It was funny how Nora had to leave home to appreciate it.

It was only later, when the food had been eaten and goodnight kisses had been given and prayers had been said; when Nora had lay down in bed and pulled the cover to just under her nose that she placed her hand over her heart and let herself think of Katherine. She reached under her pillow and closed her fingers around her medallion. The knowledge that the picture of Katherine and Nightingale Prancer was inside, gave her immense comfort.

Chapter Thirty-Four

The leaves under Frankie's Dream's hooves filled the forest with noises of crunch. Katherine was wearing her thickest jodhpurs, jumper and jacket. She had borrowed her big brother's red scarf and put it several times around her neck and then her helmet on top. She didn't always wear a helmet but the ground had felt frozen this morning and harder than usual.

She ran her fingers through his short hair just above the saddle. She let the reins be long and stretched her back. Frankie's Dream and her worked a lot together but they had never skipped training and just gone out. Katherine imagined that the horse enjoyed it as much as she did. His neck became very long and his steps more relaxed. Sometimes riding him felt like sitting on a much smaller horse, with his short steps and bumpy walking. Now, in the forest, his steps lengthened and his walk became comfortable. Katherine let go of the stirrups and moved her toes back and forth. She wanted to remember that she had felt like this before. *Relaxed. Unfocused.*

The sun was shining through the orange and brown leaves, illuminating the clearing where Nora, Martha and Katherine had been on Nora's birthday. It wasn't so long ago and yet it looked like another world now. It had gotten colder since then and nature had quickly caught up. Katherine was different as well. She was sad that her father had caught them. She was sad that Nora was so far away right now. The last time she had sat by that stream, she had experienced the pinnacle of happiness. She had given Nora, the love of her life, a present. They had kissed. She had felt cautious friendship towards Martha. She had dared to dream; not just plan.

Frankie's Dream raised his head and neighed. Katherine shivered. Was there deer in the woods? Who was Frankie talking too? She patted Frankie's neck. The hair on her neck was standing up.

"You're right," she said and kept her fingers on Frankie's warm back. "There is no need to stand here and talk to ghosts." She smiled. "Plus, the post should have come by now."

She turned Frankie's Dream around and shortened the reins. She forced him into a trot, wanting to leave the forest as soon as possible. If there were deer, that wasn't a problem. But one of her father's riders had been out recently and a huge elk had come out of nowhere. The horse had gotten so scared he had reared, kicked the rider off and ran home. The man was still in the hospital with a concussion.

*

After checking the post, Katherine took a long shower and got dressed in her smartest clothes, black trousers, and a white shirt. If she wanted to impress her father, looks were important. As she dried her hair she looked once more at the letter that was open on her desk. Every time she looked at it, her heart felt lighter. The letters, and more importantly numbers, on it, showed that it was possible. Her plan was possible.

She couldn't wait to tell Nora.

Once dressed, Katherine hurried to her father's study. It was at the end of the month and her father was probably busy looking over the stable's economics. It usually put him in a financially cautious mood which would serve Katherine's purpose. She knocked at his door, feeling like a much younger girl again. *Stop it, Katherine.* Katherine was an adult. And she needed to feel like one now. She would not be bullied.

"Come in."

She opened the door and hid the letter behind her back, not wanting her father to see it right away.

"Oh Katherine," her father said. He sighed, took off his glasses, and started cleaning them on his shirt. "Come in and sit down."

"Thank you." She made her way to one of the chairs in front of his desk. She moved quickly, hoping he wouldn't notice the letter still in her hand.

"Did you have a nice ride?" Her father put his glasses back on. "I heard Mr. Porter canceled."

"Yes," Katherine said. "I took Frankie's Dream out for a forest hack. It was lovely if a bit cold."

"Yes, yes." Her father nodded. He wasn't meeting her gaze but Katherine thought it was more because of a distraction than him being angry with her. They had been civil with each other lately.

"Father?" She waited until he was looking at her. *Here we go.* "I think it's time for me to move."

"Move?" He took off his glasses again even though she knew he saw better with them.

She nodded. "I'm twenty-five years old. I don't know what has taken me this long but it is time. I can't live here anymore."

"Are you going to live alone?"

She understood what he was asking. It was the closest he had ever come to asking if she was planning to live *with another woman.*

"I don't know." It was the truth. "I'm looking for investors and employers right now."

"What?" Her father's eyes widened. "Investors?" He licked his lips. "Employers?" He leaned forward.

"Yes." Katherine put the letter on her lap, in the open. "I'm not planning to be a kept woman. Of course, that's a valid choice for mother and all but that's not me. I've bought a stable."

The corners of her father's mouth were shaking. In an upwards direction. *Was he laughing?* Katherine stayed silent, waiting for his response. There was nothing in the law that said she needed his blessing. But she wanted it. Badly.

"How?" He still seemed to be laughing but there was an element of surprise in his gaze.

"Aunt Marie's inheritance," Katherine said. "And I have the funds you and Mother have been saving for me since I was a child. I have had access to them since I came of age, I just haven't found a reason to use them yet."

"They are in stocks." He shook his head. "I wasn't expecting this at all."

"They're not in stocks anymore." Katherine wanted to grin but she kept her smile civil. She lifted the letter in her hand. "I sold half of them. The other half I'm going to continue to grow."

"People are getting bankrupt left and right." His expression changed. "What are your plans?"

"I'm not sure what I want to do yet, exactly." Katherine smiled and felt the tension leave her chest when her father met that smile. It was a start. "Maybe a livery or train jumping horses or maybe stud farm. Nightingale Prancer will be my first mare. I know financially it's not completely secure but that doesn't mean I shouldn't try."

"You are your father's daughter, aren't you?"

"Huh?" Katherine didn't understand what he meant.

"I had a similar discussion with my father, back in the day." He squared his shoulders. "Well, then I can only wish you luck."

Was it really this easy? Katherine couldn't believe it was that easy. Maybe she dared to push her luck. She had a mare. Now all she needed was a...

"I'll give you ten pounds sterling for Frankie's Dream." She pressed her lips together. She had no idea what her father would say now.

He looked like he wanted to say something, his mouth opened. Something ambiguous passed through his eyes. When he was looking like this, Katherine could see herself in his face. She was more like him than she had known.

"Fine." He nodded slowly. "But I want fifteen pounds and breeding rights once a year."

Katherine bit her lip, thinking fervently. It was easy to say yes but she didn't want to give breeding rights. If she had a good stallion she wanted his offspring to come exclusively from her stud farm.

"Fifteen pounds," she said. "And discounted breeding rights. You will pay 50% of what other customers pay."

Her father grinned. *My father,* Katherine thought, *how I love him.* She forgave him for chasing away Nora. He only had one person's wellbeing in mind and that was hers. He was wrong, so very wrong. But he loved Katherine. Always had. If he didn't, there was no way he would let go of a horse like Frankie's Dream for that little. Katherine was relying on a little "daughter discount."

"You drive a hard bargain." He held out his hand and Katherine knew she had won. She bounced up from her chair and shook his hand.

Chapter Thirty-Five

Soot itches. It wraps its way around every strand of hair on your head and under your nails and into your mouth. Martha had taken a long soak in the bathtub before heading out to town with Nora; they also took their little sister Anne with them. Martha had thought she was clean enough but as they left their home and started walking towards the nearest shop, her scalp was still itching. She scratched behind her ear with one hand while holding Anne's hand with her other. She glanced occasionally at Nora and couldn't help but smile. Nora's gait was so much better. Better than Martha had ever seen it. At Waterhouse Acre Stables, Martha had never noticed - it had been another world. But here, on the same street where they had all grown up, it was so clear that Nora was a different person. Her cheeks had color, her body fuller and there was life in her eyes.

Martha wanted to ask about Katherine. She didn't know if Nora and Katherine had had any type of communication since they had left the countryside. She didn't know if Nora had any plans of reaching out or if Katherine already had. Part of her wanted to know, part of her wanted to leave them to their business. She wasn't just Nora's protective big sister anymore. She considered them friends, equals. And she was not just worried but curious for curiosity's sake.

Anne tugged at Martha's hand. "Where are we going?" It was the first time Anne had ventured out of the house since falling ill and it was good that the grocer wasn't far.

"We need to buy some groceries."

"Some ham," Nora filled in. "And eggs and that wheat flour ma prefers."

"If you get tired," Martha squeezed Anne's hand until the girl looked at her, "you must tell me so I can carry you."

"Not necessarily." Nora's words made Martha look up. "I mean," Nora continued, "the doctor told me that partly why I was so weak before is because I wasn't allowed to use my muscles."

Martha wanted to argue, tell both of her little sisters that she knew better but she kept her mouth shut. This summer she had learned that she didn't always know best. She just nodded, unsure what to say.

They kept walking down the street with Anne in the middle, holding both their hands. The autumn sun was shining above them and even though there was a slight breeze, it wasn't cold. Sometimes when some leaves rustled, or something banged into the pavement, Martha closed her eyes, pretending she was back on the farm. London just wasn't good enough.

It was during one of these moments that she had her eyes closed when she suddenly walked into someone soft.

"Martha!" Nora exclaimed. "What are you doing? I'm so, so sorry, ma'am."

Martha blinked a couple of times, unsure if she was still dreaming. In front of her stood Mrs. Allen. *The* Mrs. Allen. The woman with whom Martha had had an affair during the war.

She looked the same and at the same time not. Her brown eyes were wide as she stared at Martha, a small blush spreading over her cheeks. She had the same high cheekbones and wide, yet delicate jaw line. Her brown hair looked soft and framed in her face. Martha glanced down, noticing the dark green dress that hugged all of Mrs. Allen's curves. *Oh my, stop staring Martha.*

"What's wrong, mother?" Two kids appeared from behind Mrs. Allen's skirt. Two little boys, both carrying her piercing amber eyes.

"Nothing, dears," Mrs. Allen said. "This is Mart... Miss Lakes. She used to work in your father's auto shop, when he was in the war." She shook her head as if slowly realising what was happening. "Say hello to Miss Lakes, boys."

In a twin movement, both boys bowed and lifted their little hats for Martha.

"Yes," she coughed. "Hello." She looked up at Mrs. Allen again, wondering if her anguish could be seen through her eyes. She felt a movement in her hand.

"Oh, of course." She smiled but it was more of a grimace. "These are my sisters, Anne and Nora." She turned to them. "This is Mrs. Allen. I worked in her..." her throat turned dry... "*husband's*" she coughed, "auto shop during the war." It was insane how much she could still hate that husband, a husband she had never even met and yet a man who had changed her life forever.

Mrs. Allen bit her lip.

"Well."

"Well."

They spoke in the same time. Did Martha look as red in the face as Mrs. Allen?

"I'm sorry I walked into you." *What else can I say?* It had been years, and two sons, since they had last met. Even longer since the last time they had kissed.

"I'm sorry for everything else." Mrs. Allen's words were surprising and Martha's mouth dropped open. "I wasn't fair to you, I took advantage. I…"

Martha held her hand up. "It doesn't matter," she said. "It's been a long time since then. Clearly." She motioned towards the boys.

"Yes." Mrs. Allen smiled and put her hand on one of the boy's head. "I should get going. We are going to the park."

"Mother takes us to the park to play every day," the biggest boy said with a big grin on his face.

"That sounds nice," Nora said when Martha stayed quiet.

"Well, it was nice to meet you all." Mrs. Allen smiled one last time. Her eyes didn't leave Martha's face. "Maybe we will run into each other again."

"Probably not." Martha couldn't resist the impolite words. It had hurt to see her and to see her sons, knowing how they came to be but Martha survived it. She had survived it and wanted to put it behind her now.

As they left Mrs. Allen and continued forward, and Nora and Martha shared a look over Anne's head.

"That was…?" Martha didn't know what Nora was asking. Had they talked about this before? Did Nora know? A moment of sheer panic flew through Martha until she realised that Nora was in love with a woman and probably wouldn't judge Martha's former *indiscretions*.

She nodded, not knowing what Nora's reaction would be. Nora let go of Anne's hand, reached over and palmed Martha's cheek. The action was so tender and sweet it made Martha feel like crying.

"Are you okay?"

Martha swallowed and nodded.

"I am actually." She smiled at her best friend. "I'm ready to just forget about it now."

Nora let go of her cheek. They continued walking.

"Is she your friend?" Anne asked but Martha just answered, "no, she is no one important." If it was a story Anne needed to hear in the future, Martha would tell it, but today was not that day.

We better get to the grocer with no more surprises, Martha thought. That's when they turned the corner and came face to face with Katherine.

Chapter Thirty-Six

Nora - thump - *Nora* - thump. Katherine's heart had come up with a rhythm of its own. She couldn't even take in if there were other people next to her. Katherine's eyes just zoomed in on the object of her affection. Unable to control her actions anymore, she went over to Nora with three big strides and pulled her into a big hug. It didn't even matter that they were in the middle of the street where anyone could see them.

"Hello," she whispered into Nora's hair. She held her close and her heart soared when Nora's hands came to rest on her back.

"I can't believe it's you," Nora whispered back.

Katherine pushed Nora away, holding her at an arm's length with her hands to her shoulders. She wanted to look at her; she needed to make sure Nora was okay.

"Who are you?" A small voice made them look down.

It was a little girl; Katherine was bad at guessing ages and didn't know whether the girl was closer to 3 or seven. She wore Nora's serious expression and shared the shape of her nose. Katherine couldn't remember if she had seen her during the one time she had visited the Lakes household. That could only mean one thing.

"You must be Anne, am I right?"

At being recognized, the little girl's face shone as if somebody had lit a kerosene lamp inside her head. It made Katherine chuckle that Anne had the same facial expression to show happiness that Nora did.

"Hello, Katherine."

Katherine turned to the side and noticed that Martha was there too. Martha smiled widely and held out her hand. Katherine shook it but then turned to Nora.

She was looking so healthy and beautiful, Katherine's insides ached. She needed to hold her and kiss her; not to mention talk to her. Explain. Ask questions. She was dying to connect with Nora.

"I was hoping to run into you." There wasn't enough time. "I'm in London for a jumping show."

Nora's eyes shone. "Competing or watching?" She reached forward and touched her hand to Katherine's arm. The touch was innocent enough to a bystander but it meant everything to Katherine.

"Competing. With Frankie's Dream." *And he is mine now. Do you want to own him together?* "I wish I had more time." At her words, the sun set in Nora's eyes. "But I want to see you after the show. Come and watch? It's at…"

"We live in London," Martha bit in. "We know where jumping shows are kept."

Nora knotted her eyebrows at her sister. When she looked back at Katherine she mouthed 'sorry.' Katherine didn't care.

"Come and watch." Katherine took Nora's hands in hers. "Come and cheer me on, it would mean the world to me. And afterward, I want to talk to you." She looked at Martha. "Both of you."

"About what?" Martha asked.

"About the future." Katherine didn't take her eyes off Nora. "Our future." *Was Nora looking at her lips?* Being near her but not close enough was torture. Katherine let go of Nora's hands. "I need to go now, but you will come, right?"

Nora nodded wildly. "Of course, we will. When is it?"

"Three o'clock. I know it's sudden, but please?"

Nora looked at Martha and Martha nodded too but not as enthusiastically. "I'll come unless I don't find someone to cover tonight's shift."

"You work?" Katherine wanted to know everything. She could hardly contain her curiosity about how Nora was doing. How her life was going. How much she had missed Katherine. *If she had missed Katherine at all.*

"I work at my mother's washhouse. But I'm free today to watch Anne." Nora looked down at the little girl. "I'll take her with me."

"So, I will see you later?" They needed more time. Katherine needed more time. There would be more time. There had to be.

"You will." Katherine pulled her into another hug; she couldn't resist.

"I'll explain everything later, I promise," she whispered into Nora's hair. She held on for a little bit longer than necessary. "I love you." The words were so low Katherine didn't know if Nora had heard them but it didn't matter.

*

Frankie's Dream pranced as if he was a unicorn and stretched his neck, showing off to the audience. Katherine had never seen him act this way before and she chuckled through the nerves. She patted his neck.

"Don't just show off," she whispered. "You need to live up to it, too."

She had been training for many months now but couldn't believe they had reached this point already. Katherine had always wanted to compete but now, when she had reached that point and was riding in front of a huge London audience, she wasn't sure anymore.

Her heart was pounding in her throat and she hadn't even looked up at the stands to see if Nora was there. Part of Katherine needed her there and part of Katherine would have felt relieved if she wasn't. If something went wrong and Katherine and Frankie's Dream made a fool of themselves, she didn't want Nora to see.

They trotted around the arena like the other competitors had done too, waving at the crowd. When she had almost gone all the way around, a strange chanting reached her ears. She looked up, from beneath the hem of her black, velvet helmet.

In the stands, Nora, Martha, and Anne were sitting, chanting her name over and over. But they weren't the only ones. Katherine didn't know their names but knew that Nora had a lot of sisters and brothers. It had to be them, the five additional youngsters sitting next to Martha and chanting the same chant.

Instead of being embarrassed, Katherine was filled with pride so tangible she spurred Frankie's Dream into a gallop and felt as if they were both strutting around the arena. She was ready now, they both were, for the judge's whistle.

When it came, they left the ground and flew.

Chapter Thirty-Seven

"Aren't you sad she only got to fourth place?" Eunice was sitting closest to Nora and whispered in her ear. She placed her arm around him.

"Frankie's Dream, the horse she is riding, is a young horse and this was Miss Waterhouse's first competition. They have plenty of time to win shows, they're just starting their career."

Eunice nodded as if he understood, in his usual precarious way.

"I can't believe you have such cool friends," Rose piped up. Her voice was full of admiration instead of the usual disdain and annoyance. "I can't believe you took us all to a horse show."

"Or bought us caramel apples." Robert's face was covered in sauce.

Martha chuckled and handed him a handkerchief.

"Well," Nora said, "Miss Waterhouse took me to a horse show once and bought me a caramel apple, so it's only right I figured."

"Ugh," Emily groaned from her seat furthest away. "It's such a shame she is a woman, otherwise your friendship would have been so romantic." She looked at Nora. "Does she have any brothers she could introduce us to? It just takes one sister to make it."

Nora and Martha shared a look and Nora shook her head. The trip to the horse show *had* been romantic. If Emily only knew.

"Come on." Martha stood up and Nora followed suit. She grabbed the hand of Eunice and Martha lifted Anne up to not lose her in the crowd. "Let's go and meet Miss Waterhouse."

They all made their way down the stands and through the crowds. They found Katherine tending to Frankie's Dream, brushing the sweat out of his fur. Her helmet was off and her braid was stuck to the back of her neck, looking sweaty. Nora felt her mouth water when she thought about putting one palm underneath Katherine's hair, against the moist skin of her neck, and kissing her deeply. *Get a grip, you're among people.*

"Miss Waterhouse?" Emily was the first to speak. She walked straight up to Katherine. "Can I shake your hand? I'm so amazed at your performance, even if you didn't win. And your horse is so pretty, can I touch him?" She didn't seem to remember that Katherine had once come to their home. She also didn't wait for a reply but reached out to touch her fingers to Frankie's Dream's mule. Frankie's Dream was a gentle horse with his own will but he was tired and hungry and must have thought that Emily was offering him a treat. He sank his teeth into Emily's fingers.

"Aaaaooouuuiii." Emily yelled so loud all the nearest horses and people jumped and a guard came over to make sure no one was hurt.

"I'm sorry," Nora told the guard, taking Emily into her arms. She cradled Emily's hand in her own.

"I'm so sorry," Katherine came closer. "He has never bitten anyone before. It must be the stress from the competition, plus he is probably hungry."

Rose grinned and leaned forward, looking at Emily's hand.

"He must have thought your fingers were carrots, Em." She took a step backward when Emily gave her an ugly look.

"Not helping, Rose." Martha looked at Emily's hand. "It didn't even draw blood, I'm sure you'll be alright."

"I didn't say I was dying, did I?" Emily bit off. She shook herself free from Nora's arms. "Stupid horses, that's the last time I'm setting my foot near one, that's for sure. I'm going home, who is with me?"

"Martha and I have to stay and talk to Miss Waterhouse a bit," Nora said. "John, can you make sure everyone will get home, alright?"

*

When the children had gone and Katherine had left Frankie's Dream to be driven back to Waterhouse Acre Stables by her personnel, the three women found their way to the closest pub. Katherine ordered lemonade for all of them; they all sat down at a secluded table in the corner.

It felt romantic to sit so close to Katherine after being apart for so long, even with Martha near. Nora pulled her chair as close to Katherine's as she dared. When Katherine came to the table with the three glasses, she sat down and Nora and Martha stayed quiet. They were both equally curious at what Katherine had to say.

"There is no easy way to say this," Katherine started, making Nora worry. *What was she going to say?* "I was wondering if you wanted to come work with me?"

Nora's eyes widened and she shared a quick look with Martha. "What do you mean?"

"I have some money saved up, through stocks and a will from a late aunt." Katherine looked first at Nora, then at Martha. "I bought a farm. With fields, stables, living quarters, and everything." When no one said anything, Katherine continued. "I'm not entirely sure what I want to do with it yet. The dream would be a stud farm and I want to keep learning until I can train horses professionally."

Nora couldn't believe what she was hearing. She felt a cautious smile form on her face and opened her mouth to say something but Martha was quicker.

"How much would you pay us?"

Nora couldn't believe that that's what Martha chose to focus on. She kicked Martha under the table, feeling utterly embarrassed.

Katherine's cheeks turned slightly pink.

"Well, that's why I didn't say 'come and work for me', I said 'come and work with me'." She smiled sheepishly. "I have enough saved up to tide us over for a little while. Buy us food and the horses feed during winter. I don't have enough to offer you a wage and I'm not sure I'd want to. I want us to do this together." She locked eyes with Nora. "Darling, you haven't said a word?"

"Do you even have to ask?" Nora reached under the table to find Katherine's knee. She squeezed it. "Of course, we will say yes." She looked at Martha and released Katherine's knee to take a sip of her lemonade. She knew how much Martha hated her current job. There was no way she wouldn't jump at the chance to work at a stable again.

"I won't just be a stable girl," Martha said.

"Of course not." Katherine winked at Nora. "We will be equal. We will divide the chores and the profit equally. I mean that."

"Well, I'm not stupid enough to say no then," Martha said. "I'm in." She lifted her lemonade, tipping it in Katherine's direction. "Cheers."

Katherine laughed and Nora joined her.

"What about your parents?" Nora asked when their laughter had died down. "Were they harsh with you, after....?" She didn't know how to finish her sentence so she gestured with her hand.

Katherine's smile turned wistful. She moved stray hairs out of her forehead and put her arm around Nora's chair. It was as close as putting her arm around her as she could come.

"It was hard in the beginning. The Waterhouses aren't the most talkative bunch. We don't hug a lot and exclaim that we love each other." She sighed. "But that first week after the two of you left was the most silent my house has ever been." She moved her arm from the chair and curved her hand around Nora's shoulder.

Nora's heart skipped a beat and she quickly looked around them, seeing if anybody was looking. It was instinctive to look, a self-preservative reflex. Katherine stroked the ball of Nora's shoulder with her thumb.

"We haven't talked about it." She breathed deeply. "I don't know what he thinks or if he even cares now that I've moved out. My mother wasn't happy that I just got up and left but my father seemed relieved. He knew he couldn't control me, he just thought he should."

"Does he know you're employing us?" Martha asked.

Nora and Katherine looked at her.

"I haven't volunteered the information." The side of Katherine's mouth lifted. "If he finds out I won't deny it though. We aren't breaking any laws." Her facial expression turned serious again. "It'll be difficult in the beginning. I'm hoping we can find somebody to sponsor me as a showjumper but other than that, we will have difficult times. It won't be like my parents have it. We won't have butlers or a Mrs. Chapman or…"

Nora put her hand on Katherine's.

"We will manage."

"What about horses?" Martha asked.

Nora didn't listen to Katherine's response. Instead, she investigated, with her gaze, the planes of Katherine's face and her body. She had been wearing a smart riding outfit but it was a bit dusty now and she had pulled the cravat she had been wearing loose. She had taken the jacket off and hung it over the back of her chair. The bone-white shirt shone against the olive of her skin and black hair. Speaking of the hair, it was even messier now and Nora couldn't wait to touch it.

"… Frankie's Dream is, well a dream and together with Nightingale Prancer—"

"Where are you staying tonight?" Nora couldn't believe the audacity both at the question and the fact that she had interrupted their conversation. She felt heat rise to not just her cheeks but the whole of her face and neck as both Martha and Katherine looked at her.

Katherine's mouth fell open in the most beautiful smile that Nora had ever seen.

"Well," Katherine chuckled, "I've got a place at a hotel. Not this one but…"

"Can I come with you?" Nora felt like a different person. She turned to Martha. "You will cover for me, yes? Please? I don't care what you tell them."

Martha pursed her lips and crossed her arms. There was a twinkling in her eyes though.

I Love you, Nora Whispered

"So, I have to come up with the lie, covering for you running away with you…" Martha giggled and shook her head. "Who am I to stand in the way of young love?" She made a dismissive gesture with her hand.

"I'm older than you." Katherine wrinkled her nose. "But thank you. Of course, I'd want Nora to stay with me tonight," she coughed. "Ahem, I mean."

"We both know what you mean." Martha shook her head.

"Oh my." Nora covered her face in her hands. This was just too much.

Chapter Thirty-Eight

They said goodbye to Martha with the promise that Nora would be kept safe. Katherine took her job seriously and kept her eyes on Nora the entire time as they walked towards the hotel. Nora looked beautiful in the mellow light of the afternoon. Her hair had grown a bit longer and was falling around her shoulders in soft curls. Katherine found that she liked Nora's hair a bit longer. Around Nora's neck hung the medallion Katherine had given her for her birthday, the sight making Katherine smile. Nora usually wore dark colors but now she was wearing a green dress with little white flowers on it. It hugged around her hips in a way that… Katherine sucked in air through her teeth and bit her lip. The thoughts filling her mind would definitely *not* keep Nora safe.

As they entered the hotel, Nora slowed her step and let Katherine go first. Katherine held open the door for her. She went up to the check-in desk and informed them that she would have a friend staying with her during the night. She could have snuck Nora in but it felt too much trouble than it was worth. If they charged her more in the morning when she checked out then so be it.

The hotel was beautiful with lush carpets and ornaments on the stairwell. Katherine had been impressed when she had checked in earlier that same day but now she didn't notice any of the paintings or exotic potted plants. Now all she had eyes for was Nora.

The object of her affection, however, didn't meet her gaze as they walked up the stairs. *Why isn't she looking at me?* Was Nora so taken with the hotel? Was she feeling like this was wrong? Was she worried… was…?

Katherine unlocked the door and held it open for Nora to step inside. Nora passed by her and stared straight forward, looking at the desk, the wooden chair, and the bed.

"Do you…?" Katherine couldn't finish her sentence. As soon as the door was closed, Nora swirled around and pressed Katherine up against it. It didn't matter that Nora was almost a head shorter. Katherine let Nora push her back. *Oh, to you I willingly surrender.* Katherine's eyes fell closed when Nora captured her mouth in a very deep kiss.

"Wow," Katherine said once Nora leaned back, what felt like several hours later. "I don't know what to say."

"I couldn't even look at you before," Nora whispered, their breaths mingling in the tight space. "If I had, I would have wanted to kiss you right then and there." She giggled, the sound causing ripples deep in Katherine's stomach. "And how would that have looked."

"It would have looked lovely." Katherine captured her lips again. "People would have stopped to stare."

"Oh no." Nora laughed again but looked down. Katherine placed a kiss on her forehead. "That I couldn't bear. Not even if one of us were a man would I have liked for people to…" she turned scarlet red. "…watch us kiss."

"You are so sweet." Katherine couldn't help herself. She took Nora's face in her hands and pressed kisses all over. On Nora's nose and her cheeks, her forehead and eyelids and one, sloppy, kiss to her chin.

They laughed, standing by the door, looking at each other. Nora's smile faltered.

Kathy L. Salt

"Is this actually it?" She looked so unsure, Katherine wanted to kiss her again. "Will all our dreams come true?"

Katherine grinned. "I didn't know your dream was to live on a horse farm with me."

"I didn't either until a few months ago." Nora tugged on her hand and led her towards the bed. "But now I realise it's a dream I've had for my entire life."

Her words made Katherine's heart skip a beat. She grabbed both of Nora's hands and they fell onto the bed together with Katherine on top.

"I don't want to talk anymore." Nora fidgeted under Katherine's weight. "I love feeling you on top of me."

Katherine's blood quickened, her heart beat then a second heartbeat started somewhere lower. She remembered the last time they had been together, of having become so excited that she had been in pain. By listening to her body, she could tell that she didn't have long.

"I want to take my clothes off." Nora reached up and licked from Katherine's exposed collarbone to her earlobe.

"Oh… my…." Katherine tried to catch her breath but couldn't. "Okay." She hardly managed to get her words out. "Let's take our clothes off."

She got up and pulled Nora with her. They quickly shed their clothes and Katherine walked up to the side of the bed to pull the duvet down. When naked she had noticed that the room was chilly and she was eager to get under the sheets.

She was leaning down with her back towards Nora when she was suddenly enveloped from behind. Nora's breasts were pressed against her back, her skin was so smooth, warm, and soft that Katherine felt dizzy. Giggling

269

made Nora's body shake, enveloping Katherine in a hug, with her arms tight around Katherine's stomach.

"You look so tough sometimes," Nora spoke into Katherine's shoulder blades. "But underneath it all, you are just as soft as me."

Katherine hugged Nora's arms.

"I love you."

She convulsed in laughter when Nora started pressing butterfly kisses all over Katherine's back. They fell on top of the bed, Katherine stomach first, Nora on top.

"Oh, Mercy!"

Nora didn't care about Katherine's begging, she placed herself on top of Katherine's butt, and put her hands on Katherine's shoulder.

"Stay still for a bit."

Katherine did as she was told. She could feel Nora's wetness painting her butt cheeks and her own wetness staining the mattress. This was life. Katherine could feel her excitement rising and her insides swelling. It was pounding, close to painful and she closed her eyes, trying to just enjoy the sensation. Nora ran her hands over Katherine's back.

"You have a mole here." Nora touched a spot close to Katherine's tailbone.

Katherine hummed in agreement. She was using all her power to just lie still. When Nora whimpered on top of her and rocked her hips against Katherine's body, Katherine's discipline broke.

With a loud groan, Katherine turned around so violently that Nora fell to the side. She pushed Nora down into the mattress and wedged herself between her legs. She attacked Nora's mouth while grabbing her breast.

"You tease me too much," she muttered between their kisses. "If you keep it up, you don't know what you'll unleash in me." She nipped at Nora's bottom lip. "And I promised your sister I would keep you safe."

"Touch me," Nora moaned. She took a hold of Katherine's hand and pushed it to where she needed it the most.

"You are so wet." Katherine thought she was dying. Katherine tried to find a good angle, a way to rub her where Nora needed her.

"I want you so much." Nora's mouth was right by her ear. Her tone of voice was an octave lower than usual. "I want you...I want you inside of me."

Katherine's heart stopped at Nora's request. She had never done such a monumental thing before. She fell to the side and stroked Nora's body.

"Are you sure?"

Their gazes met and Nora nodded. "I want you to be my first."

Katherine's breath was ragged as she let her hand travel lower, towards the heart of her. Katherine's own parts were pulsing now, swollen to the point of pain. She pushed her hips into the mattress, wanting some relief.

"Katherine." Nora whimpered her name. Katherine pushed one finger inside with the most gentleness she could muster. Her discipline was wearing thin and part of her wanted to throw caution into the wind and take Nora hard and fast but she couldn't.

Nora's insides were hot, wet, and velvet. It was the best thing that Katherine had ever felt and she pressed her hips against Nora's thigh. Nora seemed to realise Katherine's dilemma and she moved one of her legs so that Katherine could ride it while moving inside her. It was getting warm and sweaty under the duvet but it made the whole situation so much sweeter.

"Can I have one more finger?"

Katherine did as she was told without a reply. Nora was pulsing around her fingers and she was holding on a razor's edge to not come herself from the sensation of just being inside of her. They were moving faster and faster. Katherine angled her own thigh to behind her hand so that she could put more force behind her thrusts. Nora's hips were moving faster and faster and Katherine was struggling to keep up.

Their mouths met in a sloppy kiss.

"I love you so much," Nora mumbled against Katherine's lips. "I love you so, so much." She groaned loudly and her hips froze mid-movement. The muscles that were around Katherine's fingers cramped as Nora cried out. Katherine's heart sped up and her own hips moved against Nora's thigh on their own accord. *Oh no, oh no, oh no.* A pulsating spread from the point where her body met Nora's and down the insides of her thigh. Her insides quaked and she fell down on top of Nora, her face in the crook of Nora's neck, exhausted and spent; her fingers still inside her.

They laid like that for a long time, just catching their breath. Nora was stroking Katherine's back slowly. The room was dark.

"Will we share a house on our farm?" Nora's chest rumbled when she spoke. She cleared her throat and chuckled. "I think I lost my voice a bit."

Katherine took her fingers out and wiped them on the sheet. She covered Nora's breast with her palm.

"I want us to share more than just a house," Katherine said. She started making circles around Nora's nipple. Round, round, round. "I want us to share a bed every night."

"Really?" Nora yawned. "What would people say?"

"I don't care." Katherine sighed contently. "It's nobody's business who sleeps where in our own house. I want…" She searched her feelings and found them to be true. "I want us to live like a married couple."

"What?" Nora sat up, pushing Katherine on to her back. There was a wondrous look in her face. "You want me to be your *wife*?" Her mouth was open, her lips plump. Her hair was very messy, standing out like a gloria around her head.

Katherine had to chuckle at the sight.

"Is that so surprising?" She propped herself up on her elbow. "Mind now that this isn't the proposal I had hoped for but…"

"Nora Waterhouse," Nora said as if tasting the word. "It sounds nice, doesn't it?"

Katherine burst out laughing and pressed a kiss to the tip of Nora's nose.

"It sounds beautiful," she said. "But I'm not sure you can actually take my last name." She grimaced. "Plus Mrs. Waterhouse is my mother, you know. I can't really imagine calling my wife that." Once she had said the word, she felt she liked it even more. The idea of pretty Nora Lakes wanting to be her wife, wanting to set up home with her *and* her horses. Just like Nora had said before; a couple of months ago, Katherine hadn't known that this was the dream. Now she knew that she had been dreaming about this moment her entire life.

She cradled Nora's cheek and kissed her deeply.

"Nora Waterhouse." She smiled. "Or Katherine Lakes. I don't care, as long as we're together."

Epilogue

Two Years Later

The air was whipping in Nora's face as she spurred Nightingale Prancer into a canter over the field. She turned around seeing if Hopper would follow. Hopper, or Our New Hope as his official name was, was the first foal born on the farm. A foal from Nightingale Prancer and Frankie's Dream. Hopper was following them easily, his gangly legs managing over the rocks and grass. Nora slowed down in a trot and then a walk, happy with the response from both horses. They had been careful with riding Nightingale Prancer since she had given birth but Nora hadn't been able to wait anymore.

She turned Nightingale Prancer around and started walking back to their home. She was up on a cliff just a few miles outside London. They weren't surrounded by forest like Waterhouse Acre Stables but rather lush, green hills where you could see for as long your eyes could reach. Nora loved this. She loved her home and still couldn't believe that they were all living there. Katherine had been extremely tenacious into putting all three of their names on the deed. Nora couldn't believe that the first to own property in their family for generations was her and Martha.

Nightingale Prancer moved her head up and down and stopped to relieve herself. Nora stood up in the saddle to give the horse's back some relief while urinating. It was a movement she never would have thought was possible but here she was. She was still going to the doctor and while he was sure that her progress was due to his treatment, Nora knew that it was thanks to Katherine and the horses.

They reached the stable yard and she sat off. She waved at Katherine who was training on Frankie's Dream in the paddock, looking very concentrated. Katherine nodded in Nora's direction but then shifted her focus back on Frankie's Dream.

Nora took Nightingale Prancer's saddle off, checked that there weren't any stones stuck inside her shoes, and then led her to the only field they had prepared. Hopper lived up to his name by hopping and prancing behind them. Once inside the field, she took the bridle off, letting Nightingale Prancer inside without a halter. She wiped the sweat off her forehead and watched as the two horses trotted as far away as possible and then stuck their heads down, grazing. Hopper was just pretending, biting randomly at the grass and then abandoning it to run around his mother. Nora grinned at the vision, wishing that there was another foal or baby animal for him to play with.

The sound of an engine told her that there was a car coming closer. She didn't need to look to see who it was because the sound gave it off. There was only one engine that could sound like it was just about to die at any minute, spluttering, struggling with the occasional explosion and stinking of a mixture of gasoline and grease. After Katherine had taught Martha to drive, Martha had saved up and bought a rusty old Hillman. Nora refused to get into it, but Martha loved it and used it to get into town whenever she needed.

It was almost dinner time and Nora picked up the saddle she had placed temporarily on the ground and walked into the stable with the tack. Not a moment later, Anne came running after her, calling her name.

As soon as Nora had put the tack away, they hugged.

"I can't believe you have gotten even taller." Anne had gone from a toddler-like chubbiness to a rather tall school-aged girl with freckles. She had needed glasses and the National Health Service had paid for them.

"Since it's Saturday ma said I could sleep here tonight if it's okay with you?" Anne's gaze left Nora as she looked around the stable. "You have so many empty boxes and not enough horses to put in them."

Nora chuckled and placed her arm around Anne's shoulder. They walked out of the stable together.

"Soon we'll have more horses. It just takes time and resources to build up a stud farm." She squeezed Anne's shoulder. "Won't the others miss you? What about Ivy?"

Ivy was the final child of the Lakes family. After having one last pregnancy, the doctor had warned their mother to never get pregnant again. Ivy had golden hair and a pair of lungs that could only belong to a Lakes sister. She loved Anne the most out of all the siblings and Anne loved feeling mature and responsible.

"Ivy keeps yelling at night so I'm irritated with her at the moment." Nora chuckled at Anne's reply. "Eunice wanted to come but when Robert said that he was going out fishing this weekend with pa, he changed his mind. Eunice, not Robert or pa of course."

"And the others?" Nora nodded at Martha in greeting as they walked over to the main building.

"Emily has moved in with Mary to help her with the new baby. She says there are more young men living there so she can find herself a husband. Rose is so jealous she hasn't come out of her room for days."

"For days?" Nora raised one of her eyebrows. "Really?" She opened the door and the three sisters went inside, making sure to take off their muddy shoes at the door.

"Maybe not days," Anne admitted.

"But Anne," Martha said. "You're not telling Nora the biggest news."

"Which one?" Anne asked.

Martha rolled her eyes.

"John is getting married!"

Nora's mouth fell open.

"Which John? Our John?" She looked first at Martha and then at Anne.

"Oh, that." Anne sighed. "Yes, he is getting married to this girl named Tilly but she is fat and boring so who cares."

"Anne!" Nora didn't know which shocked her most, the fact that her little brother was getting married or that her baby sister had called her brother's fiancée fat and boring.

Martha sighed. "Well, to be fair, Anne isn't wrong."

"Lord, what am I to do with the both of you?" Nora shook her head and walked into the kitchen. "Anne, will you help me peel the potatoes, please? We need to get dinner started, soon Miss Waterhouse will be back and I want it ready."

Anne walked into the kitchen, shaking her head.

"Sometimes you act like Miss Waterhouse is your husband, you know." Anne rolled up her sleeves and obediently waited for Nora to give her the potatoes. "At least she isn't as fat and boring as Tilly, I mean *Miss Lirth* is."

"Her last name is Lirth?" Nora looked at her.

"Yes." Anne giggled. "But Rose and Emily call her Miss *Girth* when John can't hear."

"Anne!"

"What?" Anne tilted her head to the side. "Ma laughed too."

*

Within thirty minutes, they had dinner on the table and Katherine stormed into the kitchen.

"I'm so hungry," she said and pressed a quick kiss to Nora's cheek.

"I don't care," Nora said and pointed towards the bathroom. "Go and wash up first."

Katherine pouted but did as she was told.

"See," Anne said. "She comes and kisses you on the cheek after you have prepared supper. That's what Mary's husband does when he comes home from work."

Nora and Martha shared a look. Anne was the sibling that spent the most time with them. Maybe one day she would figure it out. Nora shook her head and tucked some of Anne's hair behind her cheek.

"Don't worry about that right now," she said. "Focus on your meal. Have you washed your hands?"

Anne got up so fast that her chair almost fell backward. Nora stabilised it. Anne ran out of the kitchen the moment Katherine came in.

"Where is she going?" Katherine asked. She then glanced towards the direction where Anne had run, before kissing Nora quickly on the lips. "Hello."

"Hi." Nora smiled. "She is just going to wash-up. Let's sit down."

They sat down and Nora served them. She liked cooking and feeding people. It made her feel like a wife and every time she thought about being Katherine's wife, her heart soared.

Anne came back and they sat down to eat.

"When is Hopper going to be mine?" Anne asked after a little while.

Katherine choked on a piece of meatloaf. "Excuse me?"

"Well," Anne swallowed her bite. "Frankie is yours and Nightingale is Nora's, shouldn't Hopper be mine?"

Martha chuckled. "If Hopper is anyone's, he should be mine."

Katherine smiled and shared a look with Nora.

"Hopper belongs to all of us," she said. "After all, it's bad luck to sell the first foal born on a farm."

"I thought it was bad luck to *not* sell the first foal born on a farm," Martha said.

Katherine opened her mouth but Nora hurried to talk. She didn't want her lover and her sister to fight.

"Either way," she said. "It doesn't matter whether it's bad luck or not. Hopper belongs with his mother and father and with us." That ended the conversation.

"Speaking of horses," Martha said, "there is a horse I want to buy."

"I'm not sure we can afford one right now," Katherine said without looking up.

Nora rolled her eyes. Katherine never treated her that way but sometimes Katherine seemed like she wanted to provoke Martha on purpose. *We are going to have a conversation later.* Nora couldn't help but grin, as Anne was right. They really did act like an old married couple sometimes.

"Her owner has died," Martha said. "They're having an auction, maybe we could go."

"Martha is right." Nora had to come to her sister's defence before Katherine managed to say anything more that would lead to a fight. "We could at least go and look. If we don't find anything, we won't have wasted any money."

"And if we do, you can always sell that terrible car of yours." Katherine winked at Martha but then she sighed. "You're right though. Did I ever tell you how I bought Nightingale Prancer?"

"Tell us!" Anne leaned forward, loving story-telling more than anything.

"Well, it was the same day that Martha came to Waterhouse Acre Stables. My father had given me money to buy a couple of yearlings but the moment I laid my eyes on a small roan that was standing all by herself, I knew that I had found the one."

Nora chuckled at Katherine's dramatic tone of voice. She let the story of Nightingale Prancer fade into the background as she gathered everyone's empty plates and took them to the sink. Outside the kitchen window, the horses were grazing underneath the blue sky.

THE END

About the Author

Kathy grew up travelling around the world but is now settled with her wife in Sweden. By day she is a primary school teacher, by night, a writer, and with the little spare time she has left she enjoys cooking, playing video games and spending time with her family.

Other Titles Available From Triplicity Publishing

Loose Ends by Joan L. Anderson. After her estranged sister is killed when she falls onto the subway tracks in Paris just as a train arrives, Allison goes to Paris to deal with her sister's body and collect her things. But, after talking to the police about the accident and viewing the subway surveillance video, something seems odd about her death.

Real Love by Graysen Morgen. Leigh Myer is a trauma nurse practitioner who is not happy going through the motions of her daily life. When a friend offers up her mountain cabin for a relaxing vacation, Leigh packs her bags. She's never been to the mountains and certainly never in heavy snow. A chance meeting with a fish and wildlife officer turns her idea of a quiet, relaxing vacation…upside down. Camden Gorely loves her job and loves the mountain she works and lives on even more. She's tired of having flings with vacationers who visit for days or weeks at a time, until she meets the elusive nurse from the city. Can Leigh stop running from her past and allow real love into her heart?

Enticed by Love by Lynn Lawler. Henrietta Bailey is a mysterious woman who has spent her entire life living in the town of Crescent, a sleepy beach community in central coastal California. She loves the beach, the ocean air, and the town itself. Her simple life fulfills her. However, she spends much of her time reminiscing about her long-lost love, a woman who left her devastated. Now, another woman awaits on the horizon; a wise, intelligent, and sexy lady who is sophisticated beyond her years. This woman yearns for her soul mate and lover. Will she be able to win Henrietta's heart, or will Henrietta be fated to live the rest of her days alone?

Love Undercover by Domina Alexandra. Remi Stone never expected to get the opportunity to work undercover for narcotics. But, when the chance arrives, she takes it. With drugs coursing through a high school, Remi has only until the end of the school year to find the suspects responsible. Undercover, Remi plays her role, moving one step further into the drug industry. She never thought she'd be moving one step closer to the woman who would change her life and take hold of her heart. There is just one issue. Remi Stone is undercover as an eighteen year old high school senior. And the woman she can't seem to ignore is her History teacher. There will be a lot of challenges along the way, including one that could cost Remi her life and her heart.

Playing the Game by Graysen Morgen. Randi Rojas is a professional soccer player who seemingly has it all, a successful career, a long-term girlfriend, a loving family, and a great group of friends...until a chance meeting with an attractive woman sends her way offside, and into a whole new game. Berkley Ward lives her life to the extreme, spending her days either in the gym or four-wheeling in the woods, and her nights patrolling the streets as an officer. Affairs with taken women are easy, but after years of playing games, she's finished...until she meets a beautiful woman and a game she can't resist. Both women play a dangerously seductive game of cat and mouse, teetering on the edge of friendship and affair.

Rebel Sweetheart by Sydney Canyon. When a headstrong, country music superstar starts getting threatening letters while on tour, her manager has no other choice but to hire someone to investigate the threats, and keep her safe. Haley Nielsen is as stubborn as it gets. She does things her way, and her way only. The last thing she needs or wants is a babysitter following her every move and controlling everything she does. Shane Crowley isn't your typical private investigator, or bodyguard, for that matter. She's a former U.S. Deputy Marshal with a lot of experience, and an all or nothing attitude. Tempers flare and the energy burns red hot between the two women as they spend weeks together cooped up on Haley's tour bus, traveling the country. Will they stop resisting each other long enough to see eye to eye? Or will the letter writer make good on his threats?

A Tale of Spiders and Canned Soup by Kathy L. Salt. Living on your own can be hard, but even more so when you're dealing with haphephobia; the death of a twin sister; and a crush on your teacher. Mika is still in contact with her foster family who homes the loves of her life, three young children she would do anything for, when she begins attending University of Aberdeen and meets Pauline, an Australian that teaches Viking history. Neither woman is used to breaking the rules, and their way to each other is a hard one, especially when Mika vows to get custody of the children, whether she is ready to be a parent or not. *A story about growing up. A story about dealing with grief. A story about Mika and Pauline.*

A Night Claimed by Domina Alexandra. Bonnie Collins had plans. And being a werewolf wasn't one of them. Attacked by a rogue who was out to claim her, and facing what she now has no choice of becoming, Bonnie can't let go of her human life as a Paramedic. The last thing Bonnie needs is more challenges. However, Rikki, the Alpha of Mill City will be just that. Finding her to be possessive and ruling, Bonnie begins challenging the Alpha's every breath. Finding out her attack was no accident only makes her more angry at the situation. A group of rogues are out to get her. With no clue why, Bonnie has no choice but to seek help from the alluring Alpha and her pack, accepting the new world she was forced into.

Stunted by Breanna Hughes. Professional stuntwoman Jessie Knight takes her job very seriously and although she works in the entertainment industry, she has zero desire for fame or notoriety. She also has a very strict no-dating policy when it comes to coworkers. That is, until, she meets famous actress Elliot Chase on the set of her new film. The adrenaline rush of the stunts is nothing compared to the sparks that fly between them. After a passionate night together, a sex tape is leaked that sends Jessie and Elliot's private and professional lives into a spiral. Will the fallout be too much for them to last? Or will they find a way out of the mess together?

Mission Compromised by Graysen Morgen. Natalia Moreno is thrilled when she arrives in Fiji for a relaxing vacation. However, she soon discovers the overwater bungalow she's staying in has been double booked for the entire stay, and the resort is full. Annoyed and frustrated, she has no other choice but to share her hut with a stranger. Christian Garnier is sent to Fiji for what she refers to as a working vacation, until she finds out she has an ornery roommate for the next two weeks who is dead set on making her job twice as hard. Soon, all hell breaks loose and the two women are sent around the world on a wild goose chase.

Stargazing by Kathy L. Salt. Lissa stared open-mouthed at the GIF that played over and over on the screen in front of her. Heat flushed to her face, igniting her skin. Her heart started pounding in her chest. *Stupid internet, it should really come with a warning label.* She's never been interested in relationships or sex and as the years have gone by she has retreated more and more into her work. Everything changes when she meets Star, a porn actress with a heart of gold and a troubled childhood. *They say that opposites attract, but how much of that is true? What chance do they have when one of them is a virgin and the other one star in pornography?*

I Belong with Her by Domina Alexandra. Tajel Pierce loves the thrill of being a paramedic. Every call she goes on gives her a rush. She makes no time for a personal life. No one can ruin her love for her career. Then there is Arianna Castaldi, who just transferred to her new paramedic position in a whole new state. All she needs is a new start without any distractions. Arianna and Tajel's relationship doesn't start off perfect. Embarrassed of the one night stand Arianna believes she had with Tajel, she wants to pretend they never met and make their relationship strictly business. The only choice they have to keep from strangling each other is to go from denying their feelings to accepting them as they work through intense 911 calls.

Awakened by Fate by Lynn Lawler. Jackie is a woman living life according to her own rules. She's married, but it's the unspoken, open kind. She can have as many female lovers as she likes; she just can't talk about them. After a bizarre encounter turns her world upside down, things slowly begin to change. She finds herself in desperation as she searches for answers. What she discovers is nothing is delivered in a neatly wrapped box. Now that everything has been brought out into the open, she finds she can't run away from her truth anymore. With her new life, comes new responsibilities and a different outcome than what she was expecting. Jackie isn't alone in the story. She meets several new people who help her along her journey.

Nautical Delights by S. L. Gape. Lady Elizabeth Barrington has spent her entire life trying to please her family; constantly opting for a quiet life, she utilises her profession as a doctor to keep out of her families' clutches; bar the annual two-week Caribbean private cruise, where there is simply no budge. Confined to two weeks on board the Iconica super yacht, she intends on keeping her head down and enjoying as much of the holiday as she can, whilst keeping her family at arm's length. Until a crew member catches her eye.

Worlds Apart by S.L. Gape. Hollywood A-lister Heidi Spencer-Brady is everything you'd expect of an Idol. Loved by all, the British Beauty is graceful, talented, humble and so far removed from the 'typical' LA scene. When her husband's infidelity with his new 'leading lady' is leaked, Dawn, Heidi's best friend and manager, goes all out to protect her. She arranges for Heidi to go back to the UK and stay on her cousins farm they had visited as children, much to the disappointment of the animal fearing Heidi.

Castor Valley (Law & Order Series Book 2) by Graysen Morgen. Jessie Henry is torn when she reads about the capture of the Doyle brothers, two young men who were part of her old gang. Unable to let them hang for a crime she's sure they didn't commit, Jessie leaves her wife and the Town of Boone Creek behind, and sets out on a journey back to the one place she thought she'd never see again, *Castor Valley*. Ellie Henry watches the love of her life leave, not knowing if she will ever return. When she gets an odd telegram, nearly a week later, she fears Jessie is in trouble. With no other choice, she goes to the one person who can help her.

Fight to the Top by S. L. Gape. Georgia is a forty year old, single, Area Director from Manchester, UK who is all work and definitely no play. Having no time to socialise or spend time with her family she prides herself on being fit and well-polished. Erika is an Area Director for the same company, but in the United States. Whilst she is concentrating so heavily on the promotion she has been fighting for, she's starting to feel like her life outside of work is falling apart. The two women are exceptionally different, and worlds apart. Both of their lives are turned upside down when their jobs are snatched from under their noses, and they are suddenly faced with being thrown together by their bosses for one last major project...in Texas.

Boone Creek (Law & Order Series book 1) by Graysen Morgen. Jessie Henry is looking for a new life. She's unknown in the town of Boone Creek when she arrives, and wants to keep it that way. When she's offered the job of Town Marshal, she takes it, believing that protecting others and upholding the law is the penance for her past. Ellie Fray is a widowed, shopkeeper. She generally keeps to herself, but the mysterious new Town Marshal both intrigues and infuriates her. She believes the last thing the town needs is someone stirring up trouble with the outlaws who have taken over.

Witness by Joan L. Anderson. Becca and Kate have lived together for eight years, and have always spent their vacation in a tropical paradise, lying on a beach. This year, Becca wanted to try something different: a seven day, 65-mile hike in the beautiful Cascade Mountains of Washington state. Their peaceful vacation turns to horror when they stumble upon a brutal murder taking place in the back country.

Too Soon by S.L. Gape. Brooke is a twenty-nine year old detective from Oxford, who has her life pretty much planned out until her boss and partner of nine years, Maria, tells her their relationship is over. When Brooke finds out the truth, that Maria cheated on her with their best friend Paula, she decides to get her life back on track by getting away for six weeks in Anglesey, North Wales. Chloe, a thirty three year old artist and art director, owns a log cabin on Anglesey where she spends each weekend painting and surfing. After returning from a surf, she stumbles upon the somewhat uptight and enigmatic Brooke.

Never Quit (Never Series book 2) by Graysen Morgen. Two years after stepping away from the action as a Coast Guard Rescue Swimmer to become an instructor, Finley finds herself in charge of the most difficult class of cadets she's ever faced, while also juggling the taxing demands of having a home life with her partner Nicole, and their fifteen year old daughter. Jordy Ross gave up everything, dropping out of college, and leaving her family behind, to join the Coast Guard and become a rescue swimmer cadet. The extreme training tests her fitness level, pushing her mentally and physically further than she's ever been in her life, but it's the aggressive competition between her and another female cadet that proves to be the most challenging.

Never Let Go (Never Series book 1) by Graysen Morgen. For Coast Guard Rescue Swimmer, Finley Morris, life is good. She loves her job, is well respected by her peers, and has been given an opportunity to take her career to the next level. The only thing missing is the love of her life, who walked out, taking their daughter with her, seven years earlier. When Finley gets a call from her ex, saying their teenage daughter is coming to spend the summer with her, she's floored. While spending more time with her daughter, whom she doesn't get to see often, and learning to be a full-time parent, Finley quickly realizes she has not, and will never, let go of what is important.

Pursuit by Joan L. Anderson. Claire is a workaholic attorney who flies to Paris to lick her wounds after being dumped by her girlfriend of seventeen years. On the plane she chats with the young woman sitting next to her, and when they land the woman is inexplicably detained in Customs. Claire is surprised when she later runs into the woman in the city. They agree to meet for breakfast the next morning, but when the woman doesn't show up Claire goes to her hotel and makes a horrifying discovery. She soon finds herself ensnared in a web of intrigue and international terrorism, becoming the target of a high stakes game of cat and mouse through the streets of Paris.

Wrecked by Sydney Canyon. To most people, the *Duchess* is a myth formed by old pirates tales, but to Reid Cavanaugh, a Caribbean island bum and one of the best divers and treasure hunters in the world, it's a real, seventeenth century pirate ship—the holy grail of underwater treasure hunting. Reid uses the same cunning tactics she always has before setting out to find the lost ship. However, she is forced to bring her business partner's daughter along as collateral this time because he doesn't trust her. Neither woman is thrilled, but being cooped up on a small dive boat for days, forces them to get know each other quickly.

Arson by Austen Thorne. Madison Drake is a detective for the Stetson Beach Police Department. The last thing she wants to do is show a new detective the ropes, especially when a fire investigation becomes arson to cover up a murder. Madison butts heads with Tara, her trainee, deals with sarcasm from Nic, her ex-girlfriend who is a patrol officer, and finds calm in the chaos of police work with Jamie, her best friend who is the county medical examiner. Arson is the first of many in a series of novella episodes surrounding the fictional Stetson Beach Police Department and Detective Madison Drake.

***Mommies (Bridal Series book 3)* by Graysen Morgen.** Britton and her wife Daphne have been married for a year and a half and are happy with their life, until Britton's mother hounds her to find out why her sister Bridget hasn't decided to have children yet. This prompts Daphne to bring up the big subject of having kids of their own with Britton. Britton hadn't really thought much about having kids, but her love for Daphne makes her see life and their future together in a whole new way when they decide to become mommies.

Rapture & Rogue by Sydney Canyon. Taren Rauley is happy and in a good relationship, until the one person she thought she'd never see again comes back into her life. She struggles to keep the past from colliding with the present as old feelings she thought were dead and gone, begin to haunt her. In college, Gianna Revisi was a mastermind, ring-leading, crime boss. Now, she has a great life and spends her time running Rapture and Rogue, the two establishments she built from the ground up. The last person she ever expects to see walk into one of them, is the girl who walked out on her, breaking her heart five years ago.

Second Chance by Sydney Canyon. After an attack on her convoy, Marine Corps Staff Sergeant, Darien Hollister, must learn to live without her sight. When an experimental procedure allows her to see again, Darien is torn, knowing someone had to die in order for this to happen.

She embarks on a journey to personally thank the donor's family, but is too stunned to tell them the truth.

Mixed emotions stir inside of her as she slowly gets to the know the people that feel like so much more than strangers to her. When the truth finally comes out, Darien walks away, taking the second chance that she's been given to go back to the only life she's ever known, but she's not the only one with a second chance at life.

Meant to Be by Graysen Morgen. Brandt is about to walk down the aisle with her girlfriend, when an unexpected chain of events turns her world upside down, causing her to question the last three years of her life. A chance encounter sparks a mix of rage and excitement that she has never felt before. Summer is living life and following her dreams, all the while, harboring a huge secret that could ruin her career. She believes that some things are better kept in the dark, until she has her third run-in with a woman she had hoped to never see again, and gives into temptation. Brandt and Summer start believing everything happens for a reason as they learn the true meaning of meant to be.

Coming Home by Graysen Morgen. After tragedy derails TJ Abernathy's life, she packs up her three year old son and heads back to Pennsylvania to live with her grandmother on the family farm. TJ picks back up where she left off eight years earlier, tending to the fruit and nut tree orchard, while learning her grandmother's secret trade. Soon, TJ's high school sweetheart and the same girl who broke her heart, comes back into her life, threatening to steal it away once again. As the weeks turn into months and tragedy strikes again, TJ realizes coming home was the best thing she could've ever done.

Special Assignment by Austen Thorne. Secret Service Agent Parker Meeks has her hands full when she gets her new assignment, protecting a Congressman's teenage daughter, who has had threats made on her life and been whisked away to a Christian boarding school under an alias to finish out her senior year. Parker is fine with the assignment, until she finds out she has to go undercover as a Canon Priest. The last thing Parker expects to find is a beautiful, art history teacher, who is intrigued by her in more ways than one.

Miracle at Christmas by Sydney Canyon. A Modern Twist on the Classic Scrooge Story. Dylan is a power-hungry lawyer who pushed away everything good in her life to become the best defense attorney in the, often winning the worst cases and keeping anyone with enough money out of jail. She's visited on Christmas Eve by her deceased law partner, who threatens her with a life in hell like his own, if she doesn't change her path. During the course of the night, she is taken on a journey through her past, present, and future with three very different spirits.

Bella Vita by Sydney Canyon. Brady is the First Officer of the crew on the Bella Vita, a luxury charter yacht in the Caribbean. She enjoys the laidback island lifestyle, and is accustomed to high profile guests, but when a U.S. Senator charters the yacht as a gift to his beautiful twin daughters who have just graduated from college and a few of their friends, she literally has her hands full.

Brides (Bridal Series book 2) by Graysen Morgen. Britton Prescott is dating the love of her life, Daphne Attwood, after a few tumultuous events that happened to unravel at her sister's wedding reception, seven months earlier. She's happy with the way things are, but immense pressure from her family and friends to take the next step, nearly sends her back to the single life. The idea of a long engagement and simple wedding are thrown out the window, as both families take over, rushing Britton and Daphne to the altar in a matter of weeks.

Cypress Lake by Graysen Morgen. The small town of Cypress Lake is rocked when one murder after another happens. Dani Ricketts, the Chief Deputy for the Cypress Lake Sheriff's Office, realizes the murders are linked. She's surprised when the girl that broke her heart in high school has not only returned home, but she's also Dani's only suspect. Kristen Malone has come back to Cypress Lake to put the past behind her so that she can move on with her life. Seeing Dani Ricketts again throws her off-guard, nearly derailing her plans to finally rid herself and her family of Cypress Lake.

Crashing Waves by Graysen Morgen. After a tragic accident, Pro Surfer, Rory Eden, spends her days hiding in the surf and snowboard manufacturing company that she built from the ground up, while living her life as a shell of the person that she once was. Rory's world is turned upside down when a young surfer pursues her, asking for the one thing she can't do. Adler Troy and Dr. Cason Macauley from Graysen Morgen's bestselling novel: *Falling Snow*, make an appearance in this romantic adventure about life, love, and letting go.

Bridesmaid of Honor (Bridal Series book 1) by Graysen Morgen. Britton Prescott's best friend is getting married and she's the maid of honor. As if that isn't enough to deal with, Britton's sister announces she's getting married in the same month and her maid of honor is her best friend Daphne, the same woman who has tormented Britton for years. Britton has to suck it up and play nice, instead of scratching her eyes out, because she and Daphne are in both weddings. Everyone is counting on them to behave like adults.

Falling Snow by Graysen Morgen. Dr. Cason Macauley, a high-speed trauma surgeon from Denver meets Adler Troy, a professional snowboarder and sparks fly. The last thing Cason wants is a relationship and Adler doesn't realize what's right in front of her until it's gone, but will it be too late?

Fate vs. Destiny by Graysen Morgen. Logan Greer devotes her life to investigating plane crashes for the National Transportation Safety Board. Brooke McCabe is an investigator with the Federal Aviation Association who literally flies by the seat of her pants. When Logan gets tangled in head games with both women will she choose fate or destiny?

Just Me by Graysen Morgen. Wild child Ian Wiley has to grow up and take the reins of the hundred year old family business when tragedy strikes. Cassidy Harland is a little surprised that she came within an inch of picking up a gorgeous stranger in a bar and is shocked to find out that stranger is the new head of her company.

Love Loss Revenge by Graysen Morgen. Rian Casey is an FBI Agent working the biggest case of her career and madly in love with her girlfriend. Her world is turned upside when tragedy strikes. Heartbroken, she tries to rebuild her life. When she discovers the truth behind what really happened that awful night she decides justice isn't good enough, and vows revenge on everyone involved.

Natural Instinct by Graysen Morgen. Chandler Scott is a Marine Biologist who keeps her private life private. Corey Joslen is intrigued by Chandler from the moment she meets her. Chandler is forced to finally open her life up to Corey. It backfires in Corey's face and sends her running. Will either woman learn to trust her natural instinct?

Secluded Heart by Graysen Morgen. Chase Leery is an overworked cardiac surgeon with a group of best friends that have an opinion and a reason for everything. When she meets a new artist named Remy Sheridan at her best friend's art gallery she is captivated by the reclusive woman. When Chase finds out why Remy is so sheltered will she put her career on the line to help her or is it too difficult to love someone with a secluded heart?

In Love, at War by Graysen Morgen. Charley Hayes is in the Army Air Force and stationed at Ford Island in Pearl Harbor. She is the commanding officer of her own female-only service squadron and doing the one thing she loves most, repairing airplanes. Life is good for Charley, until the day she finds herself falling in love while fighting for her life as her country is thrown haphazardly into World War II. Can she survive being in love and at war?

Fast Pitch by Graysen Morgen. Graham Cahill is a senior in college and the catcher and captain of the softball team. Despite being an all-star pitcher, Bailey Michaels is young and arrogant. Graham and Bailey are forced to get to know each other off the field in order to learn to work together on the field. Will the extra time pay off or will it drive a nail through the team?

Submerged by Graysen Morgen. Assistant District Attorney Layne Carmichael had no idea that the sexy woman she took home from a local bar for a one night stand would turn out to be someone she would be prosecuting months later. Scooter is a Naval Officer on a submarine who changes women like she changes uniforms. When she is accused of a heinous crime she is shocked to see her latest conquest sitting across from her as the prosecuting attorney.

Vow of Solitude by Austen Thorne. Detective Jordan Denali is in a fight for her life against the ghosts from her past and a Serial Killer taunting her with his every move. She lives a life of solitude and plans to keep it that way. When Callie Marceau, a curious Medical Examiner, decides she wants in on the biggest case of her career, as well as, Jordan's life, Jordan is powerless to stop her.

Igniting Temptation by Sydney Canyon. Mackenzie Trotter is the Head of Pediatrics at the local hospital. Her life takes a rather unexpected turn when she meets a flirtatious, beautiful fire fighter. Both women soon discover it doesn't take much to ignite temptation.

One Night by Sydney Canyon. While on a business trip, Caylen Jarrett spends an amazing night with a beautiful stripper. Months later, she is shocked and confused when that same woman re-enters her life. The fact that this stranger could destroy her career doesn't bother her. C.J. is more terrified of the feelings this woman stirs in her. Could she have fallen in love in one night and not even known it?

Fine by Sydney Canyon. Collin Anderson hides behind a façade, pretending everything is fine. Her workaholic wife and best friend are both oblivious as she goes on an emotional journey, battling a potentially hereditary disease that her mother has been diagnosed with. The only person who knows what is really going on, is Collin's doctor. The same doctor, who is an acquaintance that she's always been attracted to, and who has a partner of her own.

Shadow's Eyes by Sydney Canyon. Tyler McCain is the owner of a large ranch that breeds and sells different types of horses. She isn't exactly thrilled when a Hollywood movie producer shows up wanting to film his latest movie on her property. Reegan Delsol is an up and coming actress who has everything going for her when she lands the lead role in a new film, but there one small problem that could blow the entire picture.

Light Reading: A Collection of Novellas by Sydney Canyon. Four of Sydney Canyon's novellas together in one book, including the bestsellers Shadow's Eyes and One Night.

Visit us at www.tri-pub.com